KU-150-859

AFTER FRANCESCO

BRIAN MALLOY

JOHN SCOGNAMIGLIO BOOKS
KENSINGTON BOOKS
www.kensingtonbooks.com

JOHN SCOGNAMIGLIO BOOKS are published by

Kensington Publishing Corp.
119 West 40th Street
New York, NY 10018

All Kensington titles, imprints, and distributed lines are available at special quantity discounts for bulk purchases for sales promotion, premiums, fundraising, educational, or institutional use.

Special book excerpts or customized printings can also be created to fit specific needs. For details, write or phone the office of the Kensington Sales Manager: Attn.: Sales Department. Kensington Publishing Corp., 119 West 40th Street, New York, NY 10018. Phone: 1-800-221-2647.

The JS and John Scognamiglio Books logo is a trademark of Kensington Publishing Corp.

First Kensington Hardcover Edition: June 2021

ISBN: 978-1-4967-3353-5 (ebook)

ISBN: 978-1-4967-3352-8

First Kensington Trade Paperback Edition: May 2022

10 9 8 7 6 5 4 3 2 1

Printed in the United States of America

For my husband, Terry.
In loving memory of Paul, a true artist.
And in memory of Charlie Howard, whose life mattered.

ACKNOWLEDGMENTS

For his belief in this book and for his sage editing, my deepest thanks to John Scognamiglio. Thanks to Stephanie Finnegan and Janice Rossi for their thoughtful work.

I am grateful to the manuscript's early readers, Roberta Anderson, Paul Mellblom, and Mike Malloy.

Finally, thank you to the volunteers and staff of the Minnesota AIDS Project. We are still here.

It's like living through a war which is happening only for those people who happen to be in the trenches. Every time a shell explodes, you look around and you discover that you've lost more of your friends, but nobody else notices. It isn't happening to them. They're walking the streets as though we weren't living through some sort of nightmare. And only you can hear the screams of the people who are dying and their cries for help. No one else seems to be noticing.

—Vito Russo

Chapter 1

JANUARY 1988:
THE END OF THE WORLD

Aunt Nora always says that people can still surprise you. Take today's funeral, for example: The organist was playing "*Ave Maria*," and I was thinking about how taut Brian Boitano's ass looked during last year's world championships, when Live Eddie—my gay best friend and surviving partner of Dead Eddie (the guy in the casket)—stood, walked all the way up to the altar, and demanded to be seated in the front row, next to the coffin, right alongside Dead Eddie's family.

This never happens at an "orthodox" AIDS funeral. You know, the ones where the guy died of cancer, no one mentions he was gay, and his friends and lover sit obediently in the back of the bus while the family grieves up front.

If this was a "conservative" AIDS funeral (partner a "good friend" who sits with the family; cause of death *that which must not be named*), or the increasingly popular "celebration of life" (lesbian shaman burning incense, open mic for any idiot in need of attention, family sitting next to surviving partner in stunned silence, balloon release), this wouldn't be a problem.

But it's an orthodox AIDS funeral, so it's a big fucking problem.

We can hear Live Eddie from all the way back in the gay seats: "My place is here! With him!"

Hushed voices now, probably trying to reason with him, probably trying to get his faggot-self back to steerage.

Truth be told, I didn't think Live Eddie had the balls. Yeah, Live Eddie was a jock, but Dead Eddie was the assertive one. You could really even say Dead Eddie was aggressive: When he saw Live Eddie one Friday at a Christopher Street bar, he grabbed him, stuck his tongue down Live Eddie's throat, and dry humped him right there next to the bar as men cheered. Live Eddie could have sent him sailing across the room with just one arm, but he was so flattered and embarrassed, he moved in with Dead Eddie maybe a week later.

That was the same year I met Frankie. He wanted to be called Francesco. It was the four of us back then—the Eddies, Francesco, and me—young and beautiful and living the best days of our lives, though we didn't know it. I met Francesco at a bar, too. He looked like an actor I had a crush on; I just admired him shyly. Then he noticed me looking. That smile.

Can't breathe.

Inhale. Hold.

It'll pass, always does.

Exhale. Slowly.

Inhale. Hold.

It'll pass, always does.

Exhale. Slowly.

My straight female best friend sits next to me, holds my hand, whispers, "Distract yourself. Take a look around. Catalog what you see. You know this will pass. It always does."

I look around: The church is heavy and stiff, wooden pews and marble columns. I see the backs of men's heads in the rows directly in front of me, the buzz cuts along the sides, the long hair up top. Archways surround saints, and the domed sanctuary's like half a rocket, sliced lengthwise from top to bottom. At the top, paintings of men in robes, like astronauts on countdown. 10-9-8-7 . . .

I breathe. I don't go full-blown. This one passes almost as fast as it came. I squeeze her hand. False alarm.

Up by the altar, things have gotten quiet. Funeral Home Guys have appeared, and they look like bouncers, not like the old men you usually see ushering masses. They form a wall of black suits around Live Eddie, quarantining him from the family, and they speak so softly, with such even tones, no one back in the gay seats can hear what they say.

Bouncers at a funeral. Dead Eddie's parents thought of everything.

It's almost funny: Dead Eddie, Mr. Take-Shit-From-No-One, was too petrified to tell his folks he was gay. They never knew that Live Eddie was more than a roommate until Dead Eddie died. Yeah, maybe they knew on some level, but then again, maybe not—it's not like the Eddies were middle-aged bachelors who'd lived together for decades. And his parents never once saw him sick. He never told them anything about his life that mattered. The last time I visited him—before the brain lymphoma took over—was at St. Vincent's. I nodded to Live Eddie on my way to Dead Eddie's room; Live Eddie was in the hall arguing with a nun who wanted to discharge Dead Eddie to a nursing home or hospice because of all the care he required. Live Eddie very politely shot her down, thanking her for her concern but insistent that he would take care of *his lover* in *their home*, and he had GMHC volunteers to help out. What do you get with institutional care, he asked her, and then answered his own question: Maybe aides who let him lie in his own piss and shit. Maybe they leave his meals out in the hall.

It's happened to AIDS patients before; it's happening right now. Even *if* he wanted to put Dead Eddie in a nursing home, how many of them took people with AIDS, anyway?

She shook her head. What about Beth Abraham Hospice?

But that's way out in the Bronx, and always full.

I left them in the hall, nun and lover, both trying to do the right thing for a young man who could not stand up for more than a minute before he fell over. Dead Eddie was black-and-blue from losing his balance and from the KS lesions, and so thin he reminded me of the old newsreels of concentration camp survivors. I flinched when I saw the camp liberations in war documentaries, but now I'm used to the large sunken eyes, the arms so frail you're afraid they'll shatter like glass. The room smelled like isopropyl alcohol and Clorox, and as I slid a hard chair next to his bed, I heard the occasional code announced over the intercom, the wobbly wheel of a gurney passing by the doorway like a grocery cart. He motioned me to put my ear next to his peeling lips, so I grabbed the cool bed rail and leaned down. He asked me, in that weak, dry, crackling voice you hear everywhere now, his lungs sounding like *Snap, Crackle, and Pop*: What's the hardest part about telling your parents you have AIDS?

I pretended I hadn't heard this one a million times before. I shrugged my shoulders and said, Beats me.

Convincing them you're Haitian.

I laughed for his sake.

Now, three Funeral Home Guys give up talking and grab Live Eddie, pulling him toward the vestry. Even a year ago they wouldn't have been able to move him. A fourth scopes out the pews, like a mobster checking for witnesses before his pals stuff their mark in the trunk of a Deville. Live Eddie shouts: "Get offa me!" The front pews are quiet, like they're praying, like nothing out of the ordinary's going on, like Dead Eddie wasn't gay, like he didn't die of AIDS. But then one woman screams at Live Eddie, in that shrill voice of the pious, "Show some respect for the family!"

My straight female best friend, who took the train down to Baltimore with me even though she had said after the last funeral that she couldn't go to any more of them, lets go of my hand, stands up, and shouts so loud that maybe even Dead Eddie hears: "Stop it! He belongs there!"

Gays look at each other. We're always so compliant at orthodox funerals, like the accused pleading "guilty" in hopes of leniency. But now Gay and Family, which have so successfully avoided each other for so long, are smashed together like atoms.

As a Funeral Home Guy lifts Live Eddie up in a bear hug (he wears gloves—they all do), a priest takes the podium and says into the mic—with a trace of a lisp—"Please, everyone, for the family's sake, let's calm down and remember where we are."

We're at St. Wenceslaus in East Baltimore, once a Czech neighborhood and now black, and the place they return to for their grandparents' funerals, only Eddie—Edvard Svoboda—wasn't a grandfather, or even a father, or even thirty years old yet.

"On behalf of the family," the priest continues, "I must insist—"

Okay, then, on behalf of his *real* family.

"Outta my way," I tell the stupefied gays next to me. I pimp-roll up the processional aisle, like I'm from the Bronx, and head straight for the altar. "Let him go."

The priest lisps: "Sir, take your seat or leave."

I put a sleeper hold on the bear hugger, who stinks like a gallon bucket of Stetson, and squeeze, hard. He drops Live Eddie on the floor. So now we're all huffing and puffing as Funeral Home Guys try to pull me off one of their own, and a man who looks like Dead-Eddie-before-AIDS (a brother?) jumps out of the first pew and grabs me by my one-and-only good funeral suitcoat. I hear it rip. People stand and shout or sit with their hands over their mouths, and now the gays in the back redeploy themselves up front, and I wonder if this is gonna be my first funeral riot, until we hear the voice of God, or just nearly: Laurie Lindstrom, my straight female best friend, has grabbed the microphone.

"STOP!"

We stop, all of us, gay and straight.

I let Stetson go, and the other Funeral Home Guys and Dead Eddie's look-alike let me go. Most people sit back down. All you can hear is the sound of pews creaking and people murmuring, and the gasping of Live Eddie, me, and the Funeral Home Guys. I put an arm around Live Eddie, easy to do, since he's lost so much weight. His narrow chest heaves, and his gray face is now pepper red. He blinks back tears as he says, "I want to go home."

He doesn't mean where he grew up.

People like us never do.

We come from places like Minnesota and Georgia and Pennsylvania and Missouri, but home is New York City, the place we found each other, fell in love, and only occasionally get to bury our dead.

We leave. First Live Eddie, then me, then Laurie, and then, like a recessional, the gay men and our fellow New Yorkers who came down to Baltimore to say good-bye to Eddie Svoboda, Chelsea Boy, a Muscle Mary, and the man who damned John Hinckley Jr. to hell for being such a lousy shot.

We're on the Amtrak back to New York. Live Eddie sits four or five rows behind us in the nonsmoking car, along with his sister, who flew in from Atlanta to represent his side of the family, not understanding what an orthodox funeral was or how it worked. New York gays are mostly in the smoking cars, smoking, or in the club car, drinking, catching up with friends we only run into at funerals now. Laurie looks at me bluntly through her black horn-rims when I take out a flask, Art Deco and solid sterling silver, with rose and yellow gold bands. It was Frankie's. He only ever filled it with distilled water or organic green tea. It was meant to impress.

I use it for what you're supposed to use it for.

I tell Laurie, "Cheaper than the club car."

The train rocks us side to side, and she closes her eyes. "I'm surprised there's any left."

With a sharper edge she adds: "I don't care what anyone says, you can smell vodka."

I screw the top back on, wanting more. "Didn't you bring a book to read or something? *My Friend Flicka*? *The Horse and His Boy*?" Laurie was *that* sort of girl when she was a girl.

"Be quiet." And for the hundredth time: "I want you to stop drinking."

I stare out the window. "Here's the deal. When Toshiro"— her boyfriend—"dies in *your* arms, you get to tell me to stop drinking."

We're having this back-and-forth more often. Every single time I see her, she finds an excuse to bring up my drinking, like one of those well-intentioned and earnestly bad after-school specials you've seen over and over again. But then she surprises me with "What would Frankie say?"

She's never tried that one before, at least that I can remember. There are a few times I can't remember. And there was the shameful time last fall, the time I wish I could take back and do over, when she and Toshiro rushed me to the ER for alcohol poisoning. I look at her now, really look at her, the ruby lips, the black mascara, the teased hair spilling out from under a heavy military beret, the giant blue rhinestone earring on her left, the tiny silver stud on her right. She's the one who inspired me to come to New York after she left our hometown of Minneapolis behind for college. She had gone from wallflower to rebel. I tell her: "Leave Frankie out of this."

Back in the day, when she was meek and mild and had a crush on me—maybe she still does—that would've made her blush and whimper some feeble apologies. But we're not back in the day. She says, "You're the one who constantly throws him in my face. You've been using Frankie as your excuse ever since he died, and I'm sick and tired of it. Change the record."

"You know what," I tell her as I stand, "I'm gonna stretch my legs."

She grunts. "Give my regards to the boys in the club car."

Nighttime in the East Village, or, to be more precise, "Alphabet City." Some people will tell you not to go east of First Avenue, where you'll find my neighborhood. There's Avenue A (All right), Avenue B (Bad), Avenue C (Crazy), and Avenue D (Death). It can be brutally loud or unexpectedly quiet, there can be the soft click-clack of heels on the pavement, or the piercing screams of sirens (Police? Fire? Ambulance?), and it doesn't matter if it's a weeknight or a weekend, you never know what you're going to be in for. Walking home, I can kick empty crack vials into the street, see addicts sleeping in doorways, eavesdrop as the East *Vill-ahge* artists, outfitted in irony and seeping causticness, make meaning out of their lives on street corners and front stoops. My railroad apartment—a big room, really, with a tub in the kitchen—is on the third floor of a tenement on the ravaged Avenue B side of Tompkins Square. My neighborhood's home to Puerto Rican families, junkies, gay men, white homesteaders, hustlers, lesbians, bohemians, dealers, the homeless, skinheads, dropouts, artists, drifters, hustlers, rockers, and radical priests who are all indignant about the encroaching regiments of yuppies. Police chased the junkies out of Tompkins Square Park in '83, but now it's become an encampment for people with nowhere else to go, some of them bankrupted by AIDS, along with your typical batshit crazy folks, and I wonder how long before they're cleared out, too. This neighborhood's like an old black-and-white cartoon, but instead of Felix the Cat or Oswald the Rabbit, there's Jerry the Peddler and John the Squatter, and in place of clean straight lines and round smiling suns, there's shards of broken bottles and old used needles.

Seventeen degrees was the high today—cold by New York standards—and I wonder what the Tompkins Square Park regulars will do to keep warm tonight.

My apartment isn't really my apartment, it's Frankie's.

Francesco's.

He preferred his full name. I thought that he thought that it made him more interesting in a city full of people all desperate to be more interesting, so I always called him Frankie. He was from Philadelphia, so I'd say, like I was Rocky, "'Yo! Frankieeee!'"

I'd been perfectly happy, or at least reasonably happy, or possibly occasionally happy sharing a place in Hell's Kitchen with Laurie and our various third and fourth roommates, that is, until I met Frankie. Francesco. I never wanted to live in Alphabet City, but I wanted to be with Francesco all the time because I was in love, am in love, and now that I'm on my own, I can't work up the energy or put together the cash to find a new place in a better neighborhood.

Francesco is everywhere in the apartment. There's the Art Deco murals he painted on the walls, mostly of young white men, dressed Depression-era out-of-work, dancing, kissing, and toasting one another with amber bottles of beer raised in their hands. Then, framed and hanging near the doorless bathroom, the sketch of me in pencil. I'm naked, an ankle strategically placed, a pair of *Risky Business* sunglasses on my face, because I told him it would be cool, but to be honest, I couldn't hold his gaze as he worked. Something about the way he looked at me, the slight frown, the focused concentration on my exposed skin, made me light-headed. He was everything I had ever wanted, and now that I had him, I spent my days terrified of losing him, waiting for the day he finally realized—like his artsy-fartsy East *Vill-ahge* friends insisted—that he was too good for me.

He said the portrait was dishonest, on account of the sunglasses—my fault, of course, but honesty's always been hard for me; it doesn't run in my family.

He was honest to a fault when we first met. I was on the rebound, and had worked out hard before heading to the bar by myself. I was shyly checking him out as I sucked on the world's most expensive gin and tonic. Once he noticed, he smiled, stared a hole in my head—and other parts of my body—before walking up and whispering in my ear: Would you like to make some bullshit small talk, or do you want to go to my place and fuck all night long?

I was scandalized, but I was trying to be sophisticated back then, I think all Midwesterners who wind up in Manhattan do the same, at least at first, so I told him, in a voice that I thought made me sound like I wasn't from Minnesota: Let's go to your place, fuck all night long, and *then* make some bullshit small talk.

He asked me if I was Canadian.

I had been looking at him because he resembled Joseph Bottoms, the actor I had a long-term monogamous relationship with as I held his *After Dark* magazine cover in my left hand. Francesco was stuffed in a crop top and denim cutoffs, and he had the same build and thick, wavy hair as Joseph Bottoms, but without the perfect teeth. In short order I learned that he was wearing his fuck-me-now outfit, otherwise he almost always wore snug black jeans with holes at the knees, along with platformed Doc Martens, that almost made him as tall as me. These he topped off with a black trench coat and white tank tops or ripped tees that exposed a bit of his tight stomach or just a peek of the firm curve of a pec.

That first night with Francesco was a homecoming of a kind. I had been with a few men before, even thought I was in love once or twice, but there had been no one like him. He was uninhibited, unashamed, and, most of all, fun. Sex wasn't a competition or battle for control or a talent contest. It was fun and, at the same time, as unapologetically earnest as a Hallmark card. In some ways the memory of our first night together is unbearable, I'll never live that moment in time and space again. In the morning I had chalked my euphoria up to the sex (mindblowing), and his looks (stunning), and his body (sizzling), though any one of them would have been more than enough for me.

But what made me fall in love so fast and so completely, I quickly came to realize, was his ease: with himself, with the world. This was new to me. The house I grew up in was full of secrets, there was always the risk of discovery or, worse, discovering. I had never in my life been what you would call at ease. Here was a gay man so content with just being who he was, so devoid of insecurity, that I felt like I had discovered an entirely new species of Homo sapiens.

Once he finally figured out that he was in love (with me), the fuck-me-now clothes only came out on our anniversaries. He'd pose in them, trying to make bullshit small talk, as I whistled and shouted, " 'Yo! *Frankieeee!* Hey, where's your hat?' "

I take off my funeral clothes, annoyed at the ripped suitcoat (not too noticeable—maybe I can get away with it at the next one), and lie on our futon, our Kliban comforter, the one with the drawings of cats wearing sneakers, lying on top of me. It was his last birthday gift to me, purchased and delivered by the Eddies because he was too sick to leave the apartment. He wouldn't let me use it, though, he didn't want to stain it with whatever might fly out of his mouth or his ass without warning.

I pile up the pillows and hold them in my arms.

Here, in his apartment, Francesco's with me again, his head on my shoulder and my hand stroking his thick Joseph Bottoms hair.

His voice is strong and friendly, like before.

How was Dead Eddie's funeral? he asks. Better than mine?

It was very Catholic. Not a mashup like yours.

That's what happens when your dad's Catholic and your mom's a Jew. Lots of compromises. Lots of uncertainty.

He was always intrigued by his "identity." Neither a real Italian Catholic like his dad nor a real Russian Jew like his mom. I sigh, then say, You were never uncertain about anything.

He squeezes me tighter. Sure I was.

You were certain about me.

He smirks. Master John Goodfellow (of course he'd given his dick both a first and last name) was certain about you. He required a tall, strapping Midwestern farm boy with icy blue eyes, shoulders out to there, and an ass like two basketballs overinflated. It took a little bit of time for my heart to be certain about you.

I say yet again, You know I'm not a farm boy. I grew up in Minneapolis.

That's so cute. Like it's a real city. He kisses me on a cheek.

And you were certain about the spot.

He nods. I'd seen enough of them. Remember when you

could find a bruise and just wonder how it got there instead of screaming, OH, MY FUCKING GOD, THIS IS IT!

I remember. I remember when I liked having a cold so I could stay home and eat chicken noodle soup and watch *Family Feud*.

Get a cold now and you pick out your pallbearers. Those were the good old days. Wish we'd known how happy we were. He turns to face me, his head resting on a hand propped up by an elbow. He whispers: Maybe you should go back to school. You're still a young man. You could get a degree in something that could prepare you for a career.

Like your degree did?

He ignores the comment, says, Maybe you should, you know, start seeing people again . . . and drink less. It will be two years next month, after all. That's long enough, Kevin.

You sound like Laurie.

He plops on his back, stares straight up at the water-stained ceiling that's peeling, says, She's right. What do you think?

I pat him on his stomach, not the hollow one, or the bloated one, but the one that he was so proud of. I say, Here's the thing about your funeral. I didn't know what to do. I met two of your brothers for the very first time. What was I supposed to say to them? And that one's wife, what's-his-face's wife—

Marco's wife. Suzanne.

Yeah, her. Looking at me like I was something nasty she stepped in. Wouldn't even shake my hand.

Do we *really* need to process this again?

Yeah. We do.

He closes his eyes. *Maronna mia*, you hang on to your grudges. You only met her the one time and you haven't seen her since. Don't take things so personal.

It was the look on her face. Like I killed you. Like I was the end of the world.

* * *

I work on an old donated Exxon word processor from 8:30 a.m. until 5:00 p.m., Monday through Friday. My job's personalizing gift acknowledgments for donors so they can claim their tax deductions. That is, businessmen, corporations, and stockbrokers who support Fair and Unbiased, the nonprofit I've worked for, for just over three months. Fair and Unbiased's mission is to fight bias in the media, in particular, muckraking, undercover journalism, or anything else that might embarrass the giant corporations that support Fair and Unbiased. Jews have the Anti-Defamation League, blacks have the NAACP, and Wall Street has Fair and Unbiased, fighting for social justice for America's oppressed CEOs. Fair and Unbiased publishes white papers that try to "debunk" things. For example, the connection between Agent Orange and cancer, nicotine and addiction, nuclear accidents and the end of the world.

We also host luncheons where leading thinkers and thinking leaders jerk each other off about job creation, technological innovation, deregulation, and the American dream. Some also mention God, but those are the out-of-towners in New York for business, the local talent tend to grimace when God is thanked, like dinner guests when the host's dog vomits and promptly laps up the sick.

My desk's in the middle of a big off-white room that's stocked with filing cabinets and boxes of stuff nobody uses. It's accessible by three different hallways. People walk through every couple of minutes, on their way to the copier or the bathroom or the supply closet, or maybe to the postage meter to save money when they send out their résumés. They see me putting carbon paper in my word processor, which is really just a souped-up typewriter.

The blue copy goes in the donor file.

The yellow copy goes in the "chron" (chronological) file.

The pink copy goes in the campaign file.

They also see me on the phone, attentively listening as a recorded voice tells me the correct time. I don't have a watch and there's no clock in the room, so I call time, maybe five or six times an hour. I'm always let down. They say you experience time differently depending upon the situation. Like, when you're in a car accident, everything slows down—you can see the other car, but you know there's no way to avoid it. You know the impact's coming, the shattering glass, you just don't know if it will kill you.

That's exactly how I experience time at Fair and Unbiased.

You'd think the people who work here would all be conservatives and capitalists, but there's a few left-wing artists who need health insurance, and then there's me, a college dropout who should've listened to his high-school guidance counselor and learned a trade. My straight male best friend did, and he makes three times what I do living in a city that people can actually afford to live in.

But you know, New York is sophisticated.

And the blue copy goes in the donor file.

Glamorous.

And the yellow copy goes in the chron file.

Exciting.

And the pink copy goes in the campaign file.

Dead Eddie used to say that if you love what you do, you'd never hate going to work. I told him that was the dumbest-ass thing I had ever heard in my entire life, and I went to public school. Then I told him the only thing I really loved doing was Frankie. Francesco.

Don't get me wrong—there are mind-numbing, soul-sucking jobs everywhere, not just here. And I do love New York, especially the New York I moved to in 1979. I remember being surprised by the graffiti that seemed to cover everything, even the subway cars, inside and out. By having to look straight up to see the sky. By all the people living in the streets and parks. By the movie theaters on Broadway that showed films like *Dominatrix Without Mercy* and *Sweet Throat* (not to be confused with *Deep Throat*). And by the yellow cabs with their checkered stripes, a luxury I still can't afford.

So, what made New York such a wonderland for me?

It was the place where so many of us found each other. My first month here, I met more gay Minnesotans in New York than I ever did growing up in the "Land of 10,000 Lakes."

That first year. Not looking over my shoulder afraid of who might recognize me. Talking all night with Laurie on the lumpy old mattress we shared as she diagnosed me with dissociative disorder, and I prescribed her one hundred milligrams of mind-your-own-damn-business, to be taken daily, with or without meals. Making love to a man for the first time and apologizing profusely for refusing to bottom because I thought it would hurt, and, well, not really my thing. And the not lying. That was the biggest difference between New York and Minneapolis, not lying. Using masculine pronouns to talk about someone I wanted to sleep with. Not spending so much time and energy pretending, as if I'd been mute my entire life up until New York, or maybe trying to speak a second language that I never really got the hang of.

Freedom, ecstasy, heartbreak, joy, love, danger. New York had it all.

It was a different city.

I was a different person.

"At the tone, the time will be two forty-seven p.m. and thirty-eight seconds."

The gym's my second home, more so since Francesco died. When I first arrived in New York, I worked out to make myself someone men would lust for in the bars and leave alone in the subway. But then the workouts made me feel better, centered, calmer; and even now, I work out hard, harder than before, even with a hangover. My Walkman preempts small talk and the flirtatious requests to *Spot me. Spot me real good.* For the most part the Walkman does the trick. But there's still gym rats who will tap me on the shoulder, ask me to critique their dead-lifts (*I feel like I'm arching my back*) or their barbell overhead push presses (*My abs don't feel on*). Of course their form is perfect, they're here even more than I am, and their tank tops never cover their nipples. There's a lot of attitude queens at my gym who'll look right through you if they spot any flaw or imperfection, and I'm afraid I'm getting a reputation for being one myself.

But it's not like that.

When Francesco was alive, I'd flirt and tell dirty jokes and swoon over the newest sides of beef just like everybody else. I'd talk gay politics naked in the locker room, enjoying the sexual tension, the way men would speak to me without looking at my face, and maybe go out for coffee or something to eat with a few of the regulars after we got dressed. Because I had Francesco, I could enjoy myself. I could be friendly and outgoing; I was confident because I was loved and in love. And if a guy told me I seemed tense, that I needed to loosen up, and began to rub my shoulders, and whisper seductively in my ear, I'd smile and let him know my apartment's gone condo.

If he said, *Your partner will never know,* I'd say, *I'd know.*

If he said, *I'll play safe,* I'd say, *Doesn't get any safer than not doing it.*

And off I'd go, flattered and pure as Minnesota snow, home to Francesco and his drawing table. Maybe he and his fellow penciler, and best friend Toshiro, would be pulling an all-nighter for DC or Marvel, but mostly it was just him cranking out consistent pages of illustrations for the comic book houses. He'd ask me how my workout was, and I'd tell him I upped the weight on my dumbbell lying triceps extensions or maybe I added single-leg deadlifts to my routine.

He'd say, *That's nice.*

Some nights I'd test him—telling him I was able to do thirty exterior lat parallel squats, or that I finally mastered the close grip single-arm toastie-flies.

He'd say, *That's nice, asshole.*

The Walkman's batteries die, but I leave the headphones on as I barbell squat. This is my favorite. I stoop, step under the bar on its rack, position it on my rear deltoids, gripping narrowly on either side. And then the part I like best—standing up, tightening my glutes, flexing my stomach, lining my head up with my spine, and stepping back from the rack. I love the feel of the bar, the pressure of the weights on each end. It makes me feel like I'm Atlas, able to hold the world in place, preventing disaster for just one more day. My feet are placed a little wider than my hips, my toes point slightly outward, my elbows forward, and I close my eyes as I ease down slowly, leisurely, until my thighs are parallel to the floor.

This is the world pushing me down.

Then I rise. I feel it in my heels when I come back up. I'm standing my ground, and then down again, up again, feeling the weight trying to force me into the fetal position, but I come back up every time, stand like a man, because I'm the one in control. I'm the one who can handle all the weight, stop the earth from dragging me down to its core.

Yeah, I make it sound all grandiose and melodramatic— blame it on living so long in the dumpy yet pretentious East *Vill-ahge*—but life can try to break you in so many different ways, but we still stand, and for as long as we can. I love pressing against that weight, I like keeping it balanced on my shoulders. I love letting it know who's boss.

I can't help but hear "Impressive. Wish I could squat that much." I open my eyes, look in the mirror. Standing behind me is one of the regulars, a guy who's been coming here for years, since before Francesco got sick. His name's Darius, I think.

Probably not his real name: He's an actor who gets by waiting tables, unlike all the other waiters in this city who make ends meet by acting. He's black, so all he gets cast in is crowd scenes.

I'm not done, but I set the barbell back on the rack.

"Hi, Darius."

"Davis."

Can't even get his fake name right. "Sorry."

He reaches up, puts a hand on my shoulder. "Not to worry. Here's how to remember: Bette Davis, hold the Bette."

That's stupid. I smile, nod.

He's short and overbuilt, in a nipple-exposing tank top, and his spandex shorts mold his pipeline for the basket shoppers. We used to naked-talk in the locker room, his preferred topic *Dreamgirls*, mine, anything-else-at-all. We flirted, but it was gay courtly love. We both had partners we were devoted to, and went home to, after all the double entendres and innuendos had run their course. Over the past few years, I've just nodded at the regulars, always plugged into my Walkman, even in the locker room, where I no longer shower, just change my clothes, making sure my shirts are long enough to cover me up as I put on my pants. On my way out I don't pat any naked shoulders, don't tell anyone I'll catch him later as I slap him on the ass.

Davis says, "You always seem to be on a mission. No chitchat. Straight in, straight out, if you'll pardon the expression."

I wipe my forehead. "Guess I'm just all business these days."

"You know what they say—all work and no play."

"Speaking of no play, how's the acting?" I can do bitchy when cornered.

He laughs. "Going about as well as my pickup lines."

I relax a little.

"Did you know that I'm back on the market for a very limited time?"

"I did not."

"Took me months to get over him. But good news for you—seeing you here tonight reminded me that I've always been a little sweet on you. So I was thinking, 'Wouldn't it be nice if Kevin and I went somewhere fabulous to eat, maybe followed by a bit of dancing?' "

I fold my arms across my chest. "I'm not doing the dating thing."

He looks at me seriously. He isn't hurt or embarrassed. He knows Francesco's been dead for what in the world of the gay plague seems like a very long time. So many of us die every month. Two years ago might as well be two hundred years ago, and there's only so much time available to mourn one person before it's time to mourn the next. He says, "Hey, completely understand. What do you say to the coffee-with-a-friend thing?"

I consider it, but what would we talk about? What would I say? "Sorry."

He smiles. Before he heads over to the pec deck, he touches my arm, says, "If you ever change your mind, let me know. No expectations, no pressure. Just someone to listen."

I nod.

There's a man at the rack next to mine in a full sweat suit, hood up, who I haven't seen here before. He's thin—thin like he might have it—and he balances the bar—with twenty-five-pound weights—asymmetrically, and too high on his back, nearly on his neck. His setup isn't tight, and as he descends, his heels come up off the floor, his knees push inward. He struggles to get back up.

He's going to screw up his back.

I lift the bar off his shoulders, and he holds on to the rack, gasping, and straightens himself out. When I can clearly see his face, it's narrow, and I think there's makeup, but maybe not. The lighting is cocktail-dim in this place. Maybe he doesn't have it, maybe he isn't even gay. Maybe he's just like the guy in the Charles Atlas ads on the back of my old comic books. Maybe he's sick and tired of being a scarecrow and wants to be the hero of the beach.

He says, embarrassed, "Thanks. Nearly broke my neck."

"It just takes practice," I tell him. "Let's try one together."

It's been a couple weeks since Dead Eddie's funeral, so Live Eddie called and asked me to meet him for a meal, or what he called an "AIDS widows night out," which in New York is every night of the week. We planned to meet at our regular café on St. Marks Place at nine, but it's well past that and, so far, no Live Eddie. I haven't ordered anything, so the waiter's trying to give me the bum's rush when Live Eddie finally shows up.

"You gonna order food now?" the waiter, a kid with a buzz cut, pierced nose, and acne, asks me.

I give him my alpha-male look. "When we're ready."

"Two burgers, fries, and waters," Live Eddie tells him in his Georgia accent as he unwraps his black-and-white checkerboard *shemagh*—big enough to be a tablecloth—from around his thin neck. He removes the overcoat layer next, the giant sweater layer, like he's the incredible shrinking man, right down to the gray sweatshirt, which stays on. Peeking out around the neckline is a long-sleeved thermal.

The kid huffs off as Live Eddie arranges his *shemagh*, overcoat, and giant sweater on the chair across the small table from me. He looks better, or maybe it's just the makeup he wears to cover the dark circles he usually has under his eyes. His face has that slenderness you see all over the Village, East and West, and he's still not cutting his sandy hair, which he's parted down the middle. With his scruffy beard and mustache, he looks like a scrawny, old-before-his-time Jesus, not that Jesus ever had much meat on his bones, at least the Catholic ones that Aunt Nora has nailed to their crosses.

I remember the first time I saw Live Eddie. He was wearing rugby shorts. "Looking good," I tell him as he sits.

He mutters, "No, I'm not," before adding, "These chairs are murder on my ass."

"We can go somewhere else."

"No need." He gets up, folds his overcoat on the seat, tops it off with the giant sweater, and sits on them like they're a pile of pillows. He surveys the café from his perch. "I like this—wish I was taller in real life. And you're having my burger and fries, you eat like a fullback." A rugby fullback, not a football full-back. Live Eddie was a prized player in the gay league. You should've seen his thighs back in the day. He could trap a man between them for entire weekends and they'd beg for more.

"Don't want to eat or can't eat?"

"It'll just make me *plotz*. I called to cancel, but I guess you'd already left."

"Sorry. Seriously, we can reschedule."

He doesn't say, yes, that would be a good idea, or thank me for offering the option. He, instead, just smiles sadly and looks at me, wondering, I guess, what it's like to not know one way or the other. Around us gossip, flirtation, and pretentiousness run through the café like old wiring, and the other diners' intense little conversations taste like espresso spiked with Wild Turkey. Finally he says, "I'll watch you eat."

"That doesn't sound like much fun."

He smirks. "It'll be like watching porn. Greasy hamburgers that stay down are like Jeff Stryker telling me to *tighten that ass*. Neither are going to happen, but a girl can dream." The waiter brings us water, but just barely. "Besides, it's my treat. I wanted to thank you for coming to my rescue at Eddie's funeral. Wasn't exactly my proudest moment."

I frown. "Seriously? 'Cause I was really proud of you."

"You're getting radical in your old age."

"I'm twenty-eight."

"Like I said. Gonna join ACT UP next? Shut down Wall Street?"

When the waiter returns, he drops two plates on the table with a martyr's fuck-the-tip clatter. Live Eddie takes a quick sniff before he pushes his plate in front of me. "'*Eat*, Papa, *eat*,'" he says earnestly. "'The children want a fat Santa Claus.'"

I really enjoy the meal(s), knowing Live Eddie's picking up the tab; ever since Francesco died, money's . . . I take a giant bite of free burger. My eyes roll back in my head: This is sex now.

Live Eddie says, "You're looking quite tasty yourself this evening in that tight T-shirt. Still living at the gym, I see."

I chew, swallow. "I need it after a day at Fair and Unbiased. My brain may be dead, but my body isn't. And it helps with the depression. You should come back."

He laughs. "You're kidding, right? Some days I can't lift a fork."

"I was being serious earlier—you're looking healthier."

"Don't jinx me."

"Sorry."

He watches me eat as a group a few tables down sing "Happy Birthday" sardonically. Then he says, "Isn't your birthday soon?"

"Last Tuesday."

"Shit!"

"It's okay. Laurie and Toshiro invited me out, but celebrating birthdays . . . I dunno. I went to the gym, opened a bottle of wine, and watched *Thirtysomething*."

He reaches over, squeezes a bicep, something he's always done. "Can't stand that show. They get to be in their thirties, and all they can do is whine about it. Still, Michael's fuckable. You should've called me. No, wait, I should've remembered. I'm sorry."

I dab a couple fries in ketchup. "Don't sweat it."

He holds a water glass up to his lips, but changes his mind.

"Twenty-eight years old. On the giant slide down to the big three-oh."

I nod. Thirty used to sound old. Now it sounds prehistoric.

"Still, lots of time left, yeah?"

I shrug, start in on the next burger.

He asks again, "Lots of time, yes?"

I wipe a lip; I put too much ketchup on this one.

He looks at me seriously. "Kevin, do me a personal favor and get tested. I think you need to know. I'll go with you for the test. I'll be there with you for the results. They say the Western blot's a lot more accurate." A pause. "And if you're negative, you need to start making some plans."

If I'm NEGATIVE? "If I'm *negative*, I need to start making plans? What's that supposed to mean?"

He decides he's thirsty after all, so I listen to the jumble of conversations around us as he takes careful, precise sip after careful, precise sip of his water. There's talk of John Sex and Howard Beach. Drag queens debate who can pass as an RG (real girl).

At last, Live Eddie puts his glass down, says, "Well, that was stupid. Now I'll be going to the bathroom all night."

"Answer my question," I say before another huge bite.

He winks, taps my nose with a finger, says, "*Beep!*" Then again: "*Beep-Beep!*"

"Answer my question," I repeat, mouth full.

He pulls his long hair behind his head. It's so thin now, as if each strand's anorexic, like Karen Carpenter on her last holiday special. "If you're negative, you should go back to school, get a degree in something useful. It's never too late. Without Frankie . . ."

He doesn't finish the thought.

I know what he's trying not to say, but I make him say it, anyway. " 'Without Frankie,' what?"

"Nothing." He reaches over to beep me on my nose again, but I grab his finger.

"Ouch! Jesus, don't bend it."

I let go. " 'Without Frankie,' what?"

He folds his bony arms over his bony chest. "Without Frankie . . . I worry you'll end up broke. And to be honest with you, a raging alcoholic."

As the Minnesota Lutherans say when they're upset: *interesting*. If they're really pissed, they'll add, *different*.

Even though we lived in a dump in a neighborhood that's a dump (no, it's not *gritty* and *real*, it's a fucking dump), Francesco was the one who was good with money. He was in demand for his illustrations, and freelanced with Marvel and DC and Charlton. He worked late nights under a single lamp clamped on his drawing table, penciling books as I slept, titles like *The Legion of Super-Heroes* (a favorite thanks to Shadow Kid's revealing costume) and *Swamp Thing* (not a favorite because of the hot-girl-loves-tortured-monster trope [monster being a stand-in for nerdy, frustrated straight boys everywhere]). His parents also liked to help him out with money: His father was a South-Philly-made-good Italian who was, as his mother put it, *comfortable*. My parents? That's a story for another day.

I try to keep an even tone, but I know I sound pissed. "I'm a big boy. I can take care of myself."

He surrenders, changes the subject: "My parents want me to move back to Atlanna now that Eddie's gone."

"Will you?"

"Oh, hell no. I mean, you're here, and Laurie and Toshiro are here, and . . ." He stops. Everyone else is dead. He sighs. "Maybe your parents," but then he stops himself, remembers my mom's Ford Galaxy hit the ice and fell into the Upper Mississippi when I was still in high school, and that my dad disappeared going on ten years now.

The rest of the dinner's quiet, but I eat so fast that it really doesn't matter; besides, Live Eddie spends most of it in the bathroom.

When we get outside, Live Eddie's bundled up against the cold, for me a New York winter just means a navy surplus deck jacket and a wool cap. We walk beneath tenements, five stories high, past the homeless and the yuppies, the avant-garde East *Vill-ahgers* and the peddlers with their blankets laid out on the sidewalk, covered with old magazines like *Honcho* and *National Geographic*, along with the hot bikes and stolen boom boxes they sell.

"Night's young," I say. "Wanna go to the Pyramid?" It's a club on Avenue A, where Francesco took me to dance all night to DJ Ivan Ivan as we basted in our own sweat.

Live Eddie puts his hand on my back as he looks up at me and says, "Really? You want to go clubbing?" He shakes his head, but then he asks, "Is Lowlife playing?" But before I can answer, he shakes his head again. "I have to go home. Come with me and spend the night."

I stop and look at him. It's cold enough that I can see my breath. "What're you doing?"

Live Eddie shakes his head. "It's *me*, Kevin. Jesus. I just miss human contact, don't you? I just want to hold on to you. I want you to hold on to me. We used to cuddle all the time before Eddie and Frankie, remember? If that's too weird for you now, I suppose I get it. Not really, though."

Apart from a hug here and there, I haven't held anything but a stack of pillows for going on two years. "Yeah. I mean, sure, I'll come over—not 'yeah, it's too weird.' "

A weathered white man dressed in rags and blankets wanders over, his creased and tattered cardboard sign telling us VIETNAM VETERAN ANY AMOUNT HELPS GOD BLESS. We ignore him, so he shuffles on.

Live Eddie smiles at me. "Thanks." He blows on his hands

despite the gloves. "I've seen faggots do some stupid shit when they're lonely. I swore to Eddie that I wouldn't do stupid shit after he was gone. No grief sex." He drops the smile as he adds: "And no self-medicating."

I nod like he's talking about anyone else but me.

He says, "Maybe holding on to each other's the healthiest thing we can do."

Live Eddie lives in Chelsea, in a place we used to call—back in our urbane days—*"le pied-à-terre des les Eddies."* During the cab ride (his treat), he told me he doesn't like living in the neighborhood anymore: He's sick of the buff and overstyled Chelsea boys who display themselves on the streets, and his frail frame, beard, and long hair mark him as an outcast or a dissident or an untouchable or maybe all three. Rewind a little, and he *was* that Chelsea boy he now finds so annoying. But the idea of moving is too overwhelming: He'd have to decide what to do with all of Dead Eddie's things, which remain precisely where they've always been, like he might walk through the door at any moment. Fortunately, Live Eddie can make the rent on his own, at least for the time being. That's lucky because, unbelievably, Dead Eddie never took care of the will he said he would take care of, so he died intestate, meaning everything of Dead Eddie's belongs to his parents, including his checking and savings accounts. Live Eddie might get a roommate for company if nothing else, and he floated the idea of me moving in, but I worry what would happen to Francesco's murals if I did. So, for now, he's on his own. It's more challenging than he thought. He doesn't know what to do with himself.

That makes two of us.

It's nice to be in a real bed with fresh flannel sheets and pillowcases that aren't stained. I'm in Dead Eddie's oversized candy-striped nightshirt, which sounds creepy but isn't. Yeah, Live Eddie hangs on to me tight, but he's not pretending I'm somebody else, and his hands don't wander like in the old days when we'd get carried away. He said he needs to hear a human heart beating and feel the warmth of living flesh again. It's like therapy, he tells me; he has what he calls "nighttime anxiety": When he does finally fall asleep, he wakes up with a jolt and obsesses over the fact that Dead Eddie really is gone forever, that he'll never see him again, or hear his voice again, even though he's still on the answering machine (*that* is creepy).

How we hold each other is not anything like sex: sex and death are so much the same in our minds that the idea of sperm, even wrapped up tight in latex, feels like long-hauling hazardous waste. Like one drop of the stuff could burn a hole straight through to China.

We hear the traffic along West Twenty-fifth, and overhead, someone running the tap.

He puts his hand back on my chest as he says, "This is nice. You know how they swaddle babies so they won't cry, so they think they're still in their mothers' wombs? This is the grown-up version."

"It's nice." And like old times, before Dead Eddie, before Francesco, before AIDS.

"I think what I miss most is talking to Eddie at the end of the day, with all the lights out. We never really talked about anything profound. It was just our little ritual. Don't freak out, but sometimes I play the answering machine just to hear his voice."

"I thought so. It's kinda strange to hear his voice when I leave a message."

"No, it isn't." He shifts a bit, asks, "Did you and Frankie have late-night talks in bed?"

"First year, all the time. After that, he'd work all night cranking out consistent pages. Then, when he got sick, well, you know, sleeping was an ordeal. His lungs."

Live Eddie strokes my shoulder. "Eddie was terrified he'd never wake up."

"All Frankie wanted was one good night's sleep. He couldn't get comfortable. His hips and legs were in so much pain."

Live Eddie reaches up, pets my hair. "The strangest thing for me was our last night together. There wasn't much left to say. Actually, there wasn't much he could say. It was just after three in the morning. I called his doc and told her that Eddie stopped breathing. I asked what I should do for that. It seemed like just one more symptom to treat, you know? He gets something new, you try something new. You give him Bactrim. Dextran sulfate. AL721. You get a blood transfusion. You try acupuncture. AZT. Meditation. You make him eat some macrobiotic crap he can't stand. But she said she was very sorry, that it was all over, and there was nothing left to do except call the undertaker."

He stops petting me, rubs his eyes. "You know, that just made no sense to me, maybe 'cause I hadn't slept in days. I thought, 'There's always been something else to try, something new to give him, even if it's just some homemade crap that everyone's talking about. There was always something I could do for him.'

"You remember what it was like. Eddie was my other job. I'd come home from work, and he was my second shift. Meals, drugs, laundry, diapers, IV, sponge bath, teeth, shave. The volunteers told me I was doing too much, that it wasn't good for my own health, but I didn't care. After he went blind, I'd read to him. His favorite was *The Boys on the Rock*, I must've read it to him half-a-dozen times. And now I come home from work and I just sit and stare. There's so much empty time now. I watch too much TV. I watch *Dolly*. I watch *Kate and Allie*. Did you know that *My Two Dads* isn't about what you'd think it's about?

"I blame myself a lot. The hardest thing is thinking he died because I didn't love him enough."

I cringe.

He says, "Sorry."

We lie there for a while, and when he's quiet, when I close my eyes, I can pretend it's Francesco next to me.

But then he ruins it when he says, "What was the hardest part for you?"

"That's morbid."

"No, it isn't. I need to talk about this stuff, and who better to talk to about it with? It helps. It makes me feel like I'm not going through this alone."

"You could go to a support group."

He pulls away. "I could, but you were one of the first gay friends I made when I came out. Remember when we would talk about anything?" He sighs, puts an arm back around me. "Sorry. Forget it. It was selfish of me. You cope your way, I'll cope mine."

That stings. My way of coping . . . What the hell? I kiss Live Eddie on the top of his head. "The hardest part for me wasn't his diagnosis, or even how scared I was at first. And I don't mean scared for him. I was scared for me. I still feel so guilty about that. And it's weird to say, but AIDS could be . . . really tedious. For both of us. Day after day, nothing changing, every day just a little bit worse or maybe a little bit better.

"But the hardest part was when we drove away from his plot.

"We just left him there, all by himself."

I choke.

And then in a voice that sounds like a sheep's baas, I tell Live Eddie, "He never would have done that to me. He never would've left me alone."

Can't breathe.

Inhale. Hold.

It'll pass, always does.

Exhale. Slowly.

Inhale. Hold.

It'll pass, always does.

Exhale. Slowly.

Live Eddie says, "Shhhh. It's okay. It's going to be okay."

No, it really isn't.

Who wants to sing it with me?

Oooooh, the blue copy goes in the donor file, and the yellow copy goes in the chron file! HEY!

And that nasty old pink copy, the one sitting right there on my desk like it owns the place? Well—and stop me if you've heard this one before—the pink copy goes in . . . wait for it, wait for it . . . the campaign file!

Nah, I ain't fucking with youse! Hand to god, the mother-fucking campaign file!

Parallel Universe 143: I win the New York Lotto, hire an ar-sonist, and burn Fair and Unbiased to the ground.

Permit me to explain: Francesco loved *Star Trek* and his favorite episode was "Mirror, Mirror," where Kirk, McCoy, Uhura, and Scotty beam into a parallel universe, and Kirk wore a sleeveless captain's shirt with a plunging neckline. In that universe the Federation of United Planets was an evil em-pire, and Spock had a goatee that made him look like a regular at the Mineshaft.

But now that I think about it, that was his second favorite episode. His actual favorite was "The Empath," where Kirk swings shirtless from chains while some woman named Gem makes all his ouchies go away.

No, scratch that. It was "Who Mourns for Adonais?"

Anyway.

He made up a game based on "Mirror, Mirror." He'd say Parallel Universe Number 4. And I'd have to tell him how that universe was different from ours. Sometimes there were small differences, like there never was a Poppin' Fresh Pies in Parallel

Universe 22, or there was a Teddy Boy dress code in Parallel Universe 14. Other times there were big differences, like Parallel Universe 3, where 90 percent of people were gay and 10 percent were straight. It was a stand-up universe, one we wanted to live in. There was a Mr. America pageant, where the swimsuit competition *was* the talent competition and every contestant played his instrument. The only plague in Parallel Universe 3 was lesbian bed death.

"Mr. Doyle."

Goddamnit.

He snuck up on me.

Again.

But then, I'm pretty easy to sneak up on these days, because my head's always somewhere else. Aunt Nora calls it being "a million miles away." I wish I were a million miles away. No, wait, probably not. I'd be floating lifeless in the vacuum of space. Then, again . . .

"Mr. Doyle."

Oh yeah. Still here. Only two people in my entire life have ever called me Mr. Doyle. The first was my high-school English teacher, and he only did it because he hated my *willful ignorance*. The other's Merritt Hastings, president of Fair and Unbiased, who picked up the habit of last-names-only at Phillips Exeter Academy, a hoity-toity boarding school whose alumni, he told me when I was first hired, include Franklin Pierce, fourteenth president of the United States, and the guy who wrote *Jaws*. Merritt's a staple on news programs, where he points his finger a lot at public interest advocates, telling them they're un-American.

"Merritt," I say, followed by "Merritt."

Merritt, aka Merritt the Wherret. "Wherret" means a slap of the face. His secretary came up with it after she found a rhyming dictionary on the subway. It's not really funny, though, because you have to explain it. It's like Merritt's name; it feels like you're always hearing it for the first time, and you're not quite sure what it's supposed to mean.

"Have you been drinking?"

Yes. "No."

"Perhaps at lunch?"

Perhaps at yesterday's lunch, but perhaps not at today's. "No."

Merritt the Wherret sniffs the air. "I smell wine."

Wine?

Wine's not *drinking*; VODKA is drinking. If you count wine, which you really shouldn't, then, yes, I had a little hair of the dog for breakfast, and it was a big old hairy dog, shedding everywhere. But it was either that or call in sick to work again, and who needs the gossip, like at the last job: *Out sick again? He must have it. I'm not working with him. Me either.*

"Well," I say, "I am wearing a new cologne. It's called Malagousia."

Merritt the Wherret tilts his head like a dog hearing its name. "Malagousia is a white wine from the Evia region of Greece. I sampled it during a Mediterranean cruise. Reminded me of Gewürztraminer."

Of course it did.

Should've known; bluebloods love their wines. And even though Francesco was a Jewlic, not a blue blood, he did hitch-hike through Europe the summer before we met, and sampled the local specialties. Malagousia was a favorite. I tell Merritt the Wherret: "Oh."

He's not really a bad guy; he's just a fifty-year-old boy who has never lived in the real world. He sticks his hands in the pockets of his wool suit, black with almost invisible white stripes. He has an odor about him, too, but it's Park Avenue. He says, "Are you drunk right now?"

Wow, he has *no* idea what drunk is. "No."

M the W says, "Drinking on the job is a serious issue" (except for Fair and Unbiased's luncheons), and he means it (except for the luncheons). Jobs are serious things to MtW. He has to work because his grandfather's 50-million-dollar fortune was divided four ways, and then two more before it finally made its way to him. He really needs this job so his inheritance can grow to a comfortable amount. Nothing ostentatious, just comfortable. One simply does not touch one's principal.

Before he walks away, he says, "Meet me in my office at five."

Five.

Quitting time.

Or firing time.

And not for the first time.

At 5:15 p.m. and fourteen seconds, I call Laurie at her office, a legal advocacy group for "youthful offenders," which makes it sound like they're just young at heart. Offenders ages sixteen to eighteen are tried as adults according to New York criminal law. As Laurie tells it, their sentences are determined by their zip codes. She's so frustrated by the system she may have to go to law school herself.

"What?" she grunts. She's having a bad day. So am I, but that's nothing new.

"I think I was fired."

A pause. "You think? You don't know?"

"Merritt the Wherret just told me I was always looking 'defeated.' That's the word he used, 'defeated.' He said it was time for me to make a change for my own good. He said life's too short to be unhappy. Maybe he thinks I have it. Then again, probably not, because he shook my hand and wished me good luck."

"Why do you not understand that you were fired?"

"But he didn't say I was fired."

"Maybe he's figured out you're gay and he's being cautious. The city's antidiscrimination law isn't even two years old. No one's sure what the usual sentence for firing gays will be. He could get fined five hundred bucks or he could spend a year in jail. Maybe both."

"Should I sue?"

"Ohmigod, no."

"Just for the go-away money?"

"God, no."

"But you always call Fair and Unbiased 'evil incarnate.' "

"And the good news is you literally did absolutely nothing at your job."

"I'm way behind on my rent."

The here-we-go-again silence on the other end.

But now, this: "Dinner, my treat. Tosh needs to catch up on his *Daredevil* pencils, so he can't come. I swear to God, that's all he does anymore, twelve hours a day, every day, hunched over his drafting table. He's going to ruin his spine."

Francesco introduced Toshiro to Laurie one night when she stopped by our apartment to tell me once again how all men were pigs—not gay men, of course (as though we weren't men at all)—and to cry on my shoulder. But she scrapped her plans once she saw Toshiro. She had that awestruck look on her face, like when she showed me one of her favorite paintings, *Still Life with Gingerpot I*, at the Guggenheim, a museum that would be an excellent place to skateboard. I hate to admit it, but at the time I thought, *Poor sad cow, he's sooo out of your league.* Strands of his long black hair had fallen over one eye, and a hand rested on his shoulder blade, just under his elegant neck, as he and Francesco critiqued each other's portfolios for consistency.

Francesco said editors love consistency. His work motto: "Crank out consistent pages." Comic book artists get paid by the page. It's a good way to go broke, but Francesco was a hard worker, and good with his money, except when he would give too much away to beggars on the street.

I ask her, "Where you wanna eat?"

She says, "Somewhere cheap near me. And I have to say, for a guy who just got fired, you don't sound panicked. So that's a silver lining, at least."

No, the panics only happened every Monday morning when I sat down at this desk and tried to face another bottomless week.

We're at a deli recommended for its giant portions, and not too far from Laurie's office in midtown. She slips a small paper napkin in the collar of her giant wool sweater as we divvy up a veggie omelet and sweet potato knishes. Our waitress is not well pleased. Yeah, they serve breakfast 24-7, but not to share. She left the check with the plates and I know we'll never see her again.

I say to Laurie, "Her name tag said Wanda. Who's named Wanda?"

Laurie says, "She is. Probably Polish. Did you notice anything else about her?"

"Like what?"

"She has a job."

Apart from the sound of dishes, footsteps, and the occasional cough, the deli's pretty quiet, filled with lone diners who don't know how or don't feel like cooking dinner for themselves. A fat man across the aisle smokes a cigarette as he reads the *Daily News*. The headline is DEADLY NEW AIDS VIRUS: *First Such Case in U.S. Found in Jersey.*

Of course it was Jersey.

I stick a fork in a knish, a little annoyed with Laurie. "You're supposed to be supportive."

"I am. I called Tosh to let him know you'll be crashing on our couch for a couple months."

"I'm not homeless."

"Not yet."

"There are plenty of squats in my neighborhood." I have to make sure whoever gets Francesco's apartment doesn't paint over his murals. I need to keep watch over them.

"Oh yeah. No water if the city shuts off the pipes. No heat until you're burned out. Who're you going to share with? I read *The Good Terrorist*. Those places are full of addicts, schizophrenics, faux revolutionaries, and anarchist-posers."

"They're not all like that. Lots are artists."

"Ugh," she says, grimacing. "The *worst*. Frontline gentrifiers. If you think you can't afford your place now, just wait. There'll be a Gap on St. Marks Place before you know it. Then the yuppies will take over the entire East Village."

"Jeez, is there anyone you actually do like?"

"I *love* you. And Tosh. And Sarah"—my half sister and her cousin (it's a long story)—"and I loved Frankie. I'm very fond of Eddie One and was very fond of Eddie Two." (How we used to differentiate the Eddies, inspired by Dr. Seuss's Thing 1 and Thing 2.) "That's everyone I can think of."

"That's not a whole lot of people."

She salts her half of the omelet some more. "It's enough."

Maybe that's all the people she has room for. Sometimes I have to remind myself that Laurie had a tough start in life. Before me, before New York, Sarah, Francesco, and Toshiro, she had lost both parents, only loved books, *Little House on the Prairie*, and, for most of our senior year of high school, Jesus Christ, her personal Lord and Savior.

In the booth behind Laurie, a young man sits by himself, the collar up on his black overcoat, reading a paperback copy of *The Blue Star* and listening to his Walkman. Every now and then he looks up at me with an open face and a shy grin, meaning he's new in town. He's cute in a Ferris Bueller kind of way. Not so much sexy as adorable. Probably bullied in high school for being a skinny kid with a sweet face.

I hope he's negative.

I hope sex won't kill him.

More than anything else, though, I hope he finds someone healthy to share the rest of his life with. Maybe an artist, like Francesco, who'll be discovered and hit it big. They'll live in a giant loft in SoHo and eat at Chanterelle every night of the week except for when they hop the Concorde for a Paris getaway.

"Are you even listening to me?"

"What?"

Laurie looks behind her, sees Ferris Bueller, and smiles for once. She tells me, "Introduce yourself."

"What? No!"

She looks behind her again, says to the guy, "Would you care to join us?"

Fuck.

He takes off his earphones, smiles. "Love to, thanks. I hate eating alone." He picks up his hot pastrami and coffee before he slides into our booth next to Laurie and directly opposite me. Our knees touch under the table.

Laurie tells him she's Laurie and that I'm Kevin and he says in a soft voice that he's Pete. He just moved here from Kansas City for a job in publishing. He didn't feel like going to his apartment to eat, he shares it with five other editorial assistants he doesn't really know, and they live like pigs, seriously, you should see the place, you wouldn't believe it.

I hope he doesn't do stupid shit when he's lonely.

Laurie does her best to show him how much we all have in common: *Look, Midwesterners in the big city!*

It was overwhelming for Kevin, too, when he first moved here. He just showed up at the tiny place I sublet with three other girls. Just out of the blue! Remember that night, Kevin? It was fall, but it felt like summer, and there you were with your backpack and ten bucks to your name, if that! I thought you'd last a week in New York, but look at you now!

And what do you do now, Kevin? Pete asks with a kind smile.

I grieve.

Oh. I'm sorry.

We sit and eat.

Before he leaves, Pete rips off a piece of the check, writes down his work phone number and the apartment phone number, and tells me to call him if I ever need someone to talk to.

Nighttime in Alphabet City. Laurie and I stood outside the deli, and she scolded me for how rude I was to Pete—"We invited him to sit with us, after all"—but she invited him, I didn't, and she had no right. Then she said it's been almost two years— "Two years!"—since Frankie died and I needed to stop wallowing in self-pity and start living my goddamn life, so I told her that when Toshiro . . .

But she stormed off as I was in midsentence. Just in case I took deep breaths in, held them, and exhaled slowly. I took the subway to Christopher Street and sat in Sheridan Square, a small, unimpressive triangle with a few benches, but the heart of gay New York, even if that heart's pounding like a very old man who's trying not to keel over. This was the place I would come to look at the gay boys when I first moved to New York, watching them timidly at first, and then staring boldly. It was where I first met Live Eddie, even more frightened than I was. He had layered hair that covered his ears and nearly his eyes, but what had caught my attention was his legs in rugby shorts.

Anyway.

I sat in Sheridan Square, thinking I should make a plan, any plan, but all I did was watch men, of course, some in groups, others in pairs, some with canes or in wheelchairs, and then the ones like me, alone. I stared at the ones who looked healthy, wondering who was positive and who was negative, who would live and who would die, because maybe, just maybe, we all went a little crazy when we moved to New York and came out of our closets like freight trains, like we were making up for lost time, those lonely years of thinking you'd die of shame if anyone found out you were gay.

And now it all seems like a giant, fucking, cosmic *I told you so.*

It can be inside you for years, and if you look back and do the math—and we all have—some of us have long odds, others short, and some of us are sure things. Maybe that disappointing sex you had with what's-his-face back in 1980 turns out to be even worse than you thought. Maybe you even got it your very bashful first time when you were afraid you weren't doing it right—I mean, they're still not 100 percent on how you get it— so you lay awake all night, every night, wondering if you have it. You'll never know for sure until the spot appears or lungs congest or the sheets are soaked. Sure, you can get tested, but what's the point? If you're positive, you just live with the knowledge, pop some AZT if you can actually afford it, and watch the clock until AIDS kills you.

I live not knowing. But I act like I have it, like everyone has it, because maybe we all do. It's how we live now; it's how we die now.

So I didn't make any plans at the square. I just watched the men, like I did when I was nineteen. And any one of the men who walked past me so confidently, or so absentmindedly, might need a cane next week, a walker the week after that, a wheelchair the week after that, a coffin the week after that.

I walked back to Avenue B. I like to walk in New York. It's sensory overload, it takes my mind off things. So I walk.

Dad had this saying: "It's a privilege, not a right." Getting

Rex, our dog, was a privilege, not a right. Learning to drive was a privilege, not a right. Same with the license. And now, in New York, walking is now a privilege, not a right. Not everyone gets to walk anymore. Not everyone gets to get out of bed anymore.

It was a privilege to walk the half hour back to Francesco's apartment. But even having this privilege—to walk unassisted, or at all—didn't stop me from picking up a couple bottles of vodka on the way home.

I look at it this way: Locking myself in at night and twisting the cap off a handle of Popov won't get me infected. Safety first.

The first swallow burns.

I look at our weather-beaten dresser that we pulled out of a Dumpster. On it sit the *Risky Business* sunglasses, alongside my old Charlie Brown doll, with his orange baseball cap that Mom gave me when I was six.

The doll was Mom's little act of rebellion. When I had put dolls on my Christmas List—Charlie Brown, along with Captain Action (and his Batman costume)—Dad shook his head: Boys don't play with dolls. Mom said, It's not a Barbie. But Dad just repeated himself: Boys don't play with dolls. When I glumly opened my gifts Christmas morning (Erector Set, space walker shoes, a rosary from Aunt Nora), I gasped as I ripped the green-and-red wrapping paper off Charlie Brown. I looked up at Mom, my mouth opened wide. Dad didn't say anything, but Mom said, Merry Christmas, my own wee *buachaill*.

Her own little boy.

I take a long drink, put the sunglasses on in the dim light of the tiny apartment, lift the handle again, toast the men in the murals. Right over there, on that sagging futon, Francesco wore these very glasses night and day his final weeks, convinced that as his face sank into his skull, his eyes looked freakishly huge, like cartoon eyes, Tweety Bird's or Dondi's. They came off only when he shivered too violently to keep them on, or when he slept on his side, when he slept at all.

He wouldn't take them off, not even when his parents came up from Philly, or his artsy friends came by, or Toshiro or the Eddies or Laurie stopped in with some little interesting gift for him. He thought his giant eyes would scare them. But no matter how unnerved people were when they first walked through the door and saw an emaciated man in Ray-Bans, he could always put them at ease.

That last night he didn't wear them. Toshiro offered to put them on his face for him, but he said no. He needed to see the time he had left as best he could.

But for the visitors in the months before his death, he always had a joke at his own expense, like, *I took waaaay too many Dexatrims* or *This Halloween I'm going to scare the shit out of the kids!* Even with the blood tests to find out if some bacteria other than tuberculosis was causing the fevers, he'd just tell the person drawing blood to be sure to leave him enough to get home.

One of Francesco's East *Vill-ahge* friends, who always wore her black leather miniskirt, black stockings, and black beret like a uniform, thought she was being helpful by bringing him Louise Hay tapes, the heal-yourself guru, along with a VCR and a video of her speaking to a West Hollywood auditorium full of desperate gay men with AIDS.

Of course it's California, Francesco said.

This was a friend who hadn't seen him since he'd been diagnosed. AIDS changed Francesco, how could it not? He seethed. He didn't need some charlatan telling him to love himself. (Yes—"charlatan"—he built my vocabulary in so many ways, first by translating Gay into English for me, then giving me books to read, and then by insisting I actually read them.) *No-*

body, he said, *and I mean NOBODY, loves Francesco Conti more than Francesco Conti!*

Another swig from the handle. *I do.*

He told me, *Don't make me sad. I'm sad too much. I'm sad you have to go through this.*

A longer swallow. I still can't bear the thought of him sad. It kills me.

More Popov.

We watched the video together, Francesco talking back to the TV mostly, but to me, he said, *When I die, I hope you don't think it was because I had a bad attitude or that deep down it was what I really wanted. I mean, fuck that shit.*

The videotape ended with the gay men with AIDS singing along with Louise Hay. It broke my heart, watching those men sing as best they could. But Francesco only got angrier. He made up his own lyrics:

> *"Stupid Faggot am I*
> *My fault if I die*
> *Just did not try."*

I told him he was funny at the time, but I thought he was kinda heartless. He always had a wicked sense of humor, but until AIDS, it had never been at anyone else's expense. He said a lot of things he didn't mean when he was in pain, frustrated, helpless, afraid. I couldn't do anything to protect him from what was happening to his body and his mind. And we were becoming at odds—I wanted to keep him safe and comfortable; he wanted his independence and autonomy—over his own body, over his own life. His world had been reduced to the apartment, waiting rooms, hospital rooms.

Oh, waiter. More Popov, po-please.

I feel warm. Is it hot in here, or am I just having intermittent fevers?

*   *   *

Miss Ross had the sweetest hangover, but mine's a mother-fucker and a half. But, unlike AIDS, there's a cure for this, and I want it.

I want it. Just twist open the cap.

"I knew it, I just knew it! Call 911. Kevin, wake up. Wake up, Kevin. Kevin, goddamnit!"

Chapter 2

FEBRUARY 1988: THERE ARE NO GAY REPLICANTS

There's an IV drip in my arm when I wake up. I know what this means from the last time I had an IV drip in my arm when I woke up—they're rehydrating me. Probably glucose and vitamins.

My head. My body. It isn't a hangover, that's not the right word for it. I feel the kind of drunk you feel when the buzz is fading away. And my stomach and throat are shattered glass.

I try to raise my hands to rub my eyes, but I can't. I'm in restraints. Terrifying.

But not half as terrifying as who's standing over me.

Laurie Lindstrom.

Staring down at me. Looking like she's wearing eye black like football players do.

She says, "So here we are . . . *again*."

I watch the ceiling.

"You know, I knew it, I just knew it. I knew the second I left you outside the deli that you'd use our fight as an excuse to drink yourself sick. But this? Kevin, you nearly drank yourself *dead*. Two days you didn't pick up the phone. Do you know you were blue when we found you? Do you know if you hadn't passed out on your side, you would have drowned in your own vomit?"

I gasp, it hurts to talk: "Why am I strapped to the bed?"

"You don't like having an IV put in."

Fuck a duck. This is so much worse than last time, and last time was god-awful.

She takes a seat as Toshiro appears in the doorway with two to-go cups of coffee. He's in his uniform: long black sweater, black jeans, black scarf down to his thighs, and platform Doc Martens. His long hair is slicked back, and his striking face is haggard. He hands Laurie a cup, says to me, "I'm glad you're awake, Kevin. How are you feeling?"

"Been better. I'm really sorry."

Laurie says to Toshiro, "The doctor said to be on the look-out for tremors, but so far, so good."

On the other side of a thin curtain, someone's wheezing.

Toshiro puts a hand on my arm. "You've been drinking a lot since Francesco died, but this? This is . . ." He turns to Laurie: "自殺しそうな?"

"Suicidal," she tells him. She speaks Japanese. Don't even ask me how or why.

He pets my greasy hair.

Laurie says, "Watch out for chunks of sick."

He ignores her. "I made a promise to Francesco that I would look after you. I'm not keeping that promise. I need your help, Kevin. I want you to tell me how I can keep my promise."

I shake my head. He shouldn't blame himself; for the most part, he's kept his promises to Francesco. And he's been trying hard since Francesco died. He even took me to the National March on Washington for Lesbian and Gay Rights back in October. Dead Eddie was too sick to go and Live Eddie wouldn't go without him. Laurie was in Minneapolis helping out her aunt after her hysterectomy. People assumed Toshiro and I were lovers. So, for fun, we went to the mass wedding ceremony near the IRS building. I remember, word for word, what the officiant said: *I'm going to ask you to take a breath, totally release the past, and take one step forward into that future and your place in the world.* Toshiro held my hand and we stepped forward together, along with all the other couples, men with men, women with women, and a few women with men. *And so it is. You are together as friends, as lovers, as life mates, as partners.* I thought how much I had wanted Francesco and me to be husband and husband. But we could only marry in our alternate universe.

I asked Toshiro if it bothered him that everyone at the march assumed he was gay. He said he didn't care, people had been making assumptions about him his entire life, and other people didn't get decide who he was. Who you are, he said, is entirely up to you, whether you believe it or not. He put his arm around me as we marched with ACT UP. We chanted, "Act Up, Fight Back, Fight AIDS."

I liked pretending he was my lover that day, that I wasn't just another *surviving partner*. That I wasn't alone. I loved the entire day. I had never known what it was like to be in the majority. To just suppose almost everyone was gay because almost everyone was. I thought we should all stay in D.C., or maybe migrate like a flock and find some sanctuary just for people like us. I didn't want to go back to how things are. The march made me feel good for the first time since Francesco.

Look at me now.

Laurie says, "You can't ever drink again."

I know this sounds wrong, but the truth is a couple of shots would actually help me recover faster. Then I can stop.

A knock at the open door and in walks Merritt the Wherret. "Is this a bad time?"

Laurie stifles a laugh.

Merritt the Wherret wears earmuffs so what's left of his hair doesn't get flattened. He's made comments about how much he envies my hair, wishing he had thick dark hair that grew too fast. Male pattern baldness is his AIDS. He nods at Laurie and Toshiro as if he knows them. He tries to hand me a get-well card, but then he notices the restraints.

"Oh," he says.

He looks around. There's not a table or a dresser, so he lays the card on my stomach like it's a hot-water bottle. He says, "Your friend"—Laurie, undoubtedly—"called and asked about your insurance. We were going to cancel it this week, but . . . we'll keep it current through the end of the month. That should take care of most of"—he looks around the room—"this."

Laurie and Toshiro thank him for me. I'm too ashamed.

Merritt the Wherret stammers, "I just wanted to say . . . I hope . . . that is . . ."

Yes. It's all YOUR fault.

Laurie says, "This isn't because you fired him. His partner died two years ago this Valentine's Day."

"Oh," Merritt the Wherret says. Not sure if he even knew I was gay. It's something you don't talk about at Fair and Unbiased, except maybe with the artists who work there for the health insurance.

"His partner died of AIDS," she adds from atop the soapbox she takes with her wherever she goes. She "educates" people all the time—about AIDS, mandatory minimum sentencing, Iran-Contra, acid rain . . .

Merritt the Wherret's eyes bug out for a second, but then he recovers. "I'm very sorry to hear that." To me: "My condolences."

Once he's out the door, Toshiro frowns at Laurie. "Why did you tell him Francesco died of AIDS? The first thing he's going to do is cancel Kevin's insurance."

*   *   *

The first thing he does is cancel my insurance.

So I'm on the hook for the ambulance bill, the hospital bill, the lab bill, I'm being evicted, and the alcohol poisoning made Laurie change her mind: No, I can't crash on their couch, I've gone too far this time. I told her she went too far outing me and Francesco's death; it's gonna cost me thousands. She mumbled that I have to live an authentic life, whatever the hell that is, and that the world can't change unless I am honest. So I honestly and authentically told her to shut the hell up for once in her life.

That was a few weeks ago, now. Weeks I essentially spent just working out at the gym, because if I spend too much time in the apartment, I know I'll drink. Not enough to kill myself, but still. I never want to feel that way again. I looked for the thin man in the sweat suit at the gym, but he hasn't come back. *Bette Davis, hold the Bette* waves at me tentatively, like maybe he's not sure he's seen me, like maybe I'm a ghost.

At our make-up coffee, Laurie didn't apologize. Instead, she said I needed a clean break from New York, my home for the last nine years, because if I stay, I'll just end up drinking myself to death the next time. I told her there wasn't going to be a next time; to which she replied, if she and Toshiro hadn't found me, the last time would have *really been* the last time. All of which points to one course of action, she told me: I have to move back to Minnesota to clean up my act. She assured me that lots of people go to Minnesota to sober up. I reminded her I wasn't Liza Minnelli and I couldn't afford Hazelden. She said that Toshiro thinks it's for the best. So does Live Eddie.

Of course they've all discussed this among themselves.

Maybe they're right.

I mean, even if I wasn't getting evicted from Francesco's apartment, it's probably not good for me to spend my nights pretending he's next to me on the futon while I stare at his murals for hours on end.

Laurie has been talking nearly every day to my aunt Nora since I downed the handles of Popov. So now I have a place to stay for as long as I need: Aunt Nora's half of a duplex in South Minneapolis. I lived there with her once before, after Dad sold our house because he had this brilliant idea that he'd move to Alaska and make a fortune. That was ten years ago, which was also when he married, and then promptly walked out on, his second wife, Laurie's aunt Carol, right before she gave birth to Sarah, my half sister.

Dad just vanished.

For good, if the past decade's any indication.

I've made attempts over the years to understand my father. Francesco encouraged me to go look for him, but if Dad wanted a reunion, we would've had one by now. Francesco's father was a decent man. He didn't understand his son, but that never stopped him from loving Francesco, even when Francesco's brothers did. My dad? He was long gone by the time I came out. I've come to believe that he was flawed, like everybody else is flawed, and it's not like he didn't try to be a good father and husband and provider.

He just kept giving up. First with my mom, then with Laurie's aunt.

Aunt Nora had despaired of him. She thought he was Peter Pan, the little boy who never grows up. She would say: *One day he wants to go to university, the next he enlists and they pack him off to West Germany. He wants a wife and a boy of his own, but then he feels trapped. Oh, it was one crisis after another with your da, never knowing what he wanted to do when he grew up. How your mam was able to stand it for as long as she did, I'll never know. She was a saint.*

Live Eddie's helping me pack up the apartment, the place where Francesco and I lived, he died, and I almost drank myself to death. After his funeral I gave some of Francesco's art to Toshiro, along with his doodles to friends of ours who have since died themselves, or have dropped me from their lives because, well, either I reminded them too much of Francesco or I was too big a pain in the ass to deal with anymore. The jobs they got me, the money they loaned me, the moral support, I guess it just got to be too much in a city where everyone seems to be sick or dying, or taking care of the sick or dying, or angry as hell that everyone's sick or dying.

Fortunately, Live Eddie never gave up on me, even when he was taking care of Dead Eddie. "What about this?" he asks as he holds up the sketch of me wearing Ray-Bans and nothing else.

I'm sitting on the futon, overwhelmed. I can't stop thinking about the murals, panicked that someone will paint them over. Why did I get myself fired? I should be staying right here, preserving Francesco's work. One day people will tour this apartment to see it. Francesco's things—even this stained futon—will all need loving homes, people who will take good care of them. They can't end up in a Dumpster, not even the cracked coffee cup he stole from the Times Square Howard Johnson's. It all needs to be carefully cataloged and preserved. It needs an archivist.

The sketch of me, though? "You can have it. Something to remember me by."

Live Eddie shakes his head. "It's not as if you're never coming back. A few months out West will clear your head."

" 'Out West'? I'm not panning for gold."

"Too bad, you could really use some." He looks at the sketch, says, "You've always had a killer "—he stops himself, tries again—"a bodacious body. I'm glad he drew a nude of you for posterity. When you're an old man, you can look back and remember how you drove all the boys wild."

When I'm an old man. There's a possibility I've never really considered.

Live Eddie carefully sets the sketch on the dresser. "I myself was majorly boner-inducing, once."

I want to tell Live Eddie that he seems to be doing a lot better, healthwise, but I don't want to jinx him.

He says, "You should have Toshiro hold on to the artwork. He'll know how to store it."

What about the murals? We just can't leave them.

"I've never understood why he's with Laurie. He's so laid-back, and she's so Laurie. Plus, he's too handsome to be straight."

"But he is."

"Why Laurie, then? He could have any woman he wanted, and I include lesbians. Green card?"

"They'd have to get married for that. Besides, he already has one, somehow."

"Well, if you ask me, it's a terrible waste of a stunningly beautiful man."

"Laurie tells me it's not wasted. They're trying to get pregnant."

When it comes to Laurie and Toshiro's relationship, Live Eddie's not saying anything I didn't say myself to Francesco. But whatever Toshiro and Laurie have works, and they have more in common than most people think. After Laurie and I graduated high school, she left Minnesota behind for NYU and never looked back. When I showed up begging for a place to stay, she had already become who she is, leaving her old self— the unpopular girl with only books for friends—far behind. And Toshiro just grimaces when you ask him about Japan. He says it's no place for someone like him. When I asked him what he meant by that, he said, *A nonconformist. An uncooperative person.*

Under the sink Live Eddie's not happy with the empty bot-

tles. "I sincerely hope all of these are from *before* your most recent trip to the ER."

"Yeah."

He looks at me where I sit helplessly on the futon, and then
back at the bottles. "You're telling the truth? You haven't had
any alcohol since you got out?"

I shake my head.

"Okay. We'll leave the empties for the next person to deal
with."

So far, we've packed my Kliban comforter, my Charlie
Brown doll, Francesco's come-fuck-me outfit, and his favorite
Doc Martens. I'm useless, so Live Eddie says, "I can ask some
of Eddie's GMHC volunteers to pack up the rest and ship it to
Minneapolis. When Eddie died, they all said *if there's anything
I can do*—so they can do this."

He pets my hair. "Let's get out of here, I'm beat. You can
stay with me tonight and we'll go to LaGuardia tomorrow.
Toshiro and I can handle Frankie's sketches."

LaGuardia? I can't leave until I know the next tenant will
take care of Francesco's murals. I'm about to tell him, but I
stop. He looks half-dead.

He looks half-dead, and he's taking care of me. I say, "I don't
have the cash for a plane ticket. I'll take the bus to Minnesota,
once I save up enough."

He shakes his head. "Save how? You don't have a job. Your
aunt paid for a one-way direct to Minneapolis. Your friend
Tommy will meet you at the airport and take you straight to
her house."

Oh.

He adds, with jazz hands: "Surprise!"

I guess this is really happening.

Outside, a siren.

I can't stop thinking about the murals.

*   *   *

That next afternoon at LaGuardia, Live Eddie gives me a tight hug, tells me that he loves me. Toshiro does the same, and I give him a key to Francesco's apartment, asking if anything can be done about the wall murals. He just sighs, and apologizes for Laurie. In spite of our make-up coffee, she's still pissed, and this is her passive-aggressive Minnesota way of letting me know.

It's my second time flying. The other time was when I spent all the money I made from my after-school job bagging groceries at Red Owl, along with the money Dad gave me after Mom died, and bought a one-way ticket to New York. It was the fall of 1979 and I couldn't afford to go to General College at the U anymore. No, scratch that, I could've taken out loans, but college really wasn't my thing, and by that time Dad had disappeared, so it didn't matter as much if I fulfilled his dream of being the first Doyle man to go to college. I was tired of the remedial courses and the no-credit prep classes I had to take because I was a giant burnout in high school who lived for keggers.

But mostly I dropped out because I wanted to get laid so bad, I thought I'd lose my mind.

Makes sense, they say guys peak sexually at nineteen. And there I was on the summit all by myself. I was terrified to get laid in Minneapolis in case somebody found out. Was not ready for that. I had always been an alpha, and once they find out you're gay, you're not an alpha, you're a joke.

I'm in the smoking section because I wanted an aisle seat and the ticket guy at the gate said that this was all that was left. The guy next to me by the window keeps lighting up. He told me he's ex–Army Ranger and that the only thing in life that scares him is flying. He said he wished he was more like me; it didn't seem to bother me at all.

I said it doesn't bother me because I don't give a shit if the plane lands in Minneapolis or Lake Michigan.

He's not saying anything now.

He just lights new cigarettes off the butts of old ones. He scowls at me every few minutes, like I've put a curse on our flight. His face tells me that if we do end up at the bottom of Lake Michigan, it will be all my fault. When he closes his eyes, he looks like he's praying.

I close my own eyes and breathe in his smoke. This wasn't supposed to be my second time flying.

Francesco always dreamt that we'd fly to Italy to explore his roots. His summer in Europe, he had been too busy with wine and food and men to dig into his past, and he came to regret the missed opportunity. From Italy he planned for us to go on to Gomel in the Soviet Union, to see where his maternal grandparents had come from. If they hadn't fled before the war, he told me, his mother probably would've died during the Nazi occupation, like so many Jews did. It made him think about how a chain of events makes us who we are today. How his grandparents leaving Russia meant that we could meet and fall in love.

He imagined we could stretch out the trip, maybe even stay on a year or more, while he sold sketches to tourists on the Left Bank and I worked an under-the-table job as a waiter or bartender in some little Parisian café. I'd steal food to bring home to our candlelit squat just off the Seine. He wanted us to visit Ireland, too, since my mother was from Westport. Maybe my grandmother—or some aunts and uncles I'd never met—could put us up for a while.

I tried to imagine a gay couple in County Mayo and couldn't do it.

But he could.

He made everything seem easy: A trip to Europe or a walk around the block, they were the same thing. He was open and unafraid of whatever may come next.

Until AIDS came next.

He was enough for me; in fact, he was all I had ever wanted.

I told him that, and I'm glad I did. There's a lot I can reproach myself for, and one thing I'll never be able to forgive myself for, but not telling Francesco I loved him enough isn't on the list. I told him every day. So, if this plane does go down, that won't be one of my regrets.

I have to say that even now, even after all the time I've spent reliving our life together, I'm still not sure what I was to him. Somebody to take care of? He did want kids, and I've been told more than once that I act like one. Francesco saw me differently, though. He said deep down, I had a good heart, I just needed to make it beat loud enough so other people could hear it, the way he could. He was kind. I loved that about him, his kindness, even when it would occasionally piss me off, like when he would give his last dollar to a bum on the street. But then AIDS took his kindness away from him, along with everything else that made him who he was.

He's buried at Holy Sepulchre in Philly.

I rode with his parents in the limo, his brothers and their wives and kids followed in their own cars. His parents are good people. They tried for his sake. The driver made some comment about how you can tell the Irish section from the Eye-talian section because your Eye-talians love their mausoleums. As we drove away from Francesco's plot, I felt myself suffocating: It was the worst kind of betrayal to leave him there all by himself, locked tight in a box. I screamed at the driver to turn around, go back, because my Francesco was alone and scared and couldn't breathe and I could see him, claustrophobic and struggling.

Francesco's mother gave me one of her valiums.

I cough from the smoke and a stewardess offers me a new *Time* magazine. On the cover is an old man and woman in sweat suits, beaming. *And now for THE FUN YEARS! Americans are living longer and enjoying it more.*

The stewardess comes back, asks me if I want to switch to nonsmoking, since she hasn't noticed me light up. She has an aisle seat set aside for me if I want it. When I get situated, she whispers so the other passengers won't hear: "Would you like a beer or some wine?"

I consider it.

She repeats herself, thinking I hadn't heard.

I tell her, "Just a pop, please."

She pats my hand. "Coming right up."

The older woman in this window seat is reading a thick paperback and not talking to me, which is how I like it.

We don't fall into the lake. We land and the chain-smoking ex–Army Ranger looks like he's gloating as we pass through the Jetway, like he prayed us back down to earth safely. I make my way out of the gate, still reeking of his Barclays.

There, waiting for me, is my straight male best friend, Tommy. Picture 1975 Gregg Allman without the fuzz under his lip or the sideburns and you might as well be looking at Tommy Grabowski. We've been tight since we were little. He wears his long dirty-blond hair parted down the middle and pushed behind his ears, a pack of Camels in his flannel shirt pocket, and a pair of old faded jeans with road-salt stains ringing the frayed cuffs.

In a world full of change, there's always Tommy, and Tommy's always Tommy. This is why I love him. Not gay-love him, brother-love him.

He holds his arms out wide, smiles lazily. "Hey, it's my main man. Been too long, Kev."

We hug tight and slap each other's backs hard, because we mean it. He says, "Whoa, you on steroids? It's like hugging a brick shithouse."

He's filled out a little since the last time I saw him. At Francesco's funeral. "Just working out like it's my job. 'Cause I don't have a job."

"Enjoy it while it lasts."

I close my eyes, squeeze him tighter.

"Can't breathe."

"Sorry."

I came out to Tommy on Christmas Eve, 1982.

It was my first time back in Minneapolis since I'd immigrated to New York. Francesco was down in Philly visiting his parents, aunts, uncles, cousins, brothers, sisters-in-law, and their kids; Laurie and I had taken the bus to spend the holidays with our families, small as they are, and our common relative, my half sister on my dad's side and her cousin on her mom's side, Sarah. Tommy was still living in the apartment that we had shared over a Laundromat. He'd finished his classes at Dunwoody, a vo-tech, and got a load of mechanic's certifications, so even though the economy was in a recession, he was working steady because no one was buying new cars. He was even able to put some money away every paycheck, he wanted to start his own business.

We celebrated our reunion by listening to *Dark Side of the Moon*, getting stoned, and doing shots of peppermint schnapps, which you always drink in Minnesota in the winter.

I had no plan to come out, no speech prepared, nothing rehearsed, it just happened.

We were talking about the movie *Blade Runner*, which we thought was the coolest damn film ever made, seriously, *ever made*, and ended up wondering how anyone could know for sure if they were real or a replicant.

Tommy said, real or not, he would fuck Pris until her four years were up.

But I got kinda paranoid. Seriously, man, what if *we are* replicants? Maybe our childhood memories are false, just like Rachel's were. Jesus, how could we even tell?

Is it possible to remember things that never happened?

What if you're real and I'm not? Or I'm real and you're not?

But replicants have hopes and dreams, just like us, so they must be real, even if they were made in a lab.

What is reality, anyway?

So we were laughing and freaking out and laughing and freaking out.

And eating. Frosted Flakes, right out of the box.

Then my epiphany: They don't make gay replicants, so I have to be real!

Tommy couldn't breathe. Gay replicants! Ha, ha, ha.

I'm serious. It's the truth.

They don't make gay replicants?

No, I'm gay. Oh, and yeah, they don't make gay replicants.

We laughed and laughed until we couldn't breathe, finished the Frosted Flakes, ripped open a box of Velveeta, and I came out to him all over again.

He asked I don't know how many times: You putting me on?

No.

You putting me on?

No.

On your mother's grave?

Yeah.

You putting me on?

And then, after he thought about how I had never talked about getting laid the way he did, he believed me. We'd been sitting on his couch, the one we'd hauled out of a Dumpster years before. He stood up and took a few steps back, weaving slightly. He looked at me like he had never seen me before in his life.

He stammered: Are you in gay love with me?

No, man, you're like my brother. I had tears in my eyes. You're my brother, man. You can't be in gay love with your own brother. Just can't. That's FUCKING wrong! I took a photo of Francesco out of my wallet, pointing and shouting: I'm in gay love with him!

Tommy sobbed, Kevin, you're my brother! You're my brother, man!

At the baggage carousel he says, "So Laurie said you were pretty fucked-up."

"She said 'fucked-up'?"

"Nah, but that's what she meant. Alcohol poisoning. Twice, huh?"

I can't look at him. "Yeah."

"Weak tit. I've been to the ER four times that I can remember. Were you getting drunk every day?"

"No."

"So, what's the problem? You just take it easy during the week, only get fucked-up Friday and Saturday, and recover on Sunday. Back to work Monday, like nothing happened."

I see my bags pop down the chute. "No, I really, really fucked-up. Almost died fucked-up."

"Yeah, gotta say, that's pretty fucked-up."

On the drive to South Minneapolis, he tells me he's probably gonna get married. He loves this one and, besides, he's knocked her up. This'll be kid number three (that he knows about, anyway). Number one was put up for adoption after we barely graduated from high school. Number two is three years old and living with her mom's parents up on Fond du Lac.

Laurie and Toshiro have been trying to get pregnant, but no luck. But one glance from Tommy and wham-bam: Eggs are good to go.

Tommy says if he does marry this one, there's just gonna be a justice of the peace, no church and no reception, but he wants me there as his best man. Maybe godfather, too; his brothers are giant pains in his ass.

The second she sees me, my mom's sister, my aunt Nora O'Connor, grabs me and hugs me real hard. I mean really, really hard. I've always thought she could've been one of those lady wrestlers, like the mean one who fights dirty when the ref isn't looking and everybody hates. I can hear the announcer as she enters the ring: *And here she is, the champ-eee-on, the killing machine from the Isle of Green, the sassy lassie who's plenty nasty, the mean colleen who'll make you scream, Noooooraaaaah!*

I see the crowds booing and waving angry homemade signs: *Send Nora to Gommarrah!*

No Honor in O'Connor!

Irish You Would Die!

At the ringside announcers' table, "Mean" Gene Okerlund tells the television audience: *She absolutely makes me SICK to my stomach! And I think that these people here, and a lot of people around the whole wrestling world, have had just about enough of this woman!*

Anyway, that's the impression she often makes on most people.

I am not most people.

"My darling boy," she says. "My poor, poor darling boy!"

We're on the front porch of her half of a Powderhorn Park duplex, a south Minneapolis neighborhood aka Dyke Heights, not that Aunt Nora's a lesbian, even if everyone thinks she is. Irish women are butcher than American women, and Mayo women are the butchest of all.

"I'm fine, Aunt Nora, really."

She steps back, gives me the once-over. "Jaysus, you're bigger? You're not trying to become like that Incredible Hulk, are you?" Aunt Nora used to love the TV show with Lou Ferrigno. I told her it was because he was covered in green like Mayo and it made her all hot and bothered. She told me to stop acting the maggot.

"Just trying to stay healthy." Plus, you know, gay men and gyms. It's a whole, enormous thing, especially in New York, which is a highly competitive market. Or used to be.

"Healthy? Healthy! Laurie told me you've been making a holy show of yourself."

Tommy rescues me, says, "Hey, Miss O'Connor."

Aunt Nora has always adored Tommy, mostly because he was the only one apart from me with the balls to give her shit. "Tommy, my deadly lad, thank you for bringing Kevin back to me safe and sound." She wraps her big man arms around him and rubs his back like she's trying to warm him up or burp him.

"You gonna let us in, or what?" I ask her. It's warm for late February in Minnesota, and there's only maybe an inch of snow on the ground, but still.

"Oh! Oh, do come in, it's just the excitement of seeing the pair of you! Mind the cats."

Tommy and I haul my bags in as Aunt Nora shoos the cats from the door. Her place is just like it was back when I had lived with her: The enormous crucifix with an agonized Jesus nailed to it hangs on the wall of her little sitting room, and there's still the shrine to the Kennedys and Martin Luther King Jr. in her tiny dining room, candles lit. On the coffee table is a stack of *Catholic Bulletins*, *People*, this week's *TV Guide*, and a copy of *Time Flies* by Bill Cosby, which she's borrowed from the library.

"Now, Tommy, don't you disappear on me. I'll just put the kettle on and then you can catch me up on all your news."

Tommy says, "Sorry, Miss O'Connor, gotta book. I'm taking my girlfriend out to Jax Cafe."

"Oh, very fancy indeed. Must be serious, then?"

I answer for him: "Their love grows with each passing day."

Aunt Nora smiles. "Ah, lovely. Good for you, Tommy. It's high time you settled down and started a family of your own."

I say, "Past it, more like."

Tommy smacks the back of my head before he leaves.

Aunt Nora says, "You'll have your old room. Get yourself settled then, and we can have a proper visit."

Upstairs I discover she's stocked my room with the stuff I stored in her basement after Dad had sold our house. There's my grade school boxing trophies on a shelf over the twin bed, boxing being my thing before I moved on to partying in high school. Aunt Nora encouraged me, since my teachers have said since kindergarten that I lacked discipline and didn't work up to my potential. She taught me Irish step dancing to help me with my footwork, since you have to know how to distribute your weight to pack the hardest punch. My coaches always told me, "Be first. Throw your punches before the other kid can." My specialty was stick and move, and since I knew how to throw a deadly punch, no one ever challenged me when I got up to high school. Those were my alpha male days, lived from deep inside my closet.

Fag bashings and muggings are an everyday thing in New York, so I tried to teach Francesco how to stand, bob and weave, and the correct form for a hook, cross, and an uppercut. Of course fights outside the ring are a very different thing, so I also tried to teach him how to use the heel of his hand on a nose, fingers on an Adam's apple, and knee on a crotch. I'd say, "Come at me, faggot," but he would just wrap his arms around me tight and shout, "Yo! Who wants a smooch?" as he kissed my neck. Sometimes he'd vamp Pat Benatar's "Hit Me with Your Best Shot," bending over when he got to the line "'Fire away!'" Other times he'd sing "Hit Me with Your Rhythm Stick."

On the bed itself are old clothes, freshly washed and folded, and on top of the stack is the T-shirt Tommy's mother gave me at commencement. Printed in black letters across the chest is HI SKOOL GRADYOUATE. On the dresser is a picture of Mom in a silver frame. She's back in our old house in Northeast, smiling for the camera as she holds our dog, Rex, in her lap. There's no pictures of Dad, or as Aunt Nora referred to him: *that worthless piece of shite you call Da.*

There's even Laurie's Northeast High yearbook that she gave me as a Christmas gift when she was visiting after her first semester in New York. It only had a few signatures, things like

Wish we could have gotten to know each other better! and *Hope to see you sometime!* She said she didn't want it; she wasn't that person anymore. Since I had been popular, I should have it.

So that in the years to come, I could look back and reminisce about when I had peaked.

New York made her a smart-ass in no time at all.

Nineteen seventy-eight was an awful year: Thanks to Anita Bryant, St. Paul repealed its gay rights law in the spring. Harvey Milk was assassinated in the fall. Not that I was aware of any of it at the time. My priorities began and ended with *cool*, and you can see where that's gotten me. I wish someone had told me back then what a complete waste of time *cool* was, but then it's a sure bet I wouldn't have believed them, anyway.

I sit on the bed, flip through the yearbook's pages at random, but I know exactly where I'll end up.

And there he is: Jon Thompson. The boy I had a desperate crush on, with his big eyelashes and chocolate-colored hair, posing in a tie and suitcoat. I remember tackling him when we played snow football so I could feel his body underneath mine. Just for a moment.

God, how I'd fantasized about him from the depths of my closet. More like a bunker, really.

He was the boy I called "faggot" and "cocksucker" while I beat the crap out of him. I was yelling at myself, he just got in the way.

I cringe, flip forward until I get to Allison Minczeski's picture. She was my girlfriend. The one I imagined marrying and never having to have sex with. Because she wouldn't mind because, you know, being married to me would be enough.

Jesus.

Yeah, it's hard to be nostalgic about 1978, because popular or not, it was a totally heinous year and I could be a totally heinous person. If that was peaking, the alcohol poisoning makes perfect sense.

I unpack my Kliban comforter and toss it over the bed. My Charlie Brown doll and the Ray-Bans go on the dresser, next to Mom and Rex. The giant envelope full of pictures of Francesco and our life together in New York I put on the pillows for later tonight. I'm going to organize them in a leather photo album, a yearbook that will actually mean something and one that I can be proud of.

I can't resist and pull out a picture.

Francesco holds a cup of coffee at Veselka, a Ukrainian diner on Second Avenue. We had been out all night dancing with the A-listers under the dome of the Saint. A bouncer who had the hots for us and wanted a three-way got us in—the membership fees were so pricey. When we wouldn't put out, our free nights at the Saint came to an end.

You see, once Francesco decided he was in love with me, that was that.

No more wandering through the enchanted forest of gay men like he was the fairy king. There would be nobody else for either of us. The plan was that we'd grow old together, and if we lost interest in sex—so what—we'd still have each other. Francesco said good company eventually becomes more important than good sex. With the time we saved, we could read all the writers you were supposed to read, like Toni Morrison and James Joyce. Rent videos and spend our days watching foreign films with subtitles. Maybe finally take our trip to Europe and sip lattes on the Avenue des Champs-Élysées. I'd be Eliza Doolittle leaving my Cockney past behind as Francesco's art career took off and launched us into high society.

Or not. No matter what happened, he said, we'd always have each other, and he was so grateful that we'd always have each other. So was I, more than I ever truly knew.

Aunt Nora shouts up the stairs: "What's the holdup, then? Come down so we can have a proper chat!"

I try to remember what Francesco and I talked about that

morning at Veselka, coffee in his hand, head leaned against the wood paneling, the wisp of cigarette smoke floating into the frame from the woman puffing away at the table next to ours.

I don't know.

I hate not remembering moments with him, it's like losing my wallet down a sewer grate, and everything important is inside.

Downstairs, Aunt Nora has laid out her Belleek pot full of tea and good china cups, a sugar bowl, milk in a cream pitcher, and a plate of chocolate-covered digestives on the dining-room table. Cats form an obstacle course as I make my way to join her, where she's already poured her own cup and mine, fixing them to her taste. When I sit across from her, she sighs. " 'Tis himself, at last. I'm gasping."

She takes a careful sip as I reach for a digestive. Maybe we can start off discussing her job at Norwest, the bank where she's worked since it was Northwestern National. Maybe she has a new cat she'd like to talk about, or maybe she wants to remind me again how that "clean-on buck" Johnny Logan won Eurovision for the second time last year.

What she does say is: "Your life's in tatters. Laurie tells me you're always sloshed."

Aunt Nora was never one to ease into a sensitive subject. "My life's *not* in tatters. And I let my drinking get out of hand a couple of times, is all. Nothing worse than anybody else. Given the circumstances, you'd think I'd get a pass."

"Is that Arthur Guinness talking?"

"I'm stone-cold. I just came back to take a break from things."

She picks up a ginger tom that's jumped on the table and drops him on the floor with the rest. "And what sort of things would those be? Laurie told me you were made redundant."

Thank you, Laure Lindstrom. Wish I hadn't have gotten to know you better. "They did me a favor. It was a dead-end job that was turning me into a zombie. I'll find something else."

"Here or there?"

"There." Duh.

She pulls one of her old sweaters tightly around her as if she's chilled, the neckline bedazzled with pink rhinestones. Her face collapses as she says, "Oh, you don't mean to tell me you're going back to that awful place. Why on earth would you?" Aunt Nora's knowledge of New York extends only as far as *Fort Apache, The Bronx*, which she saw only because Paul Newman, as she puts it, *sends* her.

"My friends are there." What's left of them.

"You have friends here! There's me, and there's Tommy, and you shouldn't forget your wee sister."

The mention of her stings. I haven't been a good big brother, or any kind of brother, really. I tell myself it's because of the age difference—I was eighteen when she was born. I tell myself it's because I moved to New York before she was even a year old. I tell myself it's because her mom isn't my mom. I don't tell myself it's because she has Down syndrome, epilepsy, and congenital heart disease. The last time I saw her was when Francesco and I rode the Greyhound to Minneapolis, enduring the bathroom and the hostility of our fellow travelers because of Francesco's frequent and extended stays.

When we finally got to Minnesota, I was afraid Sarah wouldn't remember me, but she made a big fuss and hugged me, and then Francesco, and then me again, over and over. I was touched until her mother, with a bit of an edge in her voice, told me she'll hug anyone, *even complete strangers*.

I take a sip of my tea, milky with sugar, before I ask, "How is Sarah?"

"I've no idea, I can't bear to speak to that mother of hers. She's healthy, God willing. And don't change the subject."

"You brought her up."

"I was only making the point," she says as she carefully tops off her cup (the Belleek is only for special occasions), "that there are good reasons for you to move back here, permanent-like. You can search high and low and won't find a drop in the house. I've cleared out all the alcohol so you'll never be tempted. I won't charge you a penny's rent while you get yourself sorted, and you can stay as long as you please."

I don't know what to say to that. It used to embarrass me to be her *darling boy*, but now I really need to be someone's darling boy, and for all her quirks, she's the one person I want on my side more than anyone else.

She reaches over, holds my hand in hers. "I know what it's like. When your mam died, I thought I'd never recover. The grief was simply too much to bear. And I haven't recovered—I know now I never will, but I can bear the grief. Most days."

Mom was everything to Aunt Nora. They came to America together. "Really?"

She grins, like she always does when I catch her fudging the truth. "There's still some days when I can't risk the grocery store, because maybe I'll see a box of nut clusters in the checkout line and burst into tears. Because they were her favorite. So I stay home if I can and wait the worst of it out. But if I have to work that day, I act. I act like there's nothing wrong with me. I should have a whole closet full of Oscars for Best Actress."

"I've been letting people down. Frankie, most of all."

"It's the grief, is all. You haven't let a soul down."

My throat swells and I can feel the heat on my face.

She says, "Ah, my darling boy. People will tell you that you've grieved long enough, that the one you miss is in a better place. They've no business. I mean, yes, I do believe your mam's in a better place, with all my heart I do, but since she's died, *I'm* not in a better place. And neither are you since you've lost Frankie."

"I'm fine."

"No, you're not. Don't you worry, it's a place you learn to live in. I have."

Jesus Christ, tears are rolling down my cheeks. This fucking day. This fucking year.

She pats my hand. "I know you loved Frankie very much and you've been walking with grief ever since he passed. I don't care what other people think you should or shouldn't be doing. You walk slowly, my darling boy, you keep your own pace. And those that tell you to move past your grief just don't understand your journey."

Yeah, big old honking boo-hoo-hoo.

Aunt Nora gets up, walks across the table to where I sit, leans down, and puts her arms around me.

And then a cat jumps on the table. She says, "Off with you," swats it, and hugs me again.

Parallel universe 75: There's no AIDS and you didn't die. What's our life like?

Francesco says, Why do you do this to yourself?

It's your game. You made it up. Parallel Universe 75: There's no AIDS and you didn't die. What's our life like?

Francesco says nothing.

This neighborhood's so quiet. There aren't sirens, or the rancor from the street, no people shouting or glass breaking. In an odd way it makes it harder for me to fall asleep, and I either end up sleeping too much or not at all.

Let's try again, shall we? Parallel Universe 75: There's no AIDS and you didn't die. What's our life like?

Francesco surrenders. Well, he says, we go out clubbing with the Eddies, but we don't stay out all night like we used to, because we need our sleep. We complain about how the twinks have ruined the dance scene with their Samantha Foxes and their Tiffanies. Eddie 1's getting tired of Chelsea and wants to move out of the city and have a couple kids with a lesbian couple, and he's already picked out the names: Ashley for the girl, and Andrew for the boy. Eddie 2's panicking, he's not ready to be a father yet, and probably never will be. You have an okay job that you don't like, but you tolerate it, because I'm still freelancing and probably always will. I crank out consistent pages and have repetitive-strain injuries in my hand, shoulders, and back. I wrap my pencils in foam to make them less painful to grip. You don't work out anymore and your ass is starting to droop, but I don't say anything 'cause you'll just get mad. We never miss an episode of *The Golden Girls*. My sister-in-law Suzanne still hates us.

Wow, you're *really* bad at this game. You're supposed to say you hit it big as an artist. We're rich. We go to gallery openings, where everyone makes a fuss over you.

Okay, so I've hit it big. What's *your* big?

You.

We don't live in Parallel Universe 75. You need a big.

Chapter 3

MARCH 1988: DON'T RIM!

I'm surprised when I hear the man up front say, "Hi. My name's Mark and I'm an alcoholic." In near unison the men and women sitting in their metal folding chairs say, "Hi, Mark."

My first meeting, and if vodka doesn't end up killing me, then secondhand smoke will. I have to say I didn't think they really did the whole *My name is Joe Schmoe and I'm an alcoholic* thing. I thought it was a joke or an urban legend.

I'm here to make Aunt Nora happy, not because I'm an alcoholic—I'm not. She told me even if I didn't believe I was an alkie, I should hear alkie stories to see what might happen to me if I don't make some changes in my life. So I'm in the basement of a Lutheran church across the street from her duplex. According to the sign out front, I thought the only time they opened the basement up was to get the faithful to eat all the lutefisk, *klubb*, or hotdish they wanted in order to keep their summer camp open one more year.

But no, alkies are welcome, too, but all they have on offer for us is bitter coffee in Styrofoam cups, along with old cookies from Red Owl. The basement feels like an oven preheating and

I wish I'd worn shorts and a T-shirt, even though it's only March.

At the start of the meeting, they asked if anyone was here for the first time. I got some encouraging looks from what I assumed to be the regulars, but I kept my mouth shut. I don't think they would've liked to open their meeting with me explaining how I'm not some sort of pathetic drunk who chugs Grandpa's cough syrup when he's napping.

Up front, Mark the alcoholic (*Hi, Mark!*) can't seem to start his "share," so we wait quietly for a breakthrough. Over by the donation table, a woman, with red hair and pale skin, fidgets. I overheard two men talking about her before the meeting. One said she was beautiful, which she is. The other one said, "Don't even. She doesn't like herself and is desperate to tell anyone who will listen why."

Mark, on the other hand, doesn't seem to want to tell nobody nothin'.

A heavy man in the front row prompts him: "How long you been sober, Mark?"

"Not long." He doesn't say anything else, but he doesn't sit down, either.

Another helpful question from somewhere behind me: "When was your last meeting?"

He has to think about it, and even I know that's not good.

The woman with the red hair's impatient. Maybe she's trying to sound supportive, but it comes out all exasperated: "What do you want to share?"

Mark looks at his feet, and says so quietly that I can barely make it out: "The days seem to drag on forever since I got sober."

He has nothing else to add and the meeting proceeds. The woman with the red hair takes up the rest of the hour. Recovering alcoholics attempt to steer her thinking from a past none of us can change to a future she could create, if only she'd try. But she moves in tight circles, around and around her pain and her grievances and her disappointments, over and over and over again, like she's orbiting the sun. I sense the frustration in the room. A pudgy white woman sitting next to me whispers, "She could use an attitude of gratitude. It's not like she has cancer. *I* have cancer."

People with cancer get to say they have cancer, and not clear the room.

As the fading afternoon light makes its way through the glass-block windows of the basement, the woman with the red hair tells us what she needs: to set boundaries, to not make others' problems her own, to find at least one person she can be completely honest with.

A Native American man on my other side whispers, mostly to himself, "To be honest, what I need's a drink. My head's pounding."

I didn't know you could come to these meetings hungover.

At last, the meeting ends. We all stand, the alkies and me, and hold hands as we say, nearly in unison: "God grant me the serenity to accept the things I cannot change, the courage to change the things I can, and the wisdom to know the difference."

I've almost made it to the stairs when two alkies double-team me.

Over the racket of metal chairs being folded and stacked, one forcefully says, "Hi, I'm Cathy, and this is Donna." Cathy looks like a heavy Sandy Duncan who's been around the block one time too many, while Donna seems closer to my age and reminds me of the novice nuns who bail before their final vows. Like leaving Jesus at the altar. She smiles sweetly at me.

"I'm . . ." I don't even want to give them my first name. It's like walking in a gay bar for the first time all over again. ". . . John."

Ex-nun holds out her hand, and it's really warm. "Very nice

to meet you, John." Did she say "John" sarcastically? It's hard to tell with ex-nuns.

Rough-trade Sandy Duncan says, "Is this your first meeting? You should've introduced yourself. No one's here to judge you. It's all about support. We're here to support each other."

I say, "Oh, it's nothing like that. I'm just here to listen."

Alkies pass on either side of us; we're blocking the staircase. "Just to listen?"

Why would I be here just to listen? Why do you go to a gay bar if you're not gay? "I'm in grad school and I'm doing a paper on . . . alcoholic support systems."

Gangster Sandy Duncan throws her hands up, says, "Help! My support systems are alcoholic!" Then she goes, "Ha-ha-ha!" Finally: "Don't mind me. I'm on the pink cloud!"

Ex-nun says, "I wrote a lot of those papers myself, my first few meetings. They were all about *denial*." Her emphasis on the word "denial" is only mildly homicidal-rage-inducing.

Gun moll Sandy Duncan laughs like she's got a pinch between her cheek and gum, coughs a little, and finally gets out, "You two oughtta compare notes. On all those papers you wrote!" Then she winks, saying, "Not really!"

Ex-nun says, "Can I buy you a cup of coffee? Real coffee, I mean, not like the stuff they serve here. We can talk about your research."

If this was New York, she'd know better than to waste her time with me. "No, thanks, but no. I'm not in recovery."

Roughneck Sandy Duncan rolls her eyes. "You're only as sick as your secrets."

You don't know what sick is, lady.

As I turn, ex-nun says, "Maybe some other time, then. We're all in recovery from something, *John*."

Aunt Nora's impressed that I'm not drinking—I have to kiss her on the cheek when I come home from the gym or when I head upstairs to bed so she can get a good whiff of me. Since I won't go to AA or mass, her new strategy is to get me involved in something bigger than myself. So we're in the lobby—really just a big ugly room with dividers—of the Minnesota AIDS Project, or MAP, located on the second floor of a dumpy old two-story office building in South Minneapolis, next to a 7-Eleven and just across the street from a drive-in liquor store. Here we wait for the MAP volunteer coordinator to interview me.

The reception area is a mishmash of secondhand desks and chairs, and the stained ceiling drips with snowmelt. There are buckets here and there on the orange shag carpet to catch the drops. I say to the receptionist, a heavyset white man wearing a rainbow afghan-crochet sweater and a dream catcher earring, "Nice place. Haven't seen shag carpets in a while."

He doesn't look up from his typewriter, where he hunts and pecks with his index fingers. "It was a donation from the bathhouse that closed."

Glad I'm wearing my Docs.

The volunteer coordinator is named Brian, a tall skinny guy, but not AIDS skinny. We follow him into his office, a small windowless room with safe-sex posters covering the walls. Aunt Nora stares at them as Brian says, "I just need to make a copy of your application. Be right back."

One poster features a handsome gay couple, blond and white. One's taking off his shirt, and the caption says: *You won't believe what we like to wear in bed.* Another poster says, *Great sex! Don't let AIDS stop it,* along with this advice: *Don't let him come in your ass. Don't come in his. Don't come in his mouth. Don't let him come in yours,* along with *Don't rim.*

Aunt Nora asks, " 'Rim'? What's that, then?"

Jesus. "It's an Americanism."

"You'd think I'd have heard of it by now. I've been in this country over thirty years. It has to do with gay sex, doesn't it?"

"Yes, it can . . . well, straight people can do it, too, if they want."

"Gives you the AIDS, then?"

"Can we drop it, please?"

Aunt Nora frowns, shifts in her chair as she studies the poster for clues. "Since when did you become such a Holy Joe?"

I fold my arms across my chest. "I just don't want to talk about this stuff with my own aunt."

And, right on schedule to the very nanosecond, the Irish Catholic guilt enters the room like a wet, chill fog. "Would you rather I wait by myself out in the car?"

"No. I'm sorry."

She shakes her head. "Even you have to admit, I've done my best with all of this. Maybe I'm no Elizabeth Taylor, but since you told me about being gay, and about Frankie getting sick, where have I been? On *your* side. Perhaps I could have done more, but not all families would be so compassionate. And understanding."

She's right.

She's always right; it's annoying. Laurie was the first person I came out to, but she had already figured it out. Tommy, well, the pot and peppermint schnapps eased the way. But with Aunt Nora, I mean *Jaysus*, Aunt Nora . . . the years it took off my life, wondering how I would ever tell my aunt Nora. She's the strongest woman I know, and I don't mean her character. I was honestly afraid she'd knock me the fuck out.

I told her that first visit back, when Tommy picked me up to take me to the bus station. I thought it would take both of us to restrain her, and if her head exploded, it wouldn't matter. I was heading back to New York, anyway.

The three of us were standing in her front doorway. She was asking me when I'd be back next. She couldn't enjoy herself when I visited, knowing I'd be leaving again. I told her, You might not want me back.

Why on earth would you say a thing like that? You're my darling boy.

Aunt Nora, I have something to tell you, and you may be very disappointed in me.

She frowned. Sounds serious. Are you in trouble with the law?

No.

You get some New York gal up the pole, then?

No, nobody's pregnant.

And that exhausted her list of possibilities.

Tommy was having a nic-fit, so he said: He's gay. Then he lit a Camel.

Aunt Nora shook her head. Don't tease now, Tommy. Kevin's trying to tell me something important.

Tommy exhaled, his eyes closed: Yeah, that he's gay.

She looked at me and I just stared at her big man feet, I couldn't look her in the eye. She said, So you're a gay now.

I am.

A gay homosexual?

Yes.

She sucked in her lips. Her pale face turned a sort of ash. She thought about it, then said, in a whisper: Do you think it's chemical, like? I heard on the telly that may be so.

What she meant was *Do you believe sexual orientation is genetically determined?*

I said, Yeah, it's chemical.

She sighed. She kissed me on my cheek, said she'd need to pray on it.

After a few weeks she called, satisfied that being *a gay* wasn't my fault, it's the chemicals what cause it. Her advice: "Keep up with your boxing, you're going to need it."

Now she says: "I was the one, after all, who stood up during transubstantiation and told Father Stanislaus you can't get AIDS from the Communion cup."

"I'm sorry, Aunt Nora."

"When I was a girl, we'd never speak of homosexuals. If you were that way, your family sent you packing for England to be with your own kind."

"I'm *really* sorry, Aunt Nora."

We sit in silence for a minute, until she says, "So what's the 'rim'? And why shouldn't you do the 'rim'?"

Dear God, get back here, volunteer-coordinator guy.

And then, years too late, God finally decides to answer a prayer of mine. Brian appears. He smiles at me, sits behind his desk, takes another look at my volunteer application. And then he smiles at Aunt Nora, confused. "Did you want to volunteer, too?"

She pats my hand. "I'm just here to support my lovely gay nephew."

He nods slowly.

She says, "Like my own son, so he is."

"That's nice." He looks across the desk at me. "So, Kevin, could you tell me why you're interested in volunteering with us?"

Aunt Nora tells Brian: "You look Irish to me."

He looks at her, says, "My parents came over."

"Where from, then?"

He says, "Enniskillen."

Aunt Nora gasps. "Oh, you know all about the Remembrance Day bombing, then? Eleven dead. Even I can't approve of that. Ten of them were civilians, including three married couples, the poor things."

Brian says, a Minnesota frost in his voice, "Yes, I heard about it." To me, he repeats: "Why are you interested in volunteering with us?"

Because I have to do something? "I want to support my community."

"Do you have any particular skills or experience related to health education, addiction, or caregiving?"

Aunt Nora says, "He's a recovering alcoholic."

I groan. "I am not."

Brian asks, "Recovering?"

I try to sound pleasant: "An alcoholic."

Aunt Nora adds, "And he took care of his friend all through his illness. But it's far too soon for him to volunteer to do that sort of thing again. His friend's only been dead the two years."

There's something about the word "friend." Something that burns me right up. You hear it all the time at the orthodox and conservative funerals. It's code. Or a lie. Calling Francesco "my *friend*," like he was in the same league with someone I partied with in high school . . . like he's just one of many. He wasn't one of many.

He was everything.

I feel my blood pressure rise.

I say, "Frankie wasn't my 'friend.' He was my . . ." Partner? That word was never right, it doesn't do justice to what we had. Lover? Makes it sound like it was only about sex. I don't know what to call him. We were together five years. "Don't you *ever* say he was *just* my 'friend.' "

We sit. Brian stares at my application, and Aunt Nora at me.

There's all kind of silence: awkward silence, reverent silence, embarrassed silence. And then there's IRISH SILENCE. Think eye of the hurricane.

Aunt Nora stands, puts on her coat and her ski hat, grabs her giant purse with the wooden handles, says to Brian, "I'm off. Lovely meeting you."

"*Slán,*" he tells her.

She makes her exit, as only she can, like she's Ellen Ripley, last survivor of the *Nostromo*, signing off.

Brian looks at me, and Aunt Nora's right, he does look like a mick. He says, "I'm very sorry for your loss."

I nod.

Brian pulls open a drawer, hands me a tissue.

I frown, touch my face.
It's wet.

Brian agreed with Aunt Nora: It's still too soon for me to work as an emotional support buddy or a home helper, as evidenced by my spontaneous crying and alleged alcoholism.
I cry a lot lately.
So I signed on to volunteer Thursday nights doing office work, like stuffing envelopes and assembling bulk mailings.
Aunt Nora left without me, and I'm still kinda pissed at her. She can stay mad longer than anyone I know, so I call Tommy at work and he says I can crash at his place tonight. I hang out at the Nicollet Avenue McDonald's until he gets home, surprised to find that I don't have enough for a Big Mac and the fare to Tommy's, so I suck on coffee, wishing the people watching was more interesting, like it was in New York.
During the bus rides over to Tommy's place in Northeast, I look out the windows, at the dull storefronts, people dressed like it's May instead of March, and the sporadic, taxi-less traffic of Ford pickups and Cavaliers and Celebrities and Cieras. I see the flat landscape, the one- and two-story boxes of chain stores and franchises that make it impossible to tell if I'm moving forward or backward.
I didn't expect culture shock coming back to the city I grew up in.
I didn't expect to miss the bodegas, the delis, the subway (as scary as it can be), the masses of pedestrians moving deliberately, like flocks, effortlessly dodging each other in near misses, while not even seeming to look anywhere but straight ahead. I miss running into someone I know in the neighborhood. I miss 4:00 a.m. at Save the Robots on Avenue B. I even miss Alphabet City and almost all the East Village, how one block could look like a scene out of an old romantic comedy, the next overdosed

on post-Madonna fashion ("She ripped off Billy Idol's look!"),
and the one after that like London during the blitz.

But there's lots I don't miss at all. I don't miss hearing gun-
shots. I don't miss the East Village garbage, the vacant lots full
of rubble and derelict cars, the burned-out buildings, the broken glass, the posters plastered on top of each other in thick
layers, and the tags and throw-up graffiti on some blocks that
cover anything and everything that somebody standing on
somebody else's shoulders can reach.

And, to be honest, I never really could take the East *Vill-
ahge* artists with their "new avant-garde scene," speaking a language only Francesco and Toshiro could understand as their
galleries opened and closed or moved to Lower Broadway. I
don't miss the poets at the parties Francesco would take me to
with their Allen Ginsberg stories, and even less the writers discussing their works-in-progress that animated the drama of
comprehension or some such pretentious bullshit. Or the performance artists handing out passes for their one-person shows
about disordered energies at ubercool places Francesco liked to
go to before he got sick, places like Darinka or 8BC. I don't
miss the gangs of Loisaida kids shouting "*mamabicho*" and
"*puto*" at me, or the grumpy old Ukrainian women shaking
their heads as they muttered in their own language.

And there's a lot of good things about Minneapolis, like my
favorite thing as a kid, the Weatherball on top of the Northwestern National Bank building. It would change colors, and
red meant warmer weather ahead. White meant cold weather.
You could see it from fifteen miles away at night.

But the building burned down after I moved to New York.

There are other good things about Minneapolis, I just can't
think of any at the moment.

When I make it to Tommy's, I'm in a funk that's only temporarily lifted when Rick Foley opens the door, a videocassette

in his hand. He was a friend of ours from high school; Rick Foley and I saw Bruce Springsteen and Linda Ronstadt concerts when we were high as kites. He'd babble on about somehow getting Ronstadt in bed; I'd stare glassily at Springsteen wondering what it would be like to wrap my legs 'round his velvet rims. Tommy and I were going to be in Rick's wedding, but his girlfriend turned his proposal down cold. I'd lost touch with him after I left for New York.

He seems stunned to see me, like I'm a dodo, something everyone thought was extinct. I reach out to shake his hand, but he says he has a cold, better not. He pulls on his coat and says that it's good to see me, no time to catch up, he really has to go. As he leaves, he thanks Tommy for loaning him a copy of *Aliens*.

I watch him race down the stairs.

Inside, Tommy's watching the TV show *Probe*, starring the Hardy Boy who wasn't Shaun Cassidy.

"You told him," I tell Tommy.

He shrugs, walks to the kitchenette, opens two bottles of Grain Belt, and hands me one.

I look at the beer before I give it back to Tommy. "You told him."

"Oh yeah, you don't drink anymore. You sure about that? I mean, what're we supposed to do now?"

"Have them both. It's Saint Paddy's day."

He nods. "Yeah. Hate to waste them."

I repeat, "You told him."

"You didn't tell me not to tell him."

"You didn't tell me you told him."

Tommy takes a long swig out of one of the bottles before he plops back down on the couch. "Yeah, well, he was a real dick about it, so I didn't tell you I told him."

I stare at the Hamm's Beer bear poster that still covers a hole in the wall. "What'd he say?"

Tommy belches. "You know Foley. Talks a good game, but when push comes to shove, he's a priss. He's afraid he'll catch gay from you. Probably afraid he'll like it."

I sit next to Tommy, wishing I had a beer. On the television a woman's claiming to be a witch, and the Hardy Boy who wasn't Shaun Cassidy is skeptical. "That all he's afraid of catching? Did you tell him about Frankie?"

"Oh yeah! Frankie was soooo cool. I have his entire run of *Galaxy Champion* comics."

"When did you tell Rick?"

"He gave me a ride to the airport when I flew out to Philly for the funeral. He asked me why I was going, so I told him."

"And he freaked out?"

"Full-blown, lose-your-fucking-mind freak-out. 'He should be quarantined.' 'They should tattoo people like him.' 'Put 'em all on an island somewhere.' That kinda shit."

"He still live over at—"

"Leave it," Tommy says as he grabs my arm. "He's just a dumb fuck with nothing going on."

It's 3:00 a.m. I'm sleeping in my clothes on the Dumpster couch, a single blanket over me. The apartment's cold and I know I'm gonna be up all night. I want to feel my fist against Rick Foley's jaw, but that's not what's really bothering me.

I tiptoe to Tommy's bedroom and let myself in. He's asleep, so I just sit on the side of his bed and wait for him to wake up. Then I get tired of waiting, so I squeeze his nostrils shut.

He snorts, slaps my hand away, and says, "What the hell?"

I say, "I couldn't sleep."

He rubs his eyes, trying to adjust to the darkness. "Oh. Well, try. Harder."

"I need to talk."

"Now?"

I look out the window at the storefronts across the street, their windows black. Nighttime's the empty hours. "Yeah."

He pulls the comforter over his head, but I don't leave, so he pulls it down again. "You still mad at Foley?"

I shrug. "Yeah, but that's not it."

He asks, undoubtedly hoping I won't answer: "What, then?"

"Do you believe in an afterlife?"

He sits up on his elbows and I see his HARLEY-DAVIDSON GOOD WHISKEY T-shirt with the bald eagle on it. He sniffs to his left, and then his right. "You high?"

"I don't smoke anymore."

"Because if you were, it would explain a lot."

I repeat: "Don't smoke anymore. Answer my question."

His head sinks into his chest. "How the hell should I know if there's an afterlife?"

"But do you believe in it?"

"Sure, I guess."

I say, "Scoot over," and then I lie down next to him on the bed. I look up at the ceiling. "Why?"

"I dunno. Catechism, maybe? Who cares?"

I shake my head. " 'Who cares'? Seriously?"

Tommy puts a hand over his eyes. "Why do you care? We got years and years before . . . oh." We lie there until Tommy says, "You know, before you were gay, you never needed to talk about anything. I miss that."

I grunt, so he says, "Fine. Go on. Spill your guts."

My voice cracks, I can't help it. "It's just with Frankie . . . I want to believe I'll see him again."

I can feel Tommy tense up. "You might. We don't know."

"When I think about it . . ."

Can't breathe.

Inhale. Hold.

It'll pass, always does.

Exhale. Slowly.

Tommy's looking at me. "You okay?"

Inhale. Hold.

It'll pass, always does.

"Seriously, Kevin, you all right?"

I nod.

Exhale. Slowly.

He watches me, wide-awake now.

"Give me a minute," I tell him, heart pounding, and I walk in circles, stepping on shirts and socks and jeans, breathing, holding, exhaling. Tommy sits up, watching. I try—I really try—not to think about never seeing Francesco again, because when I think about it, I can't stop thinking about it, and that's when I see the plot and we're driving away and he would never do that to me. He would never leave me alone out in the cold; he would never put me in the ground. He's suffocating down there, fighting for air, and it's all my fault, I just let him struggle. I should've been a better partner to him, and I shouldn't have felt sorry for myself in that tiny apartment with him dying next to me, and I need to tell him things, a lot of things. I need to talk to him. I need to know for certain that he understands, that I tried my best to do right by him, that I'm sorry for the things I got wrong, or the times I was useless when we'd sit in silence knowing he was dying. Mostly, I want him to forgive me.

Please forgive me.

Finally I feel it lift. I sit on the edge of Tommy's bed.

Tommy says softly, "What the hell was that? You mental?"

I breathe normally. "Just happens sometimes. Comes and goes."

"You were walking in circles for fifteen minutes. Seriously, fifteen minutes. That's a long time, Kev. It's an even longer time when you're trapped in a room with a guy walking in circles."

He's exaggerating. "Sorry. Go back to sleep."

"You come in here, you wake me up, you ask me if there's an afterlife, and then you stagger around like a fucking zombie. Okay. Nighty-night."

"Nighty-night."

"Jesus," he says, "you're not going anywhere until you tell me what's wrong."

I move to the floor, sit on a pair of dirty jeans or a dirty denim shirt, I can't tell. "I freak out every once in a while. Nights are bad. I just think too much. I think it's impossible that he existed and now he doesn't. Frankie's death has to mean more than his neurons stopped firing. His life has to mean more than that. I'm worried they're going to paint over his murals in the apartment. They have to be saved. People will want to see them."

Tommy's silent for a moment or two, but then he says, "We really should be stoned for this conversation." When I don't laugh, he says quietly, "Sorry, Kev. I don't know what to tell you. Maybe cause I haven't lost anyone. And I don't know what happens when we die. Maybe that's all there is. The end. *Finito.* The big sleep. But maybe not. Maybe you'll see him again. Here's what I think. We should go on a road trip, just the two of us. Remember, back in school, when we were gonna get a couple Harleys and hit the road? I can't take that much time from work, but we could head up to the Boundary Waters for a long weekend. And if you freak out, I promise I won't kill you and dump your body in a lake. Well, I can promise to try not to. Actually, I promise I'll be quick and merciful. Quick, anyway."

I can't help it, I laugh, just a little. "Sounds okay."

He leans over, pats my head like I'm a dog. "When you laughed, just then? That's what it's all about, Kev. That's it, right there. It's all you need to know." He looks down at me, his hair falling along either side of his face. "And like when I tell you, 'I love you, Kev,' 'cause I really do—I know it's not much, but you gotta enjoy things, like what you still have, even if nothing lasts forever. Now go back to bed, and stop being mental."

I stand up. "Thanks, Tommy. I love you, too."

Instead of good night, he says, "Cool."

When Aunt Nora gets home late after work, she's PISSED. She doesn't even take off her coat. I hit the mute on *Perfect Strangers* and wait for her to detonate.

"Why didn't you come home last night?"

"Why'd you ditch me at the AIDS Project?"

She moves a cat off an overstuffed chair and sits down, coat still on. "I needed some time away from you. Why didn't you phone and let me know where you were?"

"I'm all grown up, Aunt Nora. I don't need to ask your permission for a sleepover."

She stands back up again, hands on hips. "No, you are not a grown-up, not at all. A grown-up lets his family know where he is so they don't worry themselves sick that he's lying in a ditch somewhere. A grown-up asks for help when he needs it. A grown-up doesn't try to drink himself to death when there's people doing the best they can to help. Sometimes, I swear to God in his heaven, you might as well be your . . ."

"Father? That worthless piece of shite I call Da?"

"No," she says definitively. "Your mam."

No one has ever said that to me before.

People who knew my family always said I took after my father. Even Mom saw him in me from day one. She'd say, "Just like your father"—at least three times a week, usually when I didn't do something I said I'd do or did something I promised I'd never do again. But mostly I would catch her staring at Dad and me at mealtime. It didn't matter which one—breakfast, lunch, supper—it was always the same. She'd be looking at him, and when I stabbed something with my fork, I'd feel her eyes move to me. It got worse as I got older. It began to piss Dad off so much that he'd shoot her a look when it happened. He'd say, "For Christ's sake, Eileen, do you have to do that?"

At the time I didn't understand why she did it. But after Mom died, I found out about Dad, about how he broke her heart more than once, about how he was going to leave us for Laurie's aunt Carol. She must've worried that I'd follow in his footsteps and break some poor woman's heart one day.

Obviously, she worried for nothing.

I wish I'd been a better son to her.

I was the only child she ever got to have.

Aunt Nora grieves for her every day. She believes that the car accident that killed Mom was no accident, that Mom tried to cross the Mississippi in a Ford Galaxy because Dad was going to leave her. And like all good Irish Catholics, she blames herself.

When she isn't blaming Dad.

She stares at me now; she never backs down, not once. Not even with a cat rubbing against her big man ankles, mewing for its dinner.

I tell her, like I've told her a dozen times before, "It was an accident."

Aunt Nora says, "The car or the vodka?"

"Both." Mom didn't kill herself. It was winter, and for all her years in Minnesota, Mom never really got the hang of driving on the ice and snow. These roads kill dozens of people before spring finally arrives.

Another cat meows now, which starts off the rest of them. I look away, I never could win a stare-down with her, the woman doesn't blink, barely breathes. She takes off her coat. I tell her, "You were the one who told me to walk slowly with my grief. Too big a pain in the ass for you now?"

As she pulls a hankie out of a sweater sleeve, she says, "You can be my darling boy and a big pain in my arse all at once. This isn't about losing Frankie, it's about you learning how to take responsibility for yourself and how to treat others with the respect they deserve. That bit you do get from your da. I know handsome lads get away with a lot, your da was a stunner in his day. But it's well past time you learned how to depend upon yourself. You know, Frankie used to despair about your jobs, so many I can't remember them all. One week you were going to become a personal trainer, but you give up because it's too hard to get clients. The next you're asking friends to line you up with work. It kept him up nights."

I follow her out to the kitchen, where she picks up half-a-dozen bowls from the floor. "No, it didn't. Before he got sick, he never worried about a thing."

"He wasn't up all night worrying, he was up all night working. To pay the bills."

I can feel the warmth on my face as I watch her scoop Cat Chow in bowls. "He told you all that."

The cats are yowling. "When I'd phone and you were at your gym, we'd have our little chats. He was always grateful I called you, with your mam passed on and your da . . . wherever he is."

"He never said." Neither of them did.

"He wouldn't want to upset you. I wanted to have a word, but he told me to leave it alone, that you had to find your own way. So I sent him money, but he always sent it back, with thanks. Until he got sick. Then he needed it. The both of you did."

He never said one word.

I sit down at the kitchen table as the cats crunch their chow. "He said 'leave it alone,' and *you* left it alone? When have you ever left anything alone?"

She sits across from me now. "Your mam always told me not to stir the pot. I never learned that lesson with her, but I promised myself I'd do better with you and your . . ." She doesn't know what to call him, now that I implode at the word "friend." Eventually she settles on ". . . man."

I can't look at her, so I stare at my hands. "I'm sorry, Aunt Nora."

"I know."

"Can I do anything?"

She reaches over, holds a hand. "Come to Easter Mass with me."

Fuck.

Chapter 4

APRIL 1988: I'M JUST HERE TO LISTEN

So here we are, at St. Stephen's, in Aunt Nora's old neighborhood, and the church she's returned to after the Communion cup wars at her old one. It's packed with what Aunt Nora calls, rather snootily, Easter and Christmas Catholics. All the pews are taken, so the ushers set up folding chairs along the walls. I decide to pay close attention at Easter Mass, in the hopes I might impress Aunt Nora with some Resurrection trivia.

This is a hectic time for her: she went to Holy Wednesday Mass, Maundy Thursday Mass, Good Friday Mass, Holy Saturday Night Mass (the Easter vigil), is at Easter Sunday Mass with me now, will go to Octave Masses tomorrow, Tuesday, Wednesday, Thursday, Friday, and Saturday, and complete her tour of duty on the Second Sunday of Easter Mass, aka The Divine Mercy Sunday.

On the ride over, I told her that she didn't have to bother with any of it because Easter's been canceled: They found the body.

She didn't laugh, just told me that I was some can of piss.

As my first non-funeral mass in years proceeds, the priest

tells us: "They both ran, but the other disciple outran Peter and reached the tomb first; and stooping to look in, he saw the linen cloths lying there, but he did not go in." Babies start to cry, so he speaks louder. "Then Simon Peter came, following him, and went into the tomb. He saw the linen cloths lying, and the napkin, which had been on his head, not lying with the linen cloths but rolled up in a place by itself. Then the other disciple, who reached the tomb first, also went in, and he saw and believed, for as yet they did not know the Scripture, that he must rise from the dead."

When Francesco was diagnosed, I started paying attention to religion again, thinking that maybe it could be a source of strength for us. I didn't bother with Catholicism, because Cardinal O'Connor's happy to see fags die; it's God's judgment. So I borrowed some books on New Age spiritualities, nothing too Louise Hay, which would only make Francesco angry. A lot of New Agers claimed to descend from ancient traditions and wisdoms, so I studied ancient religions next in search of one to bring us—Francesco and me, and our friends who were sick and dying—some measure of comfort. I didn't find one, but I did learn a lot.

For example, Easter is just like the pre-Christian Cybele cult. Cybele's lover was Attis, the god of ever-reviving vegetation. Attis is another virgin birth, and he died and was reborn each year. The festival honoring him began on a day of blood, called Black Friday, and ended with three days of rejoicing his resurrection. So why aren't we worshiping him? There's a lot of gods who didn't make the cut, gods like Odin, Nin, Thor (Francesco filled in on a couple issues of his comic book), and hundreds and hundreds more.

The mass ends and so we go in peace to love and serve the Lord.

On the car ride back to Powderhorn, Aunt Nora asks me what I thought about the mass.

"It was nice."

"They have a lot of lovely gay fellas at that church, did you see them all?"

"Wasn't really looking."

"A few of them were looking at you. A lovely Catholic lad might be . . ." She honks her horn at a kid on a bike who pulls right out in front of us. She rolls down her window, shouts, "You want to get yourself killed, then?" When she rolls it back up, she says, "I think it's a lovely church, a good place to meet men like yourself. Very, what's the word they use? 'Affirming.' It's very affirming."

"It was fine," I tell her.

"But?"

She knows I struggle with religion, and despise the faith I was raised in. Her own self was under the delusion for years that Mom was going to spend all eternity in hell because suicide is a mortal sin (as if Mom killed herself, as if ending your suffering sends you to hell, as if there's a hell).

And DON'T EVEN with Cardinal O'Connor—condemning condoms, railing against gay rights, calling equal protection for people like me a crime against "divine law." And if you really, really, REALLY think about it, why would you want to eat human flesh and drink human blood—literally or even metaphorically—every Sunday?

So I say, "Why are you worshiping a god who told a man to sacrifice his own son? Think about it. God tells Abraham to kill his own child. Abraham ties his kid to an altar to kill him. Go knock on your neighbor's door, ask her to sacrifice her kid to God, and see what happens. Today they lock you up if you even smack a kid."

Aunt Nora says, "No, no, no, sweetheart. Abraham doesn't sacrifice his son. God sends a messenger to stop him."

I say, "Why would a loving god put a father and his son through that?"

"To teach us that child sacrifice is wrong. They were sacrificing everything they could get their hands on back then."

"No. The messenger God sends to stop Abraham tells him, basically, 'God scared the shit out of you, and that's good!' It didn't say, *It's a sin to sacrifice a human life.*"

Aunt Nora simmers. She says, "I'm surprised you know any of this. You hardly went to Catechism, and after your mam passed, you never bothered yourself with mass."

I look out the passenger side window. What was the point of Catechism, or mass, for that matter? Why worship somebody who could've stopped Mom's car before it fell in the river? Who could've cured Francesco, but let him die? Who had the power to do anything—like free the Jews from the death camps, or feed the Irish before a million of them starved to death—but didn't? What does he do? Changes water into wine at a wedding reception to please his mother. I mean, for Chrissake!

I tell my pious aunt: "There was a lot of hours to fill in the apartment, waiting. I wanted to find something about the faith I grew up in that might help. Maybe give us some hope."

I look over at her. She nods.

I clench my fists. "But the God you worship doesn't give me hope. And that's the God everybody worships, even the Protestants, the Jews, and the Muslims. I don't get it. It's like your god's a sadist. Who tells a father to kill his own son?"

Aunt Nora looks at me deadly serious. "God was testing Abraham's faith. And tread lightly, my darling boy, because right now you're testing my patience."

My anger turns to fear when we nearly hit an MTC bus. "Please watch the road."

Aunt Nora and I have not agreed to disagree. She's right and I'm wrong, so there's nothing left to say. God will forgive me and have mercy upon my soul, as I'm still grieving my loss.

The good news is that she's lent me her car; it's an AMC Eagle, a car with four-wheel drive she bought after her Matador fell apart. After all this time in Minnesota, winter driving now makes her nervous and her *nerves can't take* getting stuck in the alley again. The downside is that four-wheel drive makes her feel like Superman, invulnerable, and I have to remind her that she isn't driving a heavy gun tank to church every holy day of obligation.

She only lent me her car because it's midmorning, so the bars aren't open, and because of my destination, which she views as an act of Christian charity. I'm going to surprise my little sister. I got her a stuffed bear for her collection, which started with the one I gave her for her very first Christmas. Well, Aunt Nora paid for the bear, like she's paid for everything else since I came back, and I need to find a temporary gig until I move back to New York.

And a way to pay off my ER bills. Still, they have to find me first. Maybe I should stay in Minnesota. The bill collectors won't think to look for me here, probably can't even find it on a map. Besides, with the eviction from Avenue B, I'm a dead end.

And I mean that literally.

Anyway, I think Sarah will love Farrell Furskin, with his overalls and red plaid shirt. I think I need a stuffed animal of my own. Something big that I can hold on to and talk to at night, instead of just the pillows.

I cross the Lake Street Bridge, and go down East River Road, the same road Mom was driving when she skidded on the ice and over an embankment. Among the things retrieved from the car were two rolls of Brawny paper towels, a jug of liquid Tide, and a bag of Old Dutch potato chips. So I know she didn't kill herself, because who does the shopping first? And the potato chips she always bought especially for me. Neither she nor Dad ate them, they liked Tid-Bits.

I wonder what Mom would think about Sarah. Sarah's mother—Laurie's aunt Carol—was *the other woman*, after all. The one Dad had carried on with for years, promised Mom he'd end it with, and finally married after Mom died and Carol got pregnant with the daughter he hasn't even met. Mom would probably love Sarah, in spite of who her mother is. Mom loved children.

I'd always wondered why I was an only child, given how off-the-boat Catholic Mom was. Before I left for New York, Aunt Nora told me after a couple of hot whiskeys with sugar that I wasn't supposed to be an only child. Mom wanted a big family, but she had secondary infertility because of endometriosis. I wonder what brothers and sisters would have been like. Maybe we could've talked about the quiet tension between our parents as we tried to fall asleep in the room we shared. Maybe I could've confided in one of them that I was gay. Or maybe they'd be like Dead Eddie's brother, who never visited him and tore my one good funeral suitcoat. Or like Francesco's brother Marco, who never visited, never called, never even sent a card. Or Marco's wife, what's-her-face with her stink eye.

Hard to say. Every kid's a crapshoot. You have these ideas about how they'll turn out, but Sarah isn't what Dad wanted. And it's even odds that neither am I, not that he stuck around long enough to find out. I mean, what man wants a gay kid?

Who cares, anyway? He was a dick to my mom. And then he just disappeared.

What a dick.

And after I protected him, when it was just him and me, during those first two years after Mom's accident, before Aunt Nora told me the truth about Dad and Carol. Before he took up with her again. I remember the Catholic widows were circling him like vultures. He had to stop going to a Catholic support group called To Live Again for people whose spouses died because he was the only middle-aged man, and the younger widows wouldn't leave him alone. They'd call him at all hours, sometimes drunk, so I was always the one to answer the phone. I'd tell them he was out and not offer to take a message, but they didn't take the hint, and they'd ask me for advice:

What does he like to do?

What's his favorite meal?

Would he like to go to a North Stars game, do you think?

I'd just stare at the receiver, feeling a little sorry for these women who'd been cheated out of a husband so early in life. I lied, told them that Dad had a girlfriend and to stop calling our house. But they didn't, not until Dad broke down and paid the extra money for an unlisted number.

When that happened, they started dropping by with little gifts for him. He had to go down the basement or hide upstairs anytime the doorbell rang. It was my job to put the widows off his scent. A lot of them brought ties, something Dad didn't need—he worked day shifts at the Highland Park Ford plant— and I wondered if all these male presents used to belong to the dead husbands.

I never see your father at mass anymore, one of the widows said to me, a brightly wrapped box of cuff links in her shivering hands.

I told her, He's converting.

With her teeth chattering—I never let the widows inside— she asked: To what?

Islam. (I was studying world religions in my history class.)

The next time she showed up at the door, she was wearing one of those veil things over her face and had a Koran with her.

Okay, so she didn't show up in a veil with a Koran. She never came back at all; I think I kind of freaked her out with the Muslim stuff. But as Aunt Nora has said, "Any story worth telling, is worth exaggerating."

And then there are some stories that need no exaggeration— that you can't bear to tell.

I drive carefully, cautiously, unlike Aunt Nora. It's been

years since I've been behind the wheel, you don't need a car in New York.

Also, my license expired.

I like the feel of the wheel in my hands. I like speeding up by hitting the gas or slowing down by tapping the brakes. I like moving at my own pace. Even though it isn't in the fifties yet, joggers are out in shorts, running up and down East River Road. Back in the day, I would've slowed down when I saw a pair of muscular legs in short shorts, imagining what they would feel like in my hands, what they would taste like as I licked them with my tongue.

Now I just drive by.

The last time I drove was here, in Minneapolis, when Francesco and I came to visit Aunt Nora and Tommy, and so he could meet my sister. The car ride was his idea, and a bad one.

Francesco liked to go out for car rides, since we never drove in New York, rarely took a taxi. It had been unseasonably warm, but I still bundled him up like an old man. As we approached a McDonald's, Francesco insisted I turn in the drive-through. I thought about what the food might do to him, but said nothing. Francesco was sick of macrobiotics and convinced that he was at the end of his life. He was nostalgic and terrified in equal measures.

So I kept my mouth shut as I unwrapped the Filet-O-Fish and handed it to him.

It wasn't more than fifteen minutes later when Francesco stuck his head out the window and vomited. In the crosswalk two teenage boys outfitted in layers of grimly colored flannel shirts and dark blue jeans pointed and laughed, the smaller one shouting at me: "Your dad's waaaay-sted!"

Francesco was only two years older than me.

I revved the engine, but the boys didn't scare. I could feel my anger mounting. Francesco swore by visualization as a technique to calm himself, so at that moment I gave it a try.

I didn't visualize a clear lake illuminated by a pink sunset or a gentle brook with smooth pebbles. I visualized the impact, the taller boy beneath the wheels, the smaller one with his tough-boy smirk tumbling over the hood, all snark and irony and blood and guts, breaking his crooked little nose on the windshield before sliding off the Matador, surviving in agony only long enough for me to put the car in reverse and do it all over again.

It worked. I felt somewhat better.

When the light turned green, Francesco whispered: "I need to change." The Filet-O-Fish had come out both ends.

Carol's place is near Beltrami Park, not far from my old house. On the front stoop there's a large VÄLKOMNA mat, and an old brass mailbox next to the front door. The house looks the same, Carol doesn't. She's stopped dying her hair blond, and it's a mop of brown and gray. She's in a red tracksuit, which makes her look like an old white hip-hop star, minus the gold chains. A cup of coffee's in her hand.

"Hello, Kevin. Laurie told me you were back in town. You should've called, let me know you were coming. Sarah's not here."

"Oh."

"Saturday mornings she has her swim class, and then they all go out for lunch. It's my 'me' time."

I look at the wrapped bear in my hands. "Sorry, I should go. This is for Sarah."

She inspects me closely. "No, please come in. There's a couple of things we need to talk about."

I frown.

"Besides, this morning was easy. Usually she has to try on five different outfits before she's ready, but today the first one was a charm."

Her sitting room is a mess of dolls, books, and videocassettes. On the wall's a color print of the Eiffel Tower and I can hear the hum of a dryer from under the floorboards.

I hand Carol my gift for Sarah, along with a Joe Cool Snoopy card.

She asks, "What's the occasion?"

"Guilt," I say. "I live so far away and I want her to like me."

"She loves everyone. What is it?"

"A stuffed bear. This one's the hillbilly postmaster of Moody Hollow!"

Carol shakes her head, hands it back. "I'm afraid it's all Barbie, all the time now. As you can see." She points to a corner where a pile of naked and clothed Barbies, black and white, lie in a pile, next to a Barbie-sized pink Corvette. "She must have a dozen of them. Laurie lectures me on how Barbie's going to make Sarah hate her own body, but she wants them. She loves to play with them, and, frankly, sometimes I just want her to entertain herself. I'm not going to picket Mattel until they make a chubby Down syndrome Barbie."

I sit next to my bear on the couch. "How's she doing?"

Carol takes an ugly worn chair. "She's loving fourth grade. She doesn't take math with the other kids, and she needs support in the mainstream classes, but she's reading the same books as the rest and she was in the school spelling bee this year."

I smile. "That's cool."

Carol sighs. "She's a good kid, so much more outgoing than Laurie at her age. Of course Laurie had her own issues." She laughs, adds, "Has her own issues. Sometimes I miss the little nerd girl with the horse books."

"You and me both."

"It's how strangers react to Sarah that burns me up. I'm sick of the looks when we're out grocery shopping, especially the pity faces on the other mothers. I want to tell them, I'd take my kid any day of the week over their spoiled little brats. But it's not just them. Yesterday some old man tried to pat her on the head like she was a dog out for a walk." She stops, smiles. "Sorry, you didn't come all the way from New York to listen to me complain."

"S'okay."

"It can be funny, too. The biggest mistake people make is underestimating her. She's delayed with her own verbal communication, but she can understand what you say, in the literal sense. And she'll remember it. And repeat it. Last year she scared her teachers when she said our next-door neighbor was going to kill the mailman. Our neighbor had said that to me when she came over for about the tenth time with my mail. People think they can say anything in front of her because she won't understand. But she does. Not exaggeration or irony, but she understands."

"And you're doing okay?"

"I'm fine. The school has excellent teachers, and she's getting a lot of individualized attention. Plus, she's made friends, and not just with girls like her. I'm already dreading junior high, though. There's nothing more vicious in the world than fourteen-year-old girls. I just hope they leave her alone. If they don't, I'm going to have to kill them."

We sit in silence and I can't think of anything else to say. Carol and I have never had what you would call a close relationship. My senior year, when Aunt Nora finally told me the truth about Carol and Dad, I guess you could say I went a little mental. Well, maybe more than a little. When Carol had the balls to show her face at the grocery store where I worked after school as a bagger, I tossed a shopping cart through the rear windshield of her Cordoba. I started calling her the "miserable old cow," like Aunt Nora did. When she married Dad at City Hall, I was the worst best man in history.

But I did make an effort after Sarah was born. It was hard to stay mad at her when she was a new mom with a baby in the

ICU and a husband who was AWOL. We even spent a Christmas Eve together as a kind of family.

But then I followed Laurie to New York and never looked back.

I stand up. "Will she be around tomorrow afternoon?"

She clears her throat a little. "Sit. Please."

I sit.

"Kevin, I really should have told you this when you were here last, but your father finally served me with divorce papers, so it's official. I'm no longer Mrs. Patrick Doyle."

What the hell? "Jesus! Why didn't you say anything?"

She hugs herself. "I was in shock. Part of me still is. I hadn't heard anything from him since he disappeared. And then the divorce papers out of the blue."

"Where is he?"

"He wound up in Alaska, after all, in Valdez. He was arrested in Fairbanks, so that's when the child support orders finally caught up to him."

"Why was he arrested?"

"He was drunk and caught with a prostitute. Guess it happens all the time up there."

"Oh."

"The good news is that he's making real money, I got a very fat check. Believe me, after years of no child support, I needed it. Now they take child support direct from his wages. He's finally doing his part for Sarah."

"Have you talked to him?"

She nearly laughs. "Oh no. Everything was done through the lawyers."

I sit there.

She reads my mind. "There wasn't any personal correspondence, either. Maybe he did try to get in touch with you, but didn't know how. And I couldn't bring myself to even write him a note."

"Has he tried to see Sarah?"

"No. He gave up all paternal rights. Even if he wanted to see her, I wouldn't let him."

"Oh."

She hugs herself harder. "And this is difficult for me to say, but I have to say it. I don't want you to see her, either."

My chest goes tight. "What?"

She stares at the pile of Barbies. "I'm very sorry for your loss. I should have sent a card or called you, but then so much time passed, I was embarrassed, so I didn't do anything . . . I'm really glad you're healthy, Kevin, really I am."

I thought she was smarter than this. "I'm not gonna give her AIDS. Jesus."

"If that was it, I never would have let her meet Frankie." She looks at me now. "That's not the reason. But Frankie's passing did get me to thinking."

I dig my nails into the palms of my hands. "About?"

"I know what happened back in New York, and I know you might be back here for a while. Maybe for good, who knows?"

"I'm not back for good."

"My point is this. Sarah has more than enough challenges already. I don't want her to fall in love with her big brother, just to lose him."

I inhale, hold it. Exhale slowly. I don't know what my voice sounds like. "I don't understand."

"You don't understand because you don't really know her. I won't even let her have a pet because she was inconsolable for weeks after the class hamster died. She feels grief in a way I can't fathom and don't know how to make better. She melts down and it scares me. Then she just shuts down. She's a lot more sensitive than other kids. Always has been. She thinks the world should be a happy place, so sad things break her heart."

This makes no sense. "She's never gotten upset when I left before. She hugs me and says good-bye. It's no big deal."

She looks at the ceiling and back down at me. "I don't mean when you go back to New York. I mean when you die."

What?

"She remembers everything. She remembers Frankie, even though she only met him the one time. She asked me for weeks after you left when you and Frankie were going to visit again. I told her you're in New York, and that's what I intend to tell her until the day *I* die."

I feel my leg shake. "I have a right to see my own sister."

"Forgive me, but, no, you don't. And you don't get to tell me how to raise my kid. It's not like you've spent a lot of time with her. You're out in New York, you're going to the clubs, you're having a fine old time, and I'm here, and I'm raising her by myself."

"You've never wanted me around."

"Hey," she snaps, "I tried. I tried damn hard! You don't get to complain about me. You were such a little bastard to me when you found out about me and your dad. I put up with the insults, the nasty looks, the silent treatments. And then when Sarah was born, I felt like maybe—*maybe*—we could get past all that, that you wanted to be a part of her life. But what do you do? You go away, just like your father. And I've been walking on eggshells around you ever since. Well, no more. You need to grow the hell up."

What's so fucking infuriating is that she's right. She did try. But I was too busy staying loyal to a dead woman to give her a real chance. I stand because my leg won't stop shaking. I play my high card: "You know, if my mom did kill herself, you were the reason."

She grimaces—this isn't the first time I've told her that. She says what she always says: "It was an accident." But then she adds: "But *if* she did kill herself, it was down to her. How anyone could do something so selfish . . ."

Selfish? "You fucking cunt."

"And just like that, we're back to where we started. Get out of my house, Kevin, and take your damn bear with you. Oh, and have a good life—what's left of it, anyway."

Long-distance is expensive as hell, and Aunt Nora has begged me not to call New York, but I have to talk to my straight female best friend.

"Your aunt" is all I get out before Laurie says, "I'm so sorry."

"You knew?"

"I call Sarah every week. When I told Aunt Carol you were back in town, she said she didn't think it was a good idea for you to visit Sarah anymore. I really, really tried to talk some sense into her, but she wouldn't listen to a word I said."

I glare at a cat pawing my shoelace. "So the class hamster dies, and I'm next. Jesus Christ. I mean, *Jesus Christ*."

"Let's give it some time, okay? She thinks she's doing what's best for Sarah. She'll come around."

"Not this time. We said shit."

I hear Laurie's deep sigh from Hell's Kitchen. "You didn't call her a bitch again, did you? First, I can't even tell you how degrading that is to—"

"Bitch would've been polite. I called her something else."

"Oh, my God, what is wrong with you? Is this about your mom? It's not like you've ever really been involved in Sarah's life."

"So now you taking *her* side?" The cat's gotten a nail caught in my shoelace.

"No, but try to understand where she's coming from. She's scared. Not of you, and not of AIDS, she's scared for her daughter."

"You might have warned me."

"I honestly didn't think she would really stop you from seeing Sarah. I told her that just because Frankie died, didn't mean you would, too."

I pet the cat. "Did you know about my dad?"

Nothing. What is it with her and her family? "So you did know. Why the hell didn't you tell me?"

"I'm really sorry. Frankie was dying. Then there never seemed to be a good time. You haven't been able to handle anything since he died."

I take off my sneaker and the cat drags it. "Stop deciding what I can handle and what I can't. Okay?"

"Okay."

"Do you know what she said to *me*?"

"Obviously, I do not."

I choke. "She told me to have a good life, whatever's left of it." Jesus Christ, I cry all the time anymore.

"Oh, honey, I'm so, so sorry. She had no right. Absolutely no right."

I sit down on the linoleum, trace the yellow and orange squares and rectangles with my foot. I'm able to say, "Just keep talking to me, please."

She does, and when she runs out of things to say, she hands the phone over to Toshiro. He says, "Hello, Kevin. Everyone in New York misses you, all seven million of us. I'm sorry you're upset. Do you know what I'm penciling right now?"

"No."

"*Who's Who in the Legion of Super-Heroes.*"

"Is Shadow Kid in it?"

"Yes. He graduates from the Legion Academy. And then he and Cosmic Boy get gay-married. Cosmic Boy is wearing his old skimpy uniform that you admire so, but in white."

I smile a little. "Where are they going on their honeymoon?"

"Trom, so they can have the entire planet all to themselves."

Trom, the planet where everyone had died years before. "How's Eddie? He hasn't called me this week."

"Oh. Fine, I think. Let me get Laurie back. She's spoken with him most recently."

"Yeah?"

"How's Eddie doing?"

"Great. I dropped by with some fresh fruit last week. He was pretty wiped, so I didn't stay long, but he said he's been gaining weight."

Thank God for that.

Thank you, God, for that.

Thursday night and I'm at the AIDS Project, sorting direct mail by zip code. The first-ever AIDS walk in Minnesota is next month and no one really knows what to expect. Will anyone show up? The conference room's crowded with folding tables and boxes of appeal letters, every one to be compiled with pledge forms and stuffed into envelopes. Once assembled, the little piles must be counted and sorted by zip codes. The "Thursday Nighters," as the volunteers prefer to be called, are an interesting group: mostly gay men, young and old, along with some straight women. They're stationed in groups of three or more around the tables. Bowls of water and small sponges for sealing envelopes sit next to homemade cookies and bars.

A boom box plays "Never Let Me Down Again" by Depeche Mode.

The group is "Minnesota Nice" and hardworking and much more reserved than your East *Vill-ahge* gays, who have to tell you what they're thinking in real time. And there's not a single drag queen in the bunch.

Brian, the volunteer coordinator, points me to a seat next to a volunteer I haven't seen before. He looks to be in his early thirties, and wears a gray suit like he just came from work. The large black retro sixties glasses are the only hint of trendiness. Take them off, along with maybe ten pounds, put him in a uniform, and he could be Jim Reed from *Adam-12*. He holds out his hand, says, "Howdy. I'm Dave." People still say "howdy."

"Kevin."

Brian says, "I wanted to talk to you two. There's a support group for surviving partners that's accepting new members. I thought you might be interested."

"There's an icebreaker," I say, but neither of them laughs.

Dave looks seriously at the brochures Brian leaves behind as I stuff pledge forms into envelopes. He reads aloud, "'A culture of grief has immersed many of us in the gay community, and multiple and chronic loss is a common experience no matter our age. The Survivors Support Group offers a safe place for you to meet other surviving partners of those who have died of AIDS, and to break the code of silence and isolation that is so often experienced at the workplace or at family gatherings. We can also help you with the uncertainties of your own health, providing support and resources to HIV-positive surviving partners and the worried well.'" Then he says, "Hmmmm."

"When did your partner die?"

I've startled him. Minneapolis ain't New York. You don't ask someone you just met something like that. He starts folding pledge forms for me to stuff, says stiffly, "It will be a year next month." He folds a few more, then asks, "You?"

"It was two years on Valentine's Day."

He frowns. "Really?"

"Nah, just fucking with youse." Then I add, "Yeah. Really."

We go back to folding and stuffing in silence as "Strangelove" plays in the background and the other Thursday Nighters laugh and talk.

Dave says, "Sorry. It's just that that's so sad."

"Was it any better in May?"

He shakes his head.

Jesus, I'm a big dick, and not in a good way. I say, "I'm sorry. I just haven't really . . . gotten back to normal." Whatever that was.

He says, never taking his eyes off his task, "You can't go back. This is normal now."

A pretty, tall, and thin woman, who's been talking and laughing since I arrived, walks over with a plate of bars, waving it under our noses. "Who's hungry?" she wants to know.

Saturday morning, and Aunt Nora has a most unfortunate surprise for me.

Her priest.

"Look who's called," she says as I come down the stairs in my bathrobe. "It's Father Michael."

He looks up from the couch, where he balances a Belleek cup and saucer on his knee.

Aunt Nora hands me a cup and saucer of my own, says, "Sit, sit. Have a nice chat with Father."

The only priest I trust is Daniel Berrigan, a Jesuit at St. Vincent's Hospital, and he spent time up the river. I say, "I haven't even had a shower."

Cats mew as Aunt Nora says, "Father has come round special for you. Sit."

"For me?" I look at the priest in his sweatshirt and jeans, his gut puts him in his third trimester.

He smiles oddly. "At your aunt's request. Nora, you didn't mention this to him?"

I answer for her. "No."

She says, "If I had, he wouldn't be here. I've told Father all about you, and how you nearly drank yourself to death. He's here to tell you, you needn't despair, that you'll see Frankie again in heaven."

For a tough old broad who's made her own way in life, Aunt Nora can be pretty damn simple.

The priest flinches, says to Aunt Nora, "Well, if that's all, it seems like you don't need me."

Aunt Nora says, "No, Father, you put things so well and he needs to hear it from the genuine article. I'll leave you to it,

then. The pot's"—she points to the little dining-room table—
"full. I'll just be downstairs doing my laundry if you should
need me."

Yeah. Up on a ladder and listening through the floorboards.

A moment or two passes before the priest says, "So tell me,
how can I help?"

I take a chair, careful of the Belleek, and get down to business. "I'm going to see my homosexual lover, who I sodomized
as much as I could, in heaven. Really?"

The priest obviously didn't sign on for this. He looks for a
place to set his cup and saucer, and finding none, sets them
carefully on the rug, where a cat takes interest. He leans in, his
elbows on his knees, and says, "You will see him again. Those
who die in God's grace and friendship enter the kingdom.
While I never met him, I can tell you that God is love. He loves
us all, gay or straight, rich or poor."

And here we go. The old *God-is-love* shtick. He's working
Berrigan's side of the street. I decide to put him through his
paces. "Prove it."

The priest smiles now, says, "It's a matter of faith, Kevin."

Of course that's what he says. "So you just wish really hard
that it's true?"

His chair creaks as he sits back. "Did your aunt mention that
I originally studied to be an astronomer when I was in school?"

What's that got to do with anything? "No."

"I wanted to discover other planets, other galaxies. Ones like
ours, with life."

He folds his arms over his belly. "Do you believe planets like
that exist?"

*Its five-year mission: to explore strange new worlds. To seek
out new life and new civilizations. To boldly go where no man
has gone before!* "Maybe."

He says, "I think so, too. The universe is a big place, so big
that even if life elsewhere is highly unlikely, the exceptions to

the rule must be in the billions." He looks thoughtful for a second before he says, "Have you ever heard of Georges Lemaître?"

I sigh. Where's he going with this? "No."

He leans in again. "He was a Belgian priest and astronomer. He applied Einstein's equations to the universe, and do you know what he came up with?"

This guy's playing twenty questions. I shake my head.

"Well, today it's known as the Big Bang theory."

I almost laugh. "I thought you were supposed to believe that God created everything in a week."

If he's offended, he doesn't show it. "The book of Genesis has two versions of the creation story. Every culture has its own version. It's understandable. It's only human to want to know where we come from. Why we're here. And what happens when we die."

"There's no evidence for life after death. Believe me, I've looked . . ." I stop, breathe.

"Well, yes, the fact of the matter, Kevin, is that there's no evidence that inconvertibly proves that we survive bodily death. Maybe there will be someday, but not today. Today all we have is faith."

I look at him honestly now. "I can't make myself believe in any of this stuff, and I've tried."

He shrugs it off. "I knew you didn't believe, the moment I saw you."

"How?"

"Experience. We're not a large parish, but we do have quite a diverse range of Catholics at St. Stephen's. There are the ones who never left, even after the freeway came through. The ones who converted, and the ones who left and then reverted. And then, we have people like you, who show up as a favor to their families every Easter and Christmas. Others were born Catholic and show up because they like the tradition, they find it comforting, even though they don't believe it. And there are the ones who don't believe in God, but feel that they should. Some of them want to hedge their bets. Others are just plain terrified."

"Of what?"

He throws his hands up in the air. "A universe that just happened by accident without purpose or meaning. That randomly resulted in a bunch of flesh bags of chemical reactions that we call people."

I take a deep breath, hold. I say to him, or maybe myself, "That's fucking depressing."

"Yes, I agree with you, it's *fucking* depressing. Bottom line, though, it's what you believe, isn't it? And for other people, it's not a depressing idea at all. They seem more than content with what time they have. In fact, for some, it's the idea of eternity that scares them. It may be true that when we die, it's over. But I don't believe it."

"Why not?"

He folds his hands together and I'm afraid he's gonna start praying. "Because, whether you believe the creation stories in the Book of Genesis, which I don't, or the equations of Georges Lemaître, which I do, something had to cause the universe to come into existence. And it seems our universe is remarkably well-ordered, because all those equations scientists come up with are able to explain how it works. If the universe is so random, it shouldn't follow any rules, but it does. If the universe is so random, scientists shouldn't be able to explain a thing about the nature of existence, it'd be impossible to do, but they do it. I take comfort in their discoveries. I take great comfort in the natural order of things. Because there's a rhyme and a reason to it. My simple brain may not be able to understand it all, but it doesn't have to."

He shoos a cat away from his cup. "I know you don't believe in, let alone celebrate, the mystery of our faith. I'm praying that you will see your partner again, but I don't know if you will. But be honest, neither do you. We learn to live with uncertainty. We need to be open to the fact that we might be wrong. Don't be dogmatic. Be open."

This coming from a priest. "So you're okay with the possibility that you could be wrong about everything you've dedicated your life to?"

He shrugs. "Don't tell the archbishop, but yes. We all live with uncertainty, whether we admit it or not." After a moment he adds, "And if nothing else, believe the voice of experience on this one—leave the vodka well alone. That stuff will kill you."

So I'm at Abbott, a South Minneapolis hospital, where the support group for surviving partners meets. I made the mistake of putting the brochure Brian gave me in the kitchen trash can before I tossed my empty Swanson's Hungry-Man Salisbury Steak dinner tray on top of it, so, of course, Aunt Nora found it, read it, and told me I had to go and meet people like myself. She says apart from hanging with Tommy, I'm spending too much time alone at the gym, but she doesn't understand that I left this city in the iron bunker of my closet and have returned a gay widower. It's a lot to explain to people who haven't seen you in a while. Besides, after my experience with Rick Foley, I'm not eager to renew old friendships that mostly revolved around drinking till we passed out, anyway. I'm skipping the Northeast High School Class of 1978 ten-year reunion, where I'd likely win the Most Changed award.

So here I am, a twenty-eight-year-old man whose aunt of indeterminable age waits in the lobby to give him a ride home. Aunt Nora wants me to be a grown-up, and yet fails to appreciate the irony.

This group is all men, except the facilitator, a lesbian volunteer with a pageboy cut, who's poured into jeans topped off with a black leather jacket. While I know squat about women, I can tell this one's a heartbreaker, a butch Bobbie Jo (the second one) from *Petticoat Junction*.

There are eight men attending in the little, anonymous, windowless room. Including Dave from the Thursday Nighters. Nobody looks to be over forty, two of them look younger than me, thin men with pierced ears, one with hair dyed blond, the other with hair dyed black, and long scarves. We sit on folding chairs arranged in a near circle. No bad coffee, no stale cookies, just the powerful stink of a Renuzit cone and some brochures from Red Door Clinic about HIV tests. Here's what I expect:

My name's Kevin and I'm an AIDS widower.

Hi, Kevin!

Then we each get a chip for the number of days we've gone without sex. The one-day chip will make us laugh as we applaud, and lead to after-meeting speculation. My two-year chip, however, will be greeted with awkward silence.

After Butch Bobbie Jo gives us the ground rules with an emphasis on *confidentiality*, she has us introduce ourselves. We're a mixed bag—one man's partner died six years ago, two of the men are not surviving partners yet, but will be any day now. Maybe even tonight.

Butch Bobbie Jo encourages Dave and me to *share our stories* as we are brand-new to the group. I look over at Dave, sitting alone with an empty chair on either side of him, not in a suit this time, but a big ugly *Cosby* sweater, jeans, and sneakers. He's wrapped tight—arms crossed, legs crossed, head down. He's not saying anything.

So I say, "I haven't been doing too well since Frankie died. I need to get my shit together. People try to help, but I'm still . . ." What's the word I want? ". . . struggling."

The guy whose partner's been dead six years says, "You can struggle with me anytime, butch."

Bobbie Jo says, "Jeff, that's sexual harassment, and this is a warning. I've warned you before, and I'm not going to again. Now you need to apologize to Kevin."

He says "sorry" with a lecherous smile as other men shoot me sympathetic looks.

Butch Bobbie Jo asks me, "Would you prefer Jeff leave?"

I can't tell whether the other men want me to boot him out or not. Guys make passes at me all the time. And, no, it ain't vain if it's true. "It's okay."

A couple of guys shake their heads. Evidently, Jeff has a history.

Butch Bobbie Jo says, "Kevin, you mentioned that people are trying to help, and that you were struggling. Lots of us struggle, even when we're surrounded by people who care about us. Would it help to tell us about your struggles?"

"Ummm. Not sure."

She tries again. "Some of us may be having the same sort of struggles."

I nod. "I don't wanna hog all the time. I'm just here to listen."

The others—except Dave, who hasn't looked up once—encourage me to open up, but Butch Bobbie Jo reminds them, "Everyone in their own time."

Next she invites Dave to share. I expect him to take a pass, but he looks up just a little, opens his mouth just a little.

He tries to say something, but it comes out as a whisper.

He struggles to breathe.

His face goes red.

And then he moans.

His shoulders tremble.

He hides his face in his hands.

He moans so loud, he sounds like a bloodhound.

Butch Bobbie Jo walks over to him, leans down, and puts a hand on his shoulder. She says, "Let it out, let it out. We're here for you."

Next the dyed-blond kid starts sobbing.

Dave manages to catch his breath, says, "Sorry, sorry" over and over.

Butch Bobbie Jo pulls out a tissue from her jacket pocket, and Dave dries his eyes, inhales and exhales, tries to pull himself together. Butch Bobbie Jo massages his shoulder slowly, purposefully, as she looks over at the dyed-black kid, Aaron, I think his name is. As if on cue, Aaron kid puts an arm around the dyed-blond kid, who's trying to gain control.

Dave adds one final "sorry" before he tells Butch Bobbie Jo, his face startled: "It's been a long time since anyone touched me."

What would Francesco do?

I stand up, take a seat next to Dave, put an arm around him, and squeeze him tight. He rests his head on my shoulder, occasionally wiping his nose and his eyes . . .

. . . As the dyed-blond kid tells us he tested positive and he's terrified to go through what his partner went through. He considered killing himself, but he's too afraid to. And he's afraid that there will come a time when he'll be too sick to kill himself. He doesn't think he will, but he wants the choice. He doesn't want to be so sick that he can no longer choose.

. . . As Aaron tells us his partner's on a respirator. He feels like shit because he wants it to finally be over. He wants his partner's suffering to come to an end.

. . . As Jeff grimaces, sucking on his clotrimazole lozenge, trying to tell us about how he still has seizure nightmares.

. . . As the other men try to lighten up the mood, discussing what we should be eating, things like steamed brown rice or steamed tofu or steamed adzuki beans, and how whole grains are the best to keep yin and yang in balance.

Jesus, I miss delis.

I kiss the top of Dave's head.

* * *

Aunt Nora's disappointed that instead of going to mass with her on Sunday, I'm at the animal shelter out in Golden Valley. She thought the priest's visit would do the trick—he is so *affirming*—but it did not. Unlike St. Stephen's, the shelter's kinda ripe (dogs, cats, disinfectant) and kinda loud.

We're here because Dave wants a dog.

And, no, this isn't a date. His sister, Tracy, is with us.

We haven't looked at more than two dogs when Dave's smitten by a big puppy, probably a German shepherd mix, who has a little bald spot by one of her eyes and another one on top of her head. Instead of a normal tail, there's just a stub, which she's wagging. She's so skinny, you can see her ribs. She's a new arrival, found wandering around North Minneapolis, not far from Brix Grocery.

Over the barking of the other dogs, Tracy, who was adopted from Vietnam, says real loud, "She's mangy. Let's keep looking." But Dave squats down and the puppy comes right up to him, and through the gate licks him on the lips. He coos, "Aw, puppy-dog kisses. What a sweetheart!"

Actually, I know something about dogs, thanks to Rex. According to the training manual I got for my sixth birthday, the puppy's licking Dave's lips so Dave will regurgitate his brunch, which the puppy wants to eat. (In this case a vegetarian omelet, green tea, and a guilty pleasure cinnamon roll with extra butter. He treated us all.)

Dave's enjoying the kisses, so I don't spoil his moment.

Tracy says, "Dave, that dog doesn't look right."

Dave says, "Aw, come on, now. Just look in her big brown puppy-dog eyes."

Tracy says, "I don't know . . . What if it's sick?" and I know what she's trying to say: *What if it dies? You can't go through that again, even with a dog. You'll fall apart.*

Dave says, "Then she'll be sick in her own nice home on her own warm bed, instead of at some institution."

Tracy doesn't say anything, just sucks in her lips, looks at me, and nods.

Now Dave tells the dog with the bald spots and the missing tail: "I'm going to name you Minnie, you moocher. You know why?" The dog's frantic to know, licking and wagging and jumping up. "Because you're a 'red-hot hoochie-coocher'!"

Chapter 5

MAY 1988: HOW NOT TO HAVE SEX IN AN EPIDEMIC: ONE APPROACH

We've been at Minnehaha Park along the Mississippi since the crack of dawn, setting up From All Walks of Life, and there are still concerns that no one will show up. Brian, the volunteer co-ordinator, tells all the gathered volunteers, including Dave, Tracy, Aunt Nora, Tommy, and me, to pretend to be walkers for the news crews if turnout is lousy.

At least we don't have to worry about rain.

Dave and I are at a T-shirt table, listening to volunteers with walkie-talkies reporting from different points along the route, which stretches over seven miles from the Ford Parkway Bridge to the Lake Street Bridge and back again, on alert for counterprotestors or, worse yet, the Berean League, trying to shut us down as they pray for our souls.

As the morning progresses, more people come to the park, and the registration tables where Aunt Nora and Tommy and Dave's sister work are doing a decent business. Worries become enthusiasm. Dogs in bandanas lie at the feet of walkers who sit on benches chatting or sipping coffee. The loudspeakers play walk songs: "These Boots are Made for Walkin'," "Walk This

Way," "You'll Never Walk Alone," "Walk on the Wild Side," "Walk Like a Man." By the time the walk's about to kick off, there's more than a thousand people, some holding signs in memory of friends and lovers, brothers and sons.

Dave looks at the dogs—not the men—longingly. He says, "I should've brought Minnie the Moocher." Her mange is clearing up and she's put on weight, both of which are miraculous to Dave, who seems to have forgotten that living things can recover from illness, heal. To tell the truth, I'd forgotten, too.

A group of skinny young giggly guys, one giving another a piggyback ride, come up for their T-shirts. The one with Jheri curls asks me what I'm doing after the walk, and his friends go "Ooooooo-oo!"

I say, "Going home. Alone."

"Ooooooo-oo!"

He puts his hands on the table, leans in. "That sounds boring," he says. "How 'bout you and I have a little party, just the two of us?"

"Ooooooo-oo!"

"Sorry. Got a date tonight with Officer Harry Truman Ioki."

One of them says, "Well, isn't that special!" and they head off, laughing, maybe at me or their friend with the Jheri curls, who my mom would have called a "brazen article."

Dave says, "How did Frankie put up with it?"

"With what?"

"All the flirting. I mean, even at a survivors' group meeting. It must have gotten pretty tedious."

"For him, yeah."

He slaps me on my arm. Then he looks straight ahead, says very businesslike, "I've given it some thought, and I've come to the conclusion that we've been celibate long enough. I think it's time to start having sex again."

I look at him.

From the backpack at his feet, he pulls out a copy of *How to Have Sex in an Epidemic: One Approach* and hands it to me.

"You realize that this is five years old now."

"It's what Gary and I used after he was diagnosed."

I flip through it. "And you realize that Michael Callen's sworn off sex entirely."

Dave sighs. "Well, call me superstitious, but Gary and I followed it to the letter. And I'm negative."

I stare at him. "You got tested? You never said."

"Gary felt so guilty. I took it three times, and when each test came back negative, I told him. It was like a weight had been lifted off his shoulders. He died knowing he didn't give it to me."

"Jeez. Congratulations. I don't have the balls to get tested." I mean, I'm barely managing as is—what would I do with a positive result? Try to kill it with another handle of Popov? Who would be left to take care of me? I can't put Aunt Nora through that, and the idea of Laurie Lindstrom changing my adult diaper as she lectures me about how it won't decompose for another five hundred years is more than just depressing.

We sit in silence, people watching for a minute or two, before Dave clears his throat, says, "You know, when I said I think we should start having sex again, I meant we should have sex with each other."

"No. I did not know that."

He watches me, but I can't look at him. He says, "This would be purely recreational. I'm not in love with you, or desperately lonely, if that's what you're concerned about."

"And that is not what I'm concerned about."

"What, then?"

"I'm not sure I remember how."

He laughs. "That's why I think we should. It's been a long time for both of us, and based on what I've learned about you from group, it's because we're both still being faithful to our partners. We would make a good coupling. We can be embarrassed together, practice, relieve some tension. Have some human touch. And since it's purely for fun, we're not being ... unfaithful. I think human contact is what we both need. We didn't die, after all. We're still young men."

"Sounds very practical."

"Yes, but that doesn't mean we wouldn't enjoy ourselves."

He stops watching dogs and looks at the bandstand now, where a beautiful young man is warming up walkers with aerobics.

I follow Dave's gaze and look at the men, some beautiful, some ugly, remembering how I used to take in gay men, the swift appraisals when I walked into the bar, the wondering if I should approach or hope to be approached, imagining what he would be like in bed. It's like looking through an old magazine I forgot I still had, and trying to decide whether to keep it or toss it.

I say, "I haven't been able to think about sex without thinking about death."

He nods, as if he's Mr. Spock and everything that I say confirms the logic of his position. "Me too. That will be part of the process. Removing the link between sex and death. Normalizing it again."

"Well, if logic dictates ... when do we start?"

He pats my hand. "I was thinking next Friday, so I can sleep in, in the morning."

Let the healing begin.

The opening number is "Shine On You Crazy Diamond," and Tommy nearly floats up to the quilted fiberglass fabric roof of the Metrodome, he's so stoned. This is my first Pink Floyd concert, and the first concert I've ever attended stone-cold sober. There's maybe fifty thousand people here for the Minneapolis stop of *A Momentary Lapse of Reason* tour, and I would estimate there's me, some of the event staff, and maybe a Narcotics Anonymous group or two in attendance who aren't completely wasted.

By the time of the "Run Like Hell" encore, Tommy's not so high, but still in straight-boy-pretend love with David Gilmour, screaming, "I'd suck that man's cock!" but I don't think Gilmour's as hot as he was in the 1970s when he was skinny and had long hair and looked all deep and moody and broody and I wanted to put a big smile on his face, along with other things.

Finally the concert ends and I wonder what category of homosexual male I fall into, I hate stadium rock (except for the Boss, Tom Petty, and Linda Ronstadt) as much as Broadway musicals (except for *West Side Story*, *Cabaret*, and *Hair*). I drive us back to our old apartment in Northeast. It's Tuesday night, and Tommy has to work tomorrow, but I've seen him pull through worse, I've pulled through worse myself. It was kind of our thing in high school.

As we cross the Mississippi, I ask him what he thinks about Dave.

"Who's Dave?"

"The guy from the AIDS Walk. You met him and his sister. She's from Vietnam, originally."

"Oh," he mutters, his eyes half-open. "Didn't really talk to him. His sister's a babe. He's okay, I guess. Why?"

"I'm probably going to have sex with him. Try to have sex with him, anyway."

"Why?"

I turn onto University Avenue. "I dunno."

He pulls his hair back into a ponytail. "You like this guy?"

I shrug. "He seems okay. He has a dog."

Tommy thinks it over. "Cool."

"He's really good-looking. Did you notice he has a dimple on his chin?"

"Really? You're asking me?"

I say, "Dimples are supposed to be attractive, but I'm kinda indifferent to it."

"So, what does this guy do?"

"I'll find out Friday."

"For a living, you moron."

"Naughty Girls (Need Love Too)" comes on the radio, so I switch it off. "He works for Cargill."

"Doing what?"

"He told me. Something with meat solutions. I dunno."

Tommy laughs. "'Meat solutions.' Is that a real thing?"

"I don't know."

"Guess you'll find out Friday."

Then Tommy's quiet and I think he may have passed out, but he says, "It must be really hard without Frankie. I mean, I only met him the once, but he was really cool. I loved his comic book stuff, he was a really cool artist. And he was cool to hang with, even when he was sick."

"Yeah. Friday's probably a bad idea."

"That's not what I said."

"I just have this empty space . . ."

Can't breathe.

Inhale. Hold.

It'll pass, always does.

I pay attention to the road and Tommy's quiet the rest of the ride. When we get to the apartment, I let Aunt Nora know I'm crashing at his place, like a good boy would. I wonder what I should tell her about Friday night. Doesn't matter. I probably won't go.

Tommy drops on his bed and is out.

It's a tight fit on the couch, but we manage. I tell Francesco that I don't think sex with Dave is a good idea, after all. I was just being polite. I tell him, He's nothing like you.

Francesco says, *You* were just being *polite*? Okay. Anyway, you shouldn't make comparisons. Dave is nothing like me, but I'm nothing like Dave, either.

I don't want to go to bed with him just because I'm lonely.

You're both lonely. He says it's just for fun, but he's lonely.

I say, His partner's only been dead a year. It's too soon for him.

Francesco shakes his head. Maybe his partner was sick a long time. Maybe Dave did his grieving while his partner was still alive. You don't know. Be curious first, Kevin, judgmental a distant second. Is there any part of you that's excited about this?

No. Every part of me feels guilty about this.

Francesco takes a deep breath, releases. Do you remember how guilty I felt about my diagnosis? The hours we spent waiting for a room to open? The endless paperwork? Giving my history over and over and over again. How it was too painful for me to sit in the tub? The not getting any sleep? The IV drips and the diarrhea and the catheter bag and the shelves full of prescriptions and how I kind of lost my mind when my entire universe was reduced to that tiny apartment? Do you remember how I could be kind and funny with everyone but you? Everyone feels guilty about something—you'd have to be a sociopath not to.

I beep him on his nose. Why remember that stuff? That wasn't us. Me watching you work. That was us. Dancing all night with the Eddies. That was us. So was the sex, the incredible sex, the letting loose like we were in some parallel universe where we shot supernovas. How you got mad at me at the Pyramid when I said if you've seen one drag queen, you've seen them all. How I got mad when you dragged me to yet another opening and I had to listen to all those artsy-fartsy types talk about their *work*. I mean, how hard is it to take a bunch of Polaroids of yourself?

You liked Keith's stuff.

Keith actually has talent.

Francesco laughs. And you have a talent for changing the subject.

I just prefer the past. Before you got sick.

Kev, Kev, Kev. Believe it or not, you're doing better now. You're not drinking yourself sick now. You're not getting fired from your job now.

I don't have one.

You know what I mean.

I cry a lot more. Have you noticed that? It's weird.

Yes, I have noticed. I've also noticed you're not locking yourself away. You're volunteering. You're going to the support group. You're hanging with Tommy. And living with Aunt Nora means you have to at least talk to one person over the course of your day. All good things, Kevin. All good things.

It's Friday night. Dave has chilled some wine, so I tell him I don't drink anymore.

He says, "Mind if I do? I need to calm down a bit." He's wearing a plain blue tee that nicely matches his canvas hiking pants. We're both very casually dressed, because tonight is like going back to the track to run a few laps after a long, hard winter. Nothing more than that.

And definitely not a date.

I nod and he heads to the kitchen with Minnie the Moocher right behind him. I inspect the living room. Not a cluttered mess of cats and books and magazines and crucifixes. Not a dumpy railroad apartment with the tub in the kitchen and beautiful Art Deco murals of young men on the walls. This place is decorated Northwoods, with pine paneling and snowshoes hung on the wall for decoration. The rug has a bear-and-tree print, and over the fireplace, on the mantel, there's a picture of Dave and Gary. Dave's stretched out on a La-Z-Boy, and Gary lies on top of him, mugging for the camera. He has blond hair and something of a pixie face, and he looks like the comedian of the two, but then, probably anyone would be if they were with logical Dave.

Francesco made me laugh.

Don't compare. Dave is Dave, and Francesco's Francesco.

I wonder if Gary was better in bed than I will prove to be.

There are mementos, too, a snow globe from San Francisco, and a kachina doll with blue fuzz coming out of its head. I pick it up for a closer look. Please, kachina doll, don't come to life and chase me around like I'm Karen Black in *Trilogy of Terror*.

Dave enters, Minnie the Moocher at his heels, says, "You like it? It's Hopi. Gary got it for me when we went to Arizona. We were just sick of the snow and made an impromptu trip."

Who goes on impromptu trips? "It's nice," I tell him.

He sits down on the couch with his glass, and Minnie the Moocher jumps up next to him, stub wagging.

But then he stands up again. "I didn't offer you anything to drink. I'm so sorry. What would you like?"

"Surprise me. Just no booze and nothing macrobiotic."

And he's off again, Minnie the Moocher right behind him.

In the corner's a CD rack, along with a shelf of albums, so I kneel down and take inventory. It's an eclectic mix. Lots of Emmylou Harris, along with Dwight Yoakam, but also Cab Calloway, Wendy Waldman, and local-boy-made-good Prince. I wonder which albums and CDs are his and which were Gary's.

When Dave and Minnie the Moocher return, he hands me a glass of sparkling water. We clink our glasses together as he says, "Better days."

"Better days."

He puts some music on and joins me on the couch, where Minnie the Moocher sits between us, our chaperone.

Emmylou Harris sings "Easy From Now On" and Dave finishes his wine in no time at all.

I try to be helpful. "Maybe we should just go to the bedroom."

He nods. "Maybe."

"Okay."

"Okay."

And we sit there.

He says, "Maybe we should talk about our likes and dislikes."

"Good idea."

And we sit there.

I say, "So . . . safety first. You have condoms, right?"

He nods, pets the dog.

"You have water-based lubricant?"

He nods, pets the dog.

"Okay. Good. Good."

He says, "I'm a top."

"Oh. Good to know. And just so you're aware, I'm not a bottom."

"That's good to know."

We sit there.

He says very suddenly, and a little too loudly, "I really don't have much experience with men. I got together with Gary pretty soon after I came out."

Now I pet Minnie the Moocher and our hands touch.

He says, "You must have had a ton of experience."

I take my hand back. "What's that supposed to mean?"

He looks at me urgently. "Oh no! I just mean, you're gorgeous. And really built. You could have anyone you wanted."

"I know I overdo the gym, but working out helps with the depression."

He says, "Sorry," before adding, "I should start working out again."

"You're really handsome. Has anyone told you that you look like . . ."

". . . Officer Reed from *Adam-12*."

"Guess they have."

He looks at his feet. "Would you like to take your shirt off?"

"With the dog here?"

He says, "Oh . . . yeah. Let me put her in her kennel."

As he leads Minnie the Moocher out of the living room, I drop, do some push-ups. When he comes back, my shirt's off.

He looks at me.

It's so strange, the way he looks at me.

Like I'm a bear that wandered into his campsite.

He keeps his distance. I hear the dog's whines.

I look over at Gary on the mantel, sitting on Dave's lap. I say, "Maybe we should have gotten a hotel room. Some neutral territory."

He blushes, says, "No, no. Here is fine." He goes to the mantel and puts the picture facedown, walks over to me, grabs my pecs in both hands, and squeezes really hard.

I gasp. The last hands on me were Francesco's.

He says, "Is this okay?"

I nod, not looking at him.

He squeezes for a while. Then his hands wander to my waist as he leans down and tries to swallow a nipple.

I should be doing something. Encouraging him. Making sounds. This is supposed to be fun. I say, "Do you want to take your shirt off?"

He comes up for air. "I prefer not to."

I lift his chin up. "What? Why not?"

"I need to lose some weight, and it makes me self-conscious. So I thought I'd keep my shirt on." His tongue works its way down my stomach, to my zipper. He kneels now, looking up at me as he unbuttons the waist and pulls the zipper down. Then he grabs the belt loops and pulls my jeans down to my ankles. He says, "Is this okay?"

Yes. No. Maybe. I nod. He runs his tongue over my thighs.

His rubs his nose on my crotch as his hands slide beneath my underwear and grab my ass, pulling my cheeks apart and pressing them back together again.

I inhale, hold it. Exhale slowly.

When he slides a finger under the waistband of my Jockeys to pull them down, I hear myself say, "Stop."

He says, "Okay." He sounds a little relieved, like I blinked first. He stands up, hugs me.

We hold each other until it feels like we've been doing it too long. So we take Minnie the Moocher for a walk and talk about Gary and Francesco.

Chapter 6

JUNE 1988: THE DROUGHT CONTINUES

We haven't had any rain and we're not going to get any anytime soon.

Since I'm back in Minneapolis, the weather is the thing to talk about, like crime was in New York.

Anyway, it's how we're starting off tonight's support group meeting. Before we fall apart into little heaps of despair, we discuss the weather. Men are dressed in shorts and tees and muscle shirts (muscled or not—mostly not) and Dave sits next to me. You think we'd avoid each other, but strange as it seems, I actually feel closer to him after our failed attempt to rediscover our homo-SEX-uality. It's like we're failures together, and we don't give a shit.

I'm wearing my cutoff jeans, because it's hot, and I still like it when men look. There's bright colors on the preppies, green and peach, and the dyed-blond kid and Aaron wear tight jeans with ripped-out knees, and white muscle tees that show off their pale, skinny arms.

Dave is Dave, in his sandals and hiking shorts, with a blue short-sleeved shirt.

Butch Bobbie Jo starts us off with the usual: ground rules, confidentiality, and an affirmation. Next we go around and do check-ins. She invites Dave to start.

"It's been a good couple of weeks. My garden's a disaster this year, so that's disappointing. Work life is fine, nothing too urgent coming down the pike."

I giggle. Meat solutions.

Butch Bobbie Jo asks, "Any anniversaries this month?"

She means things like the anniversary of the first time you met your (dead) partner, moving in together, first vacation together, things like that.

"As far as June goes, we really didn't do much. Gary didn't care for gardening, and our trips to the Boundary Waters waited until after the worst of the blackflies and mosquitos, so, no, nothing significant that I can think of. We loved the summer equinox."

Next up is Jeff, who's enjoying the exposed skin of his fellow bereaved. As he talks about his partner, who would have been thirty-seven this month, I notice the unmistakable violet-reddish-purplish lesions that have formed on an eyebrow and at his hairline. I don't think they were there last time.

When we get to me, I just talk about Gay Pride in New York, and how romantic it was to walk hand in hand up Fifth Avenue. It was the only time of year I felt safe holding Francesco's hand in public. Francesco always wanted to hold hands when we were out in the street, but I could never bring myself to do it. The other memory I share is how we flipped the bird at St. Patrick's Cathedral, just in case Cardinal O'Connor was inside. Finally I talk about how we told the counterprotestors—who held their AIDS PLAGUE FROM GOD signs in one hand as they said their rosaries in the other—to fuck off.

Butch Bobbie Jo says, "There's some anger in those memories."

"Oh. Sorry."

She says, "Absolutely nothing to apologize for. There's a lot to be angry about."

Next up is Aaron, with the dyed-black hair that I notice is growing out, exposing brown roots. He's missed a couple of meetings. His partner died after they took him off the respirator. He didn't call any of us. His partner was twenty-five. Aaron starts, stops.

Starts, stops.

This month would have been their fourth anniversary. His brother told him it's not like Aaron and his partner were actually married. Or even together all that long. His parents didn't come to the funeral.

Butch Bobbie Jo tells him, "I'm very sorry your brother said those things to you. I'm sorry you had to hear that. Your relationship is something to honor."

Men look at the floor as Aaron cries silently.

I say, "I'm sorry, too, Aaron. I know what it's like. We all do."

Aaron nods, tries to say something.

Jeff, the sexual harasser, says, "You're still really young. You'll meet someone else."

I say, "Jesus, Jeff."

He says, "What's so wrong about that? He *is* young. He doesn't even know if he's got it or not. I'm going to die soon. You think that doesn't scare the shit outta me?"

Butch Bobbie Jo says, "We're going to take a little break. Jeff, I need to see you out in the hall."

He says, "Oooooooo. I'm in for it now."

When they're gone, I stand, stretch, say, "Jesus, what a dick."

Aaron says, "He doesn't mean anything by it. I'm not even sure he knows what he's saying anymore."

Dyed-blond kid says, "He wasn't always like this. It's sad."

Sorry, Francesco. I wasn't curious first.

Our break ended, Butch Bobbie Jo and a calmer Jeff rejoin us.

Butch Bobbie Jo says, "Aaron, is there more you want to say right now?"

Aaron's twisted up like a pipe cleaner. "Yes. If I can't be honest here . . . On some level I wanted him to die. I couldn't stand it anymore. He was so sick and in so much pain and he lost his mind. I feel so bad that I wanted it to happen, you know? But I couldn't take it anymore. He fought it—oh, my God, how he fought it. He fought so hard, right up till his last breath, and that's not what I wanted. I wanted him to . . . I don't know. I wanted him to be at peace. He wasn't at peace. He was terrified. Watching him struggle with those last breaths . . ."

I sit bolt upright.

". . . it made me so angry. I wanted a peaceful death for him. They should've helped him."

Dave looks at me, whispers, "You okay?"

Aaron can't speak. He looks like he's convulsing, but not a sound comes out of him.

Butch Bobbie Jo says, "Would it help, Aaron, if we made you a cradle of support?"

Aaron nods, wipes away tears.

The group veterans stand in a circle, so Dave and I do, too.

Butch Bobbie Jo says to Dave and me, the newest additions to the group, "Sometimes there are no words. Or there are, but we're sick and tired of hearing them over and over again. So, instead of words, we hold him, physically, in our arms, which manifest our love and our support." She takes Aaron's hand and he stands next to her. Jeff tells Dave and me to join the veterans as we form two lines facing each other. Next we lean down and grip each other's wrists tightly as Aaron lies back in our arms.

We hold him up.

Butch Bobbie Jo softly sings, " 'You are my sunshine, my only sunshine,' " and the jaded New Yorker in me almost laughs out loud. But then the veterans join her and I leave my ironic cynical self behind. Aaron closes his eyes and silently weeps as we rock him back and forth, back and forth, slowly, gently, held up in our arms, he's safe to cry here, to scream here, to lose his mind here, because we have him, these fags and this dyke, and we won't let him fall.

Dave drives me home in silence.

When I walk through the door, Aunt Nora's reading *Hollywood Husbands* as her cats sleep on the couch. When she sees me, she gasps. "Have you been crying?"

Chapter 7

JULY 1988: A MAN, AN ARTIST, AND A HOMOSEXUAL WALK INTO THE MINNEAPOLIS CLUB

Back at the Metrodome. Hard to believe I was just here Wednesday night for MONSTERS OF ROCK with Tommy, disappointed but not surprised that Eddie Van Halen was the only fuckable guy in a lineup of five hair bands. It was a long, long, long night and now I'm not sure what I hate more, arena rock or East *Vill-ahge* art openings. What they have in common is that I go to please other people: Tommy now, Francesco then.

To be fair, Tommy has asked me for suggestions on things to do, but I haven't been able to come up with anything. We try to schedule our Boundary Waters trip, but he keeps getting offered overtime, and with a baby on the way, he can't afford to pass it up.

Oh. And Tommy's not getting married, after all. This week, anyway.

Today I'm at the Metrodome for the AIDS Quilt. Dave and I are dressed in all-white (don't laugh), along with the other volunteers, and our bandanas are color-coded according to who does what. I must say that Dave looks quite fetching in all-white, it contrasts his dark hair, which he's growing out in spite of the heat wave, and now he looks like Officer Reed from *Adam-12* when he was Captain Troy on *Galactica 1980*.

Our jobs will be to help unfold twelve-by-twelve-foot squares of the quilt, each square with eight panels, each home-made panel displaying the name of someone who died of AIDS. The choreography of laying out the squares is actually quite beautiful, solemn, respectful, and synchronized. They'll be laid in groups of four to make paths so people can walk through the quilt. A brochure for the event described the quilt as *a celebration of life and a way to unlock grief.*

Celebrations are for joyous occasions. And I'm still working on locking my grief up and keeping it locked up, good and tight.

And yet . . . here I am. Maybe it's only because Dave volunteered. I dunno.

By the end of the ceremony, volunteers will have unfolded the panels of nearly 3,500 people who've died of AIDS, and this is just one section of a much larger quilt that's too big for the Metrodome. I saw the entire quilt—well, the entire quilt at that time—at the March on Washington last year. Toshiro and I talked about making a panel for Francesco, but walking in the midst of so many dead men, we couldn't face the idea of adding one more name to the quilt.

When we do make our panel, it'll include some of Francesco's artwork, reproduced on the fabric by Toshiro, along with a map of Alphabet City, the place he loved more than anywhere else, with a gold star on Avenue B, our home. There will be a small Star of David and a crucifix, along with his motto: "Be curious first, judgmental a distant second."

So we have it all planned out.

We just have to make it.

I'm standing next to Dave on the main floor, where the Twins and the Vikings and the Gophers play. Dave says, "They're going to display Gary's panel for the first time. Hope I can keep it together when they read his name." Gary's panel has a drawing of cross-country skis, snowshoes, and a log cabin with smoke coming out the chimney. Also, a smiling moose wearing a Walkman.

I look out at the rows and rows of seats, imagining what it must be like for the players on game day. I say, "If you start crying, I'll start crying. I cry over anything and everything since I got back. I cried over the Ducks Unlimited ad."

He says, "Bet you didn't cry this much when you were drinking."

I think about it. "You know, you may be onto something."

He reads my mind: "Don't start drinking again. Crying is good."

I give him a quick spank. "So everyone keeps telling me. *Ooooh, unlock your grief. Ooooh, cry and be miserable. It's so healthy.* Michael Callen said we're living in wartime. How many wars have been won with tears?"

"Well, I guess we all heal in our own ways. Or not." He looks at his white sneakers. "I want to try again," he says. "You know."

I know. "Really?"

He nods. "I'm starting to feel like there's something wrong with me."

"With me, you mean."

He shakes his head. "No. With me. But I think this time we should try it at your place. A place I don't associate with Gary. I think it actually did bother me."

"Won't work. I associate my place with my aunt. If you think last time was bad . . ."

"A hotel?"

I don't say anything.

He remembers I'm an unemployed loser, says, "My treat. Friday night."

I nod. "Sounds good." I stretch, flex, trying to get in the mood for Friday. "Time to get back on that horse."

He puts his arms around my waist, and it feels good. He tells me, "I'll bring a tape player so we can have some make-out music. Any songs I should avoid?"

I grab him by the shoulders, pull him in tighter. "'I Only Have Eyes for You' by the Flamingos. It was our song. In parallel universe three it was the first dance at our wedding reception."

"Parallel what?"

"Nothing." Shut up, shut up, shut up. Parallel universes were Francesco's and my thing, you fucking idiot.

He whispers before he lets me go, "Friday will be great, no matter what." Then he slaps me on the ass.

Dave and I have been seeing each other apart from Thursday Nighters and the Survivors Support Group. He's joined me at my gym when he can, and the other thing we do together is walk Minnie the Moocher around Lake Calhoun as we talk about Gary and Francesco, and, increasingly, the other guys in our support group—Aaron in particular, because it's so fresh for him. I thought our talks were enough, but, still, along with all the weeping and moaning, I'm getting... urges. Or as Francesco would put it, *Master John Goodfellow wants to come out and play.* I thought he had died along with Francesco.

We get our cue, take our places. We hold hands with other volunteers as we form a circle around an unfolded square. As the names of the men who died are read aloud, we open the squares, lay them as instructed on the Metrodome floor.

I imagine each name they announce illuminated on the electronic scoreboard as the organist plays the "Charge" cheer. And why not? They deserve it.

Some panels are simply names sewn in fabric, full names,

first names, nicknames; other panels are decorated with a favorite shirt, an image of a beloved dog or cat, rainbows, laminated photos and poems, pink triangles, landscapes, constellations. Many are touching in how unskilled and raw the panel is; others are exceptionally beautiful, and all are more meaningful to me than any of the art in the East *Vill-ahge* galleries.

And so we listen to the names, unfurl the quilt squares, and place them gently on the floor, move on to the next set of panels. Another group is unfolding a square when I hear a woman's voice choke through the speakers: "And my brother-in-love, Francesco Conti."

Dave looks at me. "I thought you hadn't made his panel yet."

"I haven't."

"Maybe it's a different guy?"

How many Francesco Contis who died of AIDS can there be? I look at the podium, and there, in front of the microphone, is Francesco's sister-in-law, Marco's wife, what's-her-face. She's comforted by a city council member as she wipes her eyes with a tissue, and another reader takes up where she left off on the list of names.

I raise my hand and a volunteer takes my place. Dave does the same.

I pimp-roll to the podium like I'm from the Bronx. Dave follows close behind.

"Kevin, what's wrong?" More urgently now: "Hey, slow down! Hey, Kevin!"

"She never visited him! She never even sent him a fucking card! And now she's here?"

Men and women dressed in white stare at us as we make our way through the panels of dead homosexual men.

Maybe two dozen yards from the podium, Dave grabs me from behind, digs in.

I hiss, "Let go of me or I'll knock you the fuck out."

"Then you'll have to knock me the fuck out."

We stand there, with his arms locked tight around my chest,

his head resting on my back. I'm breathing too hard, too shallow. An older, official-looking lesbian with a box of tissues approaches, a worried look on her weathered face. "Are you going to be all right? Would you like to sit down? We have some grief counselors here, if you'd like to talk."

I focus on steadying my breathing. I say, "Do you know who that woman is? The one who just finished reading?"

She looks to the podium, where nearby Francesco's sister-in-law is being interviewed by a reporter.

The woman says, "That's Suzanne Huntington-Conti. She's been a reader at a few of the displays while she's on her book tour."

"'Book tour'?"

Dave's still holding me. He says, "I feel like I've heard her name before."

The woman smiles. "Yes, you may have. Her memoir just came out a month or so ago."

I say, "She wrote a memoir?" and Dave squeezes me tighter.

"Yes. Would you like a copy? She has a box of free ones for volunteers. Let me see if there's any left."

She's gone to a row of folding tables not far from the podium.

Volunteers in white glance at me as if I were overcome by grief instead of rage.

Dave says, "Kevin, what's going on?"

I don't answer his question, just say, "I changed my mind. Don't let go of me."

He says, "I won't. I'm a little turned-on, to be honest."

And we stand there until she reappears, a book in her hand. "I got you an autographed copy."

Our Sacred Journey Together: A Memoir of AIDS by Suzanne Huntington-Conti.

She says, "I haven't read it myself, but the *Times* gave it a glowing review."

Dave loosens his grip and takes the book from her.

She says, "Are you sure you're all right? Is there something I can do? You look angry, to tell the truth."

We look ridiculous, to tell the truth. I shake my head, tell her, "I thought I was ready for this." Looking at all the names that surround us, I say, "But I guess I wasn't."

She touches my arm. "Of course. Why don't you go home and get some rest. Seeing the names can be overwhelming, physically and emotionally."

Dave disengages from me entirely now. "Good idea."

The woman nods, leaves.

We stand there awhile longer. I've unlocked my grief, only to find a big old pile of smoldering rage inside.

Dave and I were going to go to an all-night HIV/AIDS vigil at the Metropolitan Mt. Sinai's chapel, but I'm too angry for solemn decorum and useless prayers. People say prayers can change the world, but they're fucking morons. What I really need to do is beat the living crap outta somebody.

Dave suggests Embers instead.

So we're sitting at a table, and I've ordered pancakes because they serve breakfast all day, and I'm not sure who's paying. Dave has the bacon cheeseburger and a shake.

He says, "You asked me to bring it in. Do you want to see it, or not?"

Our Sacred Journey Together lies facedown on the floor next to his chair.

I sip at my water. "Yeah, might as well get it over with."

He knows from my homicidal rant on the ride over that Suzanne was a stranger to me, and to Francesco's life and death in New York. His parents visited, and one of his brothers and his wife came a few times, but his brother Marco and Marco's wife, Suzanne, never came, never called. In fact, I had never met them before the funeral. Francesco didn't allow himself to be bitter until the last few weeks, when he cursed the brothers

who refused to see him before he died. It killed me to see him
so hurt. Why do that to a dying man? Your own brother? What
kind of person do you have to be?

On the cover of the book, there's Francesco's, *my* Francesco's, high-school yearbook picture, and an airbrushed studio portrait of Suzanne. The pictures are separated by a heart. If
you didn't know better, you might think Suzanne is looking up
toward heaven in her shot. But from East Village photogra-
phers, I know it's a standard pose to hide a weak chin.

I pick the book up, open the back cover, read the author's bio
aloud: " 'Suzanne Huntington-Conti was born in Washington,
D.C., and attended Wesleyan University, where she led the
fight to create the Women's Studies Program. A community
volunteer, Ms. Huntington-Conti serves on the boards of
Racial Equality Now and the Bryn Mawr Hospital Founda-
tion. She lives in Bryn Mawr, Pennsylvania, with her husband,
Marco, and their daughters, Darcy and Laurel. *Our Sacred
Journey Together: A Memoir of AIDS* is her first book. She is
currently working on a new memoir about growing up in
Georgetown, tentatively entitled *Georgetown Daughter: An M
Street Education.*' "

Dave's surprised. "How'd somebody named Huntington
wind up with somebody named Conti?"

I shrug. "Marco's done okay for himself, from what Francesco told me. He's a rising muckety-muck at PNC. It's a
bank."

Our meals arrive and I must be calming down, because I
look greedily at Dave's plate. He pushes the shake between us,
says, "We can share. And help yourself to the French fries."

In no time I'm done. Dave says, "Do you ever make yourself
ill eating so fast?"

I reach for some fries. "No."

Next he asks, "Are you going to read her book?"

I shake my head, mouth full.

"Glad to hear it. I don't think you should, it will just make you angrier. I'll read it. I think you should know if she's written anything about you. Evidently, it's a best seller." Of course it is. I nod, suck down some chocolate shake. It didn't occur to me I might be in the book, since I only met her once. He puts the book back down on the floor. "It's a pretty slim volume. I'll read it before Friday, and, if you like, we can discuss it afterward."

Anyone who *really* knows me knows that Suzanne Huntington-Conti doesn't get off so easy. I still have the phone numbers of the guy Laurie invited to sit with us at the deli, Pete, who told us he works in publishing. After an awkward reintroduction he tells me his publisher is the one that released the book, and that it was a rush job. They wanted to get it in the stores before one by a gay writer with AIDS was released. He looks up her tour information. The Twin Cities Foundation is hosting a reading tonight at the Minneapolis Club, but he says it's invitation-only.

Pete next asks me what I'm doing in Minnesota, a question all Minnesotans are used to. I tell him it's only for a while. I tell him I'll call him when I make it back to New York. He doesn't seem unhappy about it.

Tommy's going with me to the reading with a list of questions I've come up with for him to ask Suzanne, because I know she would never call on me. Question Number One: *Where the hell were you?*

The Minneapolis Club look like it belongs back East, in Philadelphia or New York or Boston. It's stone and brick covered in ivy and the doorman smiles and winks at me as he lets us in. As we walk down the paneled hallway with chandeliers over our heads, Tommy whispers, "I think this place has a dress code. I don't think he was supposed to let us in."

I say, "It's air-conditioned. Enjoy."

Tommy's dressed in his summer uniform: ratty jeans, a camouflage T-shirt, pack of Camels in the shirt pocket. I'm only slightly better—nice jeans, a black short-sleeved button-down shirt, and a giant pink triangle button.

In the big room where the event will take place, each window has eighteen panes (I count) and the ceiling is arched with wooden beams. Upholstered chairs are arranged around an oak podium with the club's crest on it. We're early, and men in suits and women in dresses—in equal numbers—drink wine and snack on hors d'oeuvres: scallops wrapped in bacon, chicken skewers in peanut sauce, little quiche-things. There's even a cake with the cover art from *Our Sacred Journey* in frosting.

Tommy, who's on his third glass of white wine, tells me to go easy on the free grub. He doesn't want us to get kicked out.

A tall woman with a sensible haircut, and wearing a gray suitcoat and matching skirt, introduces herself as we stand around with the other people who stand around, balancing little plates in one hand and wineglasses in the other. She says, "I don't believe we've met. I'm Ellen Carroll Jarrett, the foundation's vice president for stewardship."

Tommy says, "Tommy."

I say, "Kevin Doyle."

She smiles, squints at us. "I am so sorry. Are you new donors to the foundation? I feel terrible that I haven't met you before this evening."

I look at Tommy, who looks at me. Behind him, I notice two guys on the club's staff, hands folded in front of them.

I tell the truth. "Frankie was my partner." She smiles, but I can tell she doesn't know who I'm talking about, so I add, "The guy on the cake. The one who died. Of AIDS. Francesco Conti."

She gasps just a little. "Oh! Suzanne didn't mention you'd be here tonight." She adds, still not entirely convinced, "Welcome."

The club staff walks off.

Ellen Carroll Jarrett says, "Suzanne's a very courageous woman to share her story. I know her from Wesleyan. Oh, she was after my time, but I met her at one of the reunions. When she called to say she had a book coming out, and what it was about, well, I thought, here's a real opportunity to educate people."

"Uh-huh," I say.

"I haven't had the opportunity to read her memoir yet, but I am very much looking forward to doing so. The review in the *Times* was a love letter. I'm so glad. It's an important issue, one that affects us all."

I look around the room. "Seems to."

We hear a fork against a glass, like you hear at wedding receptions so the bride and groom will kiss. Ellen Carroll Jarrett says, "If you'll excuse me." Waiters top off wineglasses before the guests take their seats. And there, in one of the big upholstered chairs like a throne behind the ornate oak podium, sits Suzanne Huntington-Conti, draped in black like she was the corpse, save the red enamel heart pinned to her blouse collar. Her makeup looks professionally done, but Dead Eddie would have been able to tell for sure.

A social X-ray with apricot-colored hair speaks into the microphone. "Good evening, everyone, good evening, and welcome. It's an honor to have so many of you join us tonight for our series on issues facing the Twin Cities metropolitan region. Tonight is just one example of how the Twin Cities Foundation provides first-class service to our donors, by helping you learn more about the challenges and opportunities facing our community, and to help you, our generous donors, to express your passions through strategic philanthropy that makes a real difference. We manage charitable assets using investment strategies that are tailored to your financial priorities and giving interests. At the Twin Cities Foundation, our proven skills in

philanthropic planning and our in-depth, on-the-street knowledge of community issues help make your dollars go even fur-
ther. Each year you, our donors, support hundreds of different
causes and charities around the Twin Cities, the country, and
the world. So, please, a big round of applause for you! Our
donors!"

Wineglasses are temporarily placed on the floor as the audience applauds themselves.

The woman with apricot-colored hair continues now. "When
Ellen Carroll Jarrett, our vice president for stewardship—where
are you, Ellen?"

Ellen smiles humbly as she waves from where she stands behind the audience.

The woman with apricot-colored hair continues: "Let's give
Ellen a nice round of applause. Our donors are always telling
me just how much they appreciate all you do, Ellen, and how
they admire your commitment."

Wineglasses are temporarily placed on the floor as the audience applauds Ellen Carroll Jarrett.

The woman with apricot-colored hair continues: "When
Ellen suggested tonight's speaker for our series, I did not hesi-
tate. We may think of AIDS as a disease of homosexuals, but it
is important to understand that this disease is emerging as a dis-
proportionate threat to underserved and disenfranchised com-
munities, such as women and people of color. As leaders we are
called upon to respond with compassion to all of AIDS's victims. Just as a doctor would not withhold treatment from a
smoker with lung cancer, or deny lifesaving measures for an accident victim who hadn't been wearing a seat belt, so, too, must
we serve all the victims of AIDS. Our talented team at the Twin
Cities Foundation can provide the expertise you need to maxi-
mize the impact of your gift by combining it with the contribu-
tions of like-minded donors to agencies on the front lines of the
epidemic, from Catholic Charities to the Salvation Army.

"Our speaker tonight is a woman of enormous courage who has shared her story of caring for her beloved brother-in-law or 'brother-in-love,' as she called him, during his battle with AIDS, from his diagnosis up until his death."

Inhale. Hold.

Exhale. Slowly.

Inhale. Hold.

Exhale. Slowly.

"Their journey is one of heartbreaking debilitation, unyielding determination, and immeasurable loss. Ultimately it is the story of hope. Please join me in welcoming Suzanne Huntington-Conti."

Wineglasses are temporarily placed on the floor as the audience applauds Suzanne Huntington-Conti. Suzanne embraces the woman with apricot-colored hair, and nods to the audience.

I breathe. I hold. I exhale.

"Thank you so much for inviting me to speak to you this evening. *Our Sacred Journey Together* isn't my story—it's Francesco's story."

Inhale. Hold.

"So to give you a proper introduction to my brother-in-love, I'll read from the opening pages of *Our Sacred Journey Together*." She takes a sip from the water glass on the podium, then slips a pair of reading glasses on, the kind that hang around your neck. In a slow, practiced voice, she tells us to " 'Picture, if you will, a young woman, not such an extraordinary young woman, but not such an ordinary one, either, a kind woman, a woman not unlike many women you may have known throughout your life, perhaps a woman not so very unlike yourself.

" 'Picture this woman—myself—on a warm spring afternoon in 1985, traveling by taxi from Penn Station to a world I had never heard of, nor imagined, a place called Alphabet City, a hidden kingdom of artists and addicts, the homeless and the homesick, the resigned and the restored. It was in this place that Francesco, my brother—in love—taught me that empathy is a feeling that no painting, no sculpture, no composition, can evoke as strongly, or as powerfully, as the body horror that is AIDS. Francesco—a man, an artist, a homosexual—someone I felt I understood, was to become a living treasure in those sorrowful, wonderful days, so full of life and wisdom and pain, before they evaporated like the end of a sweet dream from which I mourned to awaken. While others desperately made their way to the American Hospital in Paris, following in the famous, oversized footsteps of Rock Hudson, Francesco and I—the two of us, together, the outsiders in his family—were content to watch the shadows on the dingy walls of his decaying rooms, a place where he taught me that the only true cure for his disease must be one that changes how we, as human beings, care for one another in our everyday lives.' "

Tommy looks at me, trying not to laugh, but whatever expression I have on my face stops him cold. He taps my arm, whispers, "Hey, you okay?"

I can't risk saying anything out loud.

When she finishes reading about herself, occasionally Francesco and no one else, she dabs her eyes, takes a deep breath, and composes herself.

And it's time for questions.

It's Minnesota, so everyone's too shy to raise their hands right away. Tommy thinks we should leave, because I look like a "fucking lunatic," but I tell him to ask my questions. Suzanne Huntington-Conti sees Tommy, notices how he's dressed, and moves on, but seeing no other hands, she gives up and points at Tommy. She asks him to stand so all can hear.

Good.

He stands, and people who hadn't noticed him do now. Here's someone who lives above a Laundromat and never went to college, but he isn't clearing their dirty plates and empty glasses. He says, not giving a shit what people think, because he's Tommy: "You never visited Frankie once in New York, and definitely not after he was diagnosed, so why are you lying about it?"

People stare at Tommy. Then they follow his gaze to Suzanne Huntington-Conti, who holds on to the podium as if it's the only thing keeping her from falling through the floor. She clears her throat, says softly, "I don't understand how you could say something like that to me. Who are . . ."

And then she sees me sitting next to him and stops talking.

Tommy looks at the list of questions I wrote. He says, "Why didn't you visit Frankie when he was sick? Are you afraid of AIDS? Do you hate gay people?"

People murmur now: *How rude, this young man has no manners; why was he even admitted dressed the way he is?*

I stand up now: "Why're you doing this, Suzanne Huntington-Conti? Tell me! You never saw him! He needed his family, but you shut him out. You wouldn't even shake my hand at his funeral. His lover! Why?"

The woman with apricot-colored hair takes charge. She stands next to Suzanne Huntington-Conti, tells me and Tommy, "Thank you for coming, young men, and offering your gay perspective, but—"

Tommy shouts, "HEY! I'm into CHICKS! My girlfriend's pregnant and I already got two kids!"

I shout, "Act Up, Fight Back, Fight AIDS!"

Suzanne Huntington-Conti staggers out of the room, leaning on Ellen Carroll Jarrett.

Staff grab Tommy by the elbows as people clear a path for their exit, and a short man with a name badge stands directly in front of me and says, "Out! Now." I'm six-two and weigh over two hundred pounds, but I'm gay, so he shoves me.

It'd be so easy to knock him the fuck out.

One punch would do it.

When I don't budge an inch, he's startled and takes a step back, looking for help. I see people watching me. They don't say anything, don't do anything, hardly seem to breathe. I recognize the looks on their faces, it's the same one Suzanne Huntington-Conti gave me at Francesco's funeral. Like I'm something she stepped in. Like I'm the end of the world.

I take a moment, take the time necessary to think things through, like butch Bobbie Jo told me to do. So this way we survivors don't do something in the heat of the moment that we might regret later: quit our jobs, have anonymous grief sex, drink a handle of vodka, try the leftover morphine.

I've done violent things in the past—beat kids up, trashed my ex-stepmother's car, knocked my dad to the floor, beat the crap out of the boy I had a crush on in high school—but this is different.

There's a ton of witnesses.

I meet Tommy outside, where he sits on the curb, watched by staff stationed at the doorway.

He tells me, "They won't call the cops if we just leave and never come back. You didn't hit anybody, did you?"

"No. Let's get the hell out of here."

"Hi, Pete. Remember me?"

In New York a young man who resembles Ferris Bueller is probably regretting the hell out of giving me his numbers. He thinks of something to say.

"Yes. We talked yesterday. And you're all anyone can talk about in marketing this morning. Did you tell her I told you about the reading? I mean, what did you do, Kevin?"

"We just asked questions. I told you her book's heinous bullshit. People need to know the truth."

"Not in marketing, they don't."

"How much did you guys give her for the book?"

"(A) I don't know. (B) Even if I did know, I couldn't tell you. Kevin, I could lose my job over this."

"Why would you lose your job? She's the one lying. She's the one pimping Frankie."

"You need to let this go."

Pete seems like a sweet guy. And he doesn't really know me at all. "You're right, you're right, I'm sorry. I lost my cool. I don't want you to get fired."

"Just promise me you won't tell anyone it was me who told you about her author event."

"Is she still in Minneapolis? Would it help if I apologized to her?"

He thinks it over. "It might. You won't make things worse, will you?"

Doesn't know me AT ALL. "No. She's family in a weird way. She's Frankie's sister-in-law. Families fight. I'm going to see her at Christmas, anyway, so we might as well clear the air now. Then this can blow over."

Pete sighs. "Let me check her schedule."

Cats investigate when I sit on the floor, and I'm getting most of their names down . . . finally. I think these three are Roger Casement, Seán Mac Diarmada, and Éamonn Ceannt.

"She's giving a talk on the post-modern rejection of grief as a singular point of view at the Walker Art Center this afternoon, and flies back to Philadelphia tonight."

"Do you have her flight information?"

"Kevin . . ."

"Or I could go to the Walker."

He gives me the flight information.

Flights are being announced, along with passenger names who are asked to report to this gate or that ticket counter. Along the concourse, elderly men and women are driven to their destinations in golf carts.

I spot her sitting at a Northwest Airlines gate, dressed entirely in black, save the heart pin she wears. She has headphones on, and writes in a black leather journal propped on her lap. She doesn't even look up when I sit down next to her. Around us, other passengers are reading books or newspapers or magazines. A few are trying to sleep on the chairs.

I stare at her, waiting.

She finally senses it, looks over at me. If she's angry or afraid, she doesn't show it. "Why are you here?"

"Why are you doing this?"

"Why am *I* doing this? Why are you stalking me? Harassing me? Defaming me? Leave me alone, or, so help me, I'll scream for airport security."

"You made all this shit up about you and Frankie. Why? I don't understand."

She slaps her journal closed, takes off her headphones. "I would think a little gratitude would be in order. I'm honoring Francesco's memory, and my book's changing hearts and minds. I'm doing important work, and what are you doing? Trying to stop me! If anything, you should be thanking me."

"Thanking you?"

"Yes, thanking me. Do you understand how much good this book's done? I've spoken about AIDS on *Larry King Live* and *Donahue* and I was on *Good Company with Steve and Sharon* just this morning. I've taken some very big risks by speaking publicly. Risks on behalf of AIDS victims."

"You're a fucking liar. Is this about money? About publishing a book? About making yourself look like some kind of Goddamn saint? 'Cause I know better."

"The book is the truth—my truth. My *emotional* truth."

"What the hell does that even mean?"

A woman in the row of seats facing us looks up. She stares, letting me know she's noticed me.

Suzanne Huntington-Conti says, loud enough for the people in the seats around us to hear, "I want you to leave me alone."

I say, even louder: "You're making money over his dead body. You hate gay people."

She stiffens, looks right at me, her face red, her voice a hoarse whisper: "How dare you! I do not hate gay people. Do you know that just last night, after your attack on me, I was talking to a waiter at the Club, *who just happens to be gay* . . ."

There oughtta be a law: They should have to jump up on a chair, scream at the top of their lungs, *"WHO JUST HAPPENS TO BE GAY,"* while doing jazz hands.

". . . and he was of the opinion that *Our Sacred Journey Together* is doing a great service for his community."

Aunt Nora has an expression: "gobsmacked." It means you can't fucking believe it. So I'm *gobsmacked* when I tell Suzanne Huntington-Conti, "Gorsh, if a gay waiter says so, maybe I got this all wrong."

She looks up and down the concourse now, probably for security. She says, "What you've got wrong is thinking I'm not going to defend my reputation against your libel. One more outburst from you or any other member of your 'community' and you'll be hearing from my attorneys, not to mention my publisher's legal team. Hope you have deep pockets. Oh, wait, you and Frankie were always broke. Is that why you're coming after me? Is this about money? How many times did Marco beg his father to stop bailing you and Frankie out? Frankie got more than his fair share. My father-in-law has grandchildren he needs to think about."

I hear my voice shake: "I'm telling the truth."

People look at us, alarmed by our tones. They glance up from their books and magazines, wondering if something's about to happen and if they should do something about it. Over the intercom a woman announces that boarding will begin shortly.

Suzanne looks at her fellow passengers, then at me. She says, "The book is doing good. I think we can both agree on that, at least. Are you mature enough to let the book do good? Or is this all about you?"

Steady Eddie hasn't called in over a week, so Aunt Nora's gives me the okay to call him long-distance. I call him "Steady Eddie" now, because so far, so good. No dramatic swings for the worse, but none for the better, either. "Steady Eddie" is an Aunt Nora-ism, and although they've never met—Aunt Nora refuses to go to New York, and sent flowers and mass cards for Francesco's funeral—Live Eddie loves to hear my stories about her, especially when I imitate her accent and say things like, *'Tis only a stepmother would blame you* or *That one suffers from a double dose of original sin.*

If he hasn't heard about it already—and I hope not—I'm not going to tell him about *Sacred Journey*, it will just make us both angry. I'm not going to tell him that Dave and I tried to have sex, or are going to try again, it might feel like a betrayal of Francesco to him. Or me.

I try to keep things light when we talk because I'm not there with him, can't put my arms around him. Topics: 1. Minnie the Moocher is fully recovered and has learned how to sit, heel, and come. Scratch that, just sit and heel. 2. The song "Dirty Diana"— really about Diana Ross? Also, Flo had the better voice, so why did Ross get to sing lead through her nose on every Supremes single?

That'll get him going. He's on Team Flo. All gay men must eventually choose.

"Hello?" He sounds faint. But I'm relieved he picks up, hearing Dead Eddie ask me to leave a message is something I just can't get used to.

"Steady Eddie! What's up, buttercup?"

He coughs. "Just took a nap."

I check the clock, add an hour. 7:34 p.m. in New York. "How ya doing?"

A short cough this time, with some throat clearing. "Steady. This summer's so damn hot, I wish it was over. If people aren't freaking out about dengue fever or syringes washing up on the beach, they're freaking out about"—he coughs, clears his throat again—"mosquitos giving them AIDS. This is a freak-out summer."

He makes a sound I recognize: spitting in a cup.

"You sure you're steady, Eddie?"

"Relax. I'm not that brave. Let's talk about something else. How's life with your aunt Nora? She turned you back into a Catholic yet?"

"Not for lack of trying." Tomorrow's Friday. I flex a bicep, I've plateaued again. Maybe I should just work on my arms before Dave and I give sex another go.

"Still volunteering?" he asks.

"Yeah. Thursday Nighters is fun. Three guys had birthdays this month, so lots of over-the-top cakes. And Dead Eddie would have loved this Lynne woman who volunteers there—she knows everything about politics and jewelry."

"'Dead Eddie'?"

FUCK. ". . . What?"

"Did you just call Eddie *dead*?"

Fuck, fuck, fuck. "I . . . It just . . . Yes."

Steady Eddie inhales. "So, does that make me 'Alive Eddie'?"

"Just 'Live Eddie,' actually . . . I'm so sorry. Jesus, I wasn't making fun . . . maybe I was. I used to drink a lot."

Finally . . . this: "Relax, Kevin. He *is* dead. Francesco's dead. Everyone's dead. I mean, what don't we joke about anymore? What do they call it? Gallows humor?"

I say in Aunt Nora's accent: "I'm mortified."

"Like I said, relax. Let's change the subject."

"Yes, please."

"I joined ACT UP."

This is news. He really must be doing well. "Who's the radical now, baby?"

He doesn't laugh. "The AZT is making me worse. Not that it really works." He inhales, hard. "Not that I have eight grand a year to blow on it. But there's nothing else out there, Kevin. Seven years into this fucking disease, tens of thousands of dead fags, and there's nothing else."

"Oh."

"Yeah, *oh*." He sighs, coughs a little. "My GMHC volunteer, the one I told you about—she used to be a lesbian separatist until the plague. She belongs to ACT UP. She told me their thing is getting drugs into bodies. I want drugs in my body, so she took me to a meeting."

"What did you think?"

"Loud. Crowded. Lots and lots of tasty guys, and lots of guys like me. Some women."

"You're still tasty. See anyone we know?"

"Maybe. So many people look different now."

"What'd you think?" I squeeze a thigh. Maybe a leg day instead.

"I'm not as out there as a lot of them, and I got sick of some of them trying to top each other with their self-righteousness, but overall what I heard made sense. I do think we're being wiped out because the government doesn't give a shit if fags live or die. Reagan keeps cutting what little funding there is. If this was toxic shock or Legionnaires, do you know what they'd be spending?"

I stop feeling myself up; this ain't our usual banter. "A lot more?"

Now he sounds pissed. "This isn't government incompetence. It's genocide, Kevin. They do nothing because they want us dead. No one gives a shit about gay men or heroin addicts. We're garbage to them."

"I don't think they want us dead . . ."

He coughs/wheezes/says, "Really? How many years is it now? How many fags are dead? And they don't *want us dead*? If they didn't want us dead, they'd fucking be doing something about it."

"But I don't think that—"

"You know what? I can't talk about this with you right now. It makes me too angry. I love you. Dead Frankie and Dead Eddie loved you, too."

I say, "Eddie, please," but he hangs up.

I walk into the sitting room, where Aunt Nora fans herself with a *Catholic Bulletin* as she reads her Danielle Steel novel. I just stand there. She asks, "What's the matter, then? Is Steady Eddie sick?"

"I don't know. He was kinda all over the place. I didn't help things. I think I fucked up big-time."

"Language. How do you mean?"

I shrug. "Yeah, well . . . I think he's going a little crazy. He says it's genocide. That the government wants gay men dead."

She closes her book, says, "He's not crazy, not even a little bit. It's nothing they haven't done before."

"What are you talking about? They're not sending us to death camps."

She shakes her head like I'm an *eejit*. "There's more than one way to try to wipe out an entire people. The potato blight."

"The famine?"

A world-class *eejit*. "In a famine there's nothing to eat. There was plenty to eat in Ireland, but it was taken by the colonizers for England. God sent the potato blight, but the English made it a famine."

Aunt Nora hates the "dirty, filthy English." I think their accents are sexy. And Rupert Everett sends me. "Come on."

She looks up to God in heaven and then back down at me. "My first-generation Yank nephew and he doesn't know his own history." She grunts, lifts herself up and out of her chair, steps over a cat, says, "You don't move a hair on your head. I'll be right back."

I watch her shuffle up the stairs as a couple of cats follow. From there I hear her pull the attic ladder down from the ceiling.

I yell from the bottom of the stairs. "Aunt Nora, I can get whatever you want up there. Please?"

A shout: "I told you to stay right where you are."

"It's too hot in the attic, you'll have a stroke."

"It'd serve you right!"

"Well, I'm not taking care of you!"

She rattles around in the attic, so I pick up a cat and turn on the TV, but it's all reruns.

Finally her grand self reappears, covered in dust and sweat, her face pinker than usual, an old book in her hands. She opens it to a dog-eared page, tells me, "You listen to this. These are the very words of that son of a bitch, Charles Trevelyan, the filthy Brit in charge of famine relief in Ireland. Bastard's second only to Cromwell. You just listen." She catches her breath before she reads: "'The judgment of God sent the calamity to teach the Irish a lesson, that calamity must not be too much mitigated ... The real evil with which we have to contend is not the physical evil of the Famine but the moral evil of the selfish, perverse and turbulent character of the people.'"

She slams the book shut. "You see now? This has all happened before, it's happening right now. You used to be handy with your fists. Why aren't you fighting?"

We're at the Saint Paul Hotel, which was hailed as the city's "million-dollar hotel" when it opened in 1910 and then became a dump in the 1970s, like everything else. But it's been restored to its former glory, and Dave chose it because we're trying to restore a former piece of ourselves.

John F. Kennedy has stayed here.

Charles Lindbergh has stayed here.

And now, Kevin Doyle, along with his grieving penis, which has stage fright on top of performance anxiety.

Dave sits on the big bed, on the phone with his sister, Tracy, who's taking care of Minnie the Moocher. He tells her, "Put the phone up to her ears, I want to kiss her good night."

Sweet and only somewhat unnerving.

He makes kissy sounds and then tells her, "You're my good girl! Yes, you are! Daddy loves his little girl! Yes, I do!"

Once he's done, he smiles at me, pats the bed, says, "Room for two."

I sit down next to him on a bed that's big enough for four people.

He says, "I forgot to bring the music, but I did remember a bottle of wine, but just now I remembered you don't drink. I'm trying to think of some other preliminaries to ease the way. We could cuddle."

That's me and Steady Eddie's thing. "We could try kissing. We didn't kiss last time."

He nods. "Just let me brush my teeth."

"You brushed them when we got here."

He exhales in my face. "Breath okay?"

"Minty fresh." I exhale in his face. "Mine good?"

"Peppermint?"

"Doublemint. 'Double your pleasure, double your fun.' "

"I like the idea of you being twins." He puts an arm around my shoulder and leans in to kiss me.

I kiss him back.

His tongue's tentative and I listen carefully for *mmmm* sounds to reassure me that he's enjoying himself.

I get nothin'.

I am an attractive man.

A DAMN attractive man, so if anyone here's enjoying himself, it should be him. Make a *mmmm* sound or sigh or something, fer Chrissake.

He pulls back. "Is this okay? My tongue in your mouth? I
didn't ask how you felt about open-mouth kissing, I'm sorry, I
really should have. I don't want to do anything without your
consent. But you should know, the risk of transmission is nil,
plus I'm negative, anyway, so it's safe. But I should have
asked."

So this is sex now—cross-check the equipment. Latex condom? Check. Water-based lubricant? Check.

Negotiate a treaty on practices and prohibitions. Morato-
rium on anal sex? Agreed. Oral sex with a condom? Agreed,
but . . . what's the point? Mutual masturbation. Agreed and
recommended.

I run a hand through his hair, which he hasn't cut since I met
him. "You still want to do this, right? I mean, if you're not in
the mood, that's fine. This bed's sex enough."

He puts his arms around my neck, and I'm a little in awe of
his face, the beauty, the intensity. He says, "Yes, I want to do
this. I don't want to push you into anything, though. Last time
you hit the brakes."

He's right. I did. But he seemed glad of it. "I want to try to
let myself go tonight. To live in the moment instead of the past.
I spend too much time in the past."

He says, "So do I. The thing is . . ."

I slide a hand under his shirt, stroke his chest. He shudders
and closes his eyes and I wish I could draw; I'd sketch that expression. I smile. "What's the thing, Dave?" My other hand
grabs his crotch. "Is this the thing?"

Jeez, I'm bold all of a sudden.

He opens his eyes with a start, grabs my hand. "The thing is,
I don't want to fall in love with you."

I pull back. "What?"

He falls back on the bed, turns, and faces the wall. "We both equate sex with death. If this works, what will I equate sex with? Love, probably. I didn't think this all the way through. I told you I didn't have much experience with men before I met Gary. It's because I fell in love with him after we had sex a few times. What if the same thing happens with you? It's just something I've been thinking about. I want sex, yeah, and I told myself this was a good idea, but when I look at you, I think maybe it isn't."

I lie down next to him, our feet on the floor, like in the old movies. "Jeez, Dave, I'm a train wreck. You're not going to fall in love with me."

Nothing.

I try again: "Let's think of this like we're gonna see a movie. You feel a lot of emotions at a good movie, but when the movie's over, you leave the theater, go back to your real life. What happened on the screen isn't your life. It's an escape from your life."

He turns his head, looks at me. "First time I saw you, I wanted to fuck you back to the Stone Age, and it made me feel bad."

I beep his nose. "I don't want you to feel bad."

"Kiss me."

I roll on top of him, hold his head in my hands, and kiss him. I finally hear *mmmmm*.

He pulls off my shirt and rolls on top of me. He says, "Stretch out your arms and close your eyes. I want to explore."

I do as he says and he carefully licks my chest as he works his way down to my jeans.

He says, "Get up. I want you to take off your pants while I watch."

I stand up, face him. He sits on the edge of the bed, his elbows on his knees, his gaze focused on my crotch. I like how his eyes feel on me even as I struggle with my jeans, I wore them too tight. I pick them up, fold them, look for a place to put them.

He says, "Just leave them on the floor."

I put them on the desk.

He says, "Now your underwear."

I look at my Jockeys, the kind Jim Palmer wears. "What about you?"

He says, "I want to make myself at home with your body first. Is that okay?"

I nod. "You *are* gonna take off your clothes, though, right?"

"Your underwear," he repeats, all business.

I hear people walking down the hall, their words muffled. When is the last time a man has seen me naked? I haven't even showered at the gym since Francesco died.

He sighs. "You don't have to. I want you to, but you don't have to."

This is as far as we made it last time, and I'm no quitter, except when it comes to my jobs. I say, "I want to." So I slide them off, thinking about how I used to make a whole big production out of it for Francesco, pulling them down, and then pulling them up again. These I pitch on the desk like a softball.

He stands up, and I'm not sure where to look. He puts his hands on my hips and they're cool from the air-conditioning. "Now," he whispers in my ear, "spread your legs as wide as you can."

He steadies me as I do. "Wider."

I stretch, slide my feet out a little more.

"Wider."

"Not without something snapping."

He smiles as he holds me in place. "Put your arms behind your head and arch your back."

I do and he lets go of me. He walks around me in slow circles, but he doesn't lay a finger on me. He kneels down in front of me and takes a close look, but his hands stay at his sides. He blows a slow, steady stream of air all over me.

"You're hard as a rock."

I sigh. "Good."

"No, it's great. Kevin, I'm not going to overthink this. I'm going to enjoy myself."

"I want you to."

"I want you to enjoy yourself."

Please touch me. "I am."

He stands up, looks me right in the eye. He says, like it's a warning, "I'm going to work you over hard. I'm gonna make you shoot across the room."

We're under the covers and Dave's clinging to me. I was finally able to get him naked, but he was very self-conscious, and I'm not sure he enjoyed being naked as much as I did. Now he has his shirt back on, but no underwear.

We were loud. Or, to be more precise, Dave was loud. For an uptight Minnesota Lutheran, boyfriend has a foul mouth. I've never heard some of that stuff before, and I went to the Mineshaft as a tourist once. I say, "I hope to God there's no one in the next room."

He says, "That was even better than I imagined it would be, and I have a pretty vivid imagination. I don't understand the guys who complain about safe sex and miss the good old days—this wore me out." He adds, in a meek voice: "I hope I didn't offend you with anything I may have said in the heat of the moment."

I have to laugh at how proper he can be after he just laid to rest a year of sexual inhibition and frustration in an obscenity-laden frenzy.

Now he says, "So I read *Our Sacred Journey Together.* Long story short, Francesco dispenses wisdom as he dies, she's fearless of AIDS and selfless, and she will never be the same. The end."

"You've got to be kiddin' me."

"She doesn't mention you anywhere. It's like you don't exist."

When I work out today, I take a shower at the gym, and give myself a good sudsing so I'm as clean as a whistle you'd blow. Tonight I talk over recent events with Farrell Furskin, the hillbilly bear I bought for Sarah that Carol refused to give her.

Because, to be honest, it doesn't seem right to discuss last night with Francesco.

So, I tell Farrell Furskin: I really enjoyed myself with Dave. I didn't think it would be as good as it was. And he was saying shit that would make a merchant seaman faint. It was all I could do to keep up with him. I mean, *wowza*.

Farrell grabs the suspenders of his overalls, tilts his bear head, says, Hush your mouth. Didn't right reckon Dave was such a dirty old foul-mouthed whore, bless his heart. Must've worn you slap out.

I slept really well for once.

Had to blow off some steam, I reckon. Dignity don't buy you coffee and a biscuit, after all. Y'all fixin' to fuck some more?

Yeah, I kinda think we have to, it was that good. Or maybe it only seemed that way 'cause it's been so long. Francesco died two years ago Valentine's Day, but we hadn't been together . . . that way . . . for months before he died.

That long? Bless your pea-pickin' little heart, you musta had a right POWERFUL hankerin'!

And then a pounding on the door like the Second Coming that makes me bolt straight up, followed by "Is that giggling I hear? Have you been drinking?"

"No! You want me to have a heart attack? *Jesus!*"

She opens the door, snaps on the light, looks at the sheet that covers me. "You have a man under there?"

"Of course not! And don't just barge in. I'm not decent."

She looks, says, "You've got your knickers on, don't you? Kiss my cheek."

"Fer Chrissake, I haven't been drinking."

"Language. If you're stone-cold, you've nothing to worry about. Kiss my cheek."

I stand up, kiss her cheek. She grabs my arms and leans up, sniffing my face.

"We good?"

She nods, and then she notices Farrell Furskin. "You've a teddy bear now?"

I shrug.

"While it's lovely to hear you laughing again, I've an early start tomorrow."

Thursday night and Dave and I sit next to each other, try to play it cool so as not to tip off the other volunteers. He's told no one about our night at the Saint Paul Hotel, not even Minnie the Moocher, and I've only told Farrell Furskin, and we both want it to stay in the closet because it's purely recreational, nothing more. You tell people you had sex during the plague and they want to know when the commitment ceremony is.

Brian, the volunteer coordinator, checks in with us. "How's the support group working out?"

We nod, mumble, break apart long strips of packaged condoms. Dave says, "Good, it's good."

He smiles, says, "I can see that," and heads to the next table.

Dave whispers, "We're not that transparent, are we?"

I sort condoms by color, saving the red ones for last. I say quietly, "Maybe we went without for so long, it's like we lost our virginity all over again. People say you look different after your first time."

Dave scans the room, looking at the Thursday Nighters am-
icably chatting as they assemble safe-sex kits (latex condoms,
little tubes of water-based lubricant, business-sized information cards with risk reduction information, along with the
AIDS hotline number). He whispers, with some urgency in his
voice, "Not so loud!"

"*You're* telling *me*, 'Not so loud'?"

It has taken forever by freight, but the boxes arrive from
New York, full of Francesco's and my life together. The cats
hopped on them, eager to get inside, but I've hauled them up to
my room and closed the door behind me. This is private.

I run my hands over the cardboard and tape, imagining
Francesco's things on a plane or a train or maybe a truck. These
possessions of his, inside these boxes, I'd catalog and recatalog,
organize and reorganize, over and over again, as I drank my
wine—and, later, my vodka. I blush when I recall how often I'd
drunkenly slow dance with his black leather jacket, moving
back and forth across the ravaged wood floor of the apartment,
"I Only Have Eyes for You" playing on our boom box. This is
what got me through a day at work: anticipating being alone
with his clothes, his books, his drawings, his Howard Johnson's mug. Invitations out became an annoyance, especially the
pity-invites from his artist friends, the ones who felt bad about
how they'd condescended to me while he was healthy or introduced him to their more intellectual, suitable, and eligible gay
friends, guys with names like Aldrich or Orson or Vance.

Fuckers.

The first box, the heaviest one, is full of books, mostly his,
but some of mine, nearly all of them ones he gave me, since
I only rarely bought books for myself, and then the ones I
did buy . . .

Books. When Francesco wasn't cranking out consistent
pages, he was making his own art, but to relax, he read. I had to

watch our little portable black-and-white TV with earphones on, since even hearing the television, let alone watching it, made him restless, like he was wasting time. He read voraciously, he was so open to words on the page, they didn't ever confuse or annoy him, the way they occasionally did me. He never skipped ahead in books, or gave up entirely the way I would when I got bored or impatient with the books he suggested by Vladimir Nabokov or Virginia Woolf or Gustave Flaubert.

The books I bought for myself and devoured were not displayed on our bookcases. Francesco was so highbrow in his reading, but he didn't read *serious* writers to impress anyone. He sincerely loved what they did with words, while I was more interested in sweet young things in love. Once I had finished *The Lord Won't Mind*, *All-American Boys*, *China House*, *Death Trick*, *Independence Day*, and *Gaywyck*, into the literal closet they went because I was worried what his artist friends would think. The books visitors could browse were titles like *Giovanni's Room*, *The City and the Pillar*, *The Well of Loneliness*, *Confessions of a Mask*.

It makes me happy to see my closet books and his showcase books packed together in a single box. The books that Francesco loved, and I never attempted, will keep me company now. Knowing I'm reading the words he had read, and turning the pages that he had turned, means I am with him again, in some small way.

The next box is full of his clothes. I sort through it carefully, holding up T-shirt after T-shirt, examining the strategic rips he tore to preview his body beneath. The black-and-white striped shirt was a favorite, always worn with black jeans, and I bury my face in it and breathe in, but it smells only of detergent and fabric softener, not of Francesco, not his mix of perspiration and tea tree oil and pencil shavings.

His Guardian Angels shirt and beret, the ones he swapped his linen WilliWear suitcoat for on a Lexington Avenue Line car. The black tee, the most recent of many, sleeveless, his uniform at punk concerts, like when he dragged me to see Black Flag because he had a crush on Henry Rollins and my ears rang for days afterward. The black vest he'd only wear with his extra-long white button-down shirt, which he never tucked in. His sleeveless yellow tee with the dropped armholes. His New Romantic black pin-striped shirt he wore with white suspenders. His shredded blue jeans that showed a lot of thigh that he always wore with his sleeveless plaid shirt. The black-studded belt he wore with his black leather pants, black fishnet shirt, and fingerless black leather gloves. A Members Only jacket. New wave skinny ties with diamond patterns. His Teddy Boy drape jacket.

There was nothing in his wardrobe that his parents would agree to bury him in, so we picked out a suit at JoS. A. Bank. It felt entirely wrong, immoral, a violation, but I had no say in the matter. I was just the surviving partner, grateful simply to be included, and, anyway, he'd lost so much weight that his mother insisted the wake be closed casket. On top of the coffin, we placed framed pictures of him from the time before AIDS.

The time before AIDS.

There will never be a time before AIDS again.

I wanted to bury him with at least one of his buttons: The Specials, Ramones Fan Club, The Beat, Pretenders, or maybe the seven buttons that, when worn together, spelled Madness. In the end I slipped a Blondie button in his suitcoat pocket.

His old toys that he had saved. Major Matt Mason with his moon base, along with NASA's "interracial gay couple," civilian Doug Davis and Lieutenant Jeff Long. The Fiat 1500 and Safari Land Rover Matchbox cars. The handless Captain Action, Action Boy, and Dr. Evil, with the exposed brain and hippie necklace.

In plastic bags specially designed for them, the comic books he had penciled for DC, Marvel, and Charlton. My favorite title to tease him with: *Soap Opera Romances*.

Ours is a soap opera romance, I would tell him.

He'd say, "No, *ours* is the real thing."

The phone rings and I make my way downstairs to the kitchen, where Aunt Nora has left a sink full of dirty dishes for me as a challenge. I make a note to get them done before she gets home.

"Is this Kevin?"

"Yeah."

"Kevin, it's Vince Meyer. Eddie's father."

I met him and Steady Eddie's mother a couple of times when they visited New York. I asked them what the courtship of Eddie's father had been like, but they didn't get the reference.

Parents calling is never good. "Is Eddie okay?"

"No. No, he ain't." His father hesitates and I think: Live Eddie, you lying son of a bitch. But then I think that parents' "okay" and gays' "okay" can often be two very different things, particularly if this is your first time around with thrush or PCP or isosporiasis or KS or encephalopathy or CMV or *Cryptococcus* neoformans or toxoplasmosis or MAC or cryptosporidiosis or TB or *Salmonella* septicemia or candida or non-Hodgkin's lymphoma or Hodgkin's lymphoma or HSV or histoplasmosis or progressive multifocal leukoencephalopathy.

I ask him, "What's wrong?"

Shouting now: "He has AIDS!"

I use my calmest voice. "I know, Vince, and I'm sorry. What I mean is, does he have trouble breathing? Do his lungs seem congested? Is he eating? Can he walk by himself?"

Vince says, "Sorry, sorry. He's got bad congestion. It makes it hard for him to breathe. And he's lost so much weight. He can't keep food down. He doesn't want to come back to Atlanna so we can take care of him. He says it would be too much for us, and that all his friends are up in New York, but . . ."

". . . a lot of them are dead."

"Yes. We can't be gone from our jobs more than a week at a time. I wanted to hire an aide, but, you know, his mother can't abide having some stranger looking after him. The volunteer gal from that gay men's place is wonderful—truly, she is—but . . . well, it's not quite the same as having a good friend look after him, someone he has a history with. And we think he needs someone who can be with him all day and all night. And my wife and I both feel . . . it would be nice if you would come back to Manhattan and stay with him."

Maybe Dave can lend me some money. Or Tommy. I can't ask Aunt Nora to do any more for me, she's done enough.

He begs now. "Eddie always calls you his best friend. He talks about you almost as much as he talks about Eddie."

"I'll be there tomorrow." Somehow.

"That's great," he says. I can hear him blow his nose. "We'll fly you out, and we can try to pay you what a PCA would cost. It's just that we're spending so much money flying back and forth. Is that okay with you?" He's thought of everything.

It's shameful, but I say it, anyway: "Of course. I wouldn't take your money, but . . ."

"Eddie told us you lost your job and your apartment. He also told us that since you've been back in Minnesota, you haven't been drinking. That's the one condition we have, Kevin, you don't drink. Nothing, not one damn drop. I need to make that absolutely clear to you. Promise me you'll stay on the wagon."

I never got drunk when I was taking care of Francesco; I'll never drink when I'm taking care of Live Eddie. "Not going to be an issue, you have my word." Then I say, with a twinge of resentment mixed with hurt, "He only tells me he's doing fine."

I picture him dabbing his eyes with a handkerchief. "That's what he's been telling us, too. My wife's up there now, and she talked to his doctor, that nice Indian lady, I can't get her name right. She said . . ."

And he falls apart, so I listen to him whimper like parents do when they're trying so hard to protect their child but understand there are some things they can't save them from. I say softly, "Eddie loves you a lot. He always says he wishes I had an old man like his old man."

A soft laugh and a little sob. "He does?"

"Yeah, all the time. He's lucky to have you for a father. And I should know."

He breathes in heavy, releases. He says, "Thank you, Kevin. Tomorrow, right?"

"Tomorrow."

Chapter 8

AUGUST 1988: $TRUMP CITY$

Aunt Nora asked if there was alcohol at Live Eddie's apartment, but I assured her that his mother probably scoured the place dry before his father even asked me to stay with their son. She's not sure it's a good idea for me to go back to New York, but I've been in Minnesota for five long months now, and all I have to show for it is sobriety, volunteering, and astounding sex.

So it's time for New York.

Dave wanted to squeeze in a conjugal visit before my flight back East and I considered it, but I decided to spend the night with Francesco's black leather jacket next to me on the bed.

We're at a Northwest Airline gate for my third flight ever, and it's the same gate where I confronted Suzanne Huntington-Conti. We sit next to each other as we wait for boarding to begin. Other couples embrace, hold hands, cling to each other at the prospect of having to part ways, even if only for a little while.

We don't.

First of all, public displays of gay affection are the unsafest sex you can have, and second of all, we're not a couple. So it's not gay love, and it certainly isn't brother love, and just the word "love" is something we've both sworn off of.

Still, I'm going to miss him and Minnie the Moocher.

The gate agent announces that boarding will begin in a few minutes. People stand around by the door to the Jetway, dragging what appears to be everything they own behind them. Dave says, "I'm sorry about your friend Eddie."

He's wearing shorts, so I'm distracted. His legs are golden brown and his *vastus medialis* is distracting. "Thanks."

He says, "How . . . how long do you think . . ."

"I dunno. Eddie tells me nothing, and his parents might be panicking prematurely."

"I'm going to miss . . . you know."

I look at his legs, sigh. I imagine running a hand up a thigh. "Me too."

Across from us a young man, wearing a Kangol hat, and a young woman poured into acid-washed jeans are playfully touching each other, occasionally kissing. It's sweet as ginger root dipped in mud.

And then, this: The man, tall and skinny and in chino shorts, gets down on one bare knee.

I say—out loud, I think—"You gotta be fucking kidding me."

Dave folds his arms, shakes his head.

A small crowd gathers as the man produces a ring. Women put their hands over their mouths; men grin and nod.

The woman looks like the girl with the husky voice in *St. Elmo's Fire*, but with taller hair. She covers her mouth like she just belched up garlic butter, and nods, eyes watering, YES! YES! YES!

Everyone at our gate applauds, save the two bitter homosexuals sitting directly across from them. Passengers walk up to congratulate them, shake their hands. The man in the Kangol hat is beaming at the well-wishers, but when he looks in our direction, all he can see is Chernobyl about to blow.

Dave sighs, says, "After this, I'm taking Aaron out to dinner."

"Anniversary?"

"Their first . . . 'date' isn't quite the word for it."

"Give him a hug for me."

"I will. Please be careful in New York."

When it's time to board, Dave and I shake hands as the newly engaged couple try to pry themselves apart. She waves to her fiancé dramatically from the Jetway, and I wonder if our plane will fall into Lake Michigan because it would serve them both right.

Of course my seat's next to hers. Fortunately, she doesn't say a word to anyone, just stares at the diamond on her finger all the way to the city that never sleeps.

I move in like a renter, on the first day of the month. Live Eddie's apartment is almost exactly as it was back in January, I mean, all of Dead Eddie's stuff is still here, and his voice is still on the answering machine. But there are some new additions: a commode next to the bed, an IV pole, the red plastic biohazard container, the dresser overloaded with prescription bottles, and the daily pill organizer.

And, of course, there's Live Eddie himself. He's gone from thin to gaunt, from gray to ashen. Most people would be shocked by the changes, but gay men have never been most people, especially now, and we've mastered the poker face, never taken aback by how much a friend has changed over the course of days, weeks, or months.

His GMHC volunteer helps out a lot, so I can go do the grocery shopping and laundry and go to the gym. She seems to know everything or how to find out everything—the best pharmacies, the best pharmacists, the best specialists, the best attorneys, the latest homemade concoctions, and if they seem to do any good, and she brings the gayest videos that we watch every day, since reading gives Eddie headaches: *Parting Glances, My Beautiful Launderette, I've Heard the Mermaids Singing.* Plus, his now-favorite, because it's so French, and, therefore, so very chic, *Entre Nous.*

Right now, it's time to change Live Eddie. I use latex gloves, just in case—just in case there's blood in his stool, just in case I have a cut on my hand. And so I don't wind up sticking my hands in bleach like a panic-stricken idiot. Like I did yesterday when I didn't bother to put gloves on and then I noticed I had a chipped nail.

Stupid.

Paranoid.

There's half-a-dozen boxes of latex gloves because of the diarrhea . . . It's like Francesco and Dead Eddie all over again. There are differences, of course—fewer visitors, since so many of our friends have died or are sick themselves or taking care of someone who's sick or dying or are mad as hell and protesting at the conventions.

And to think we used to be so shallow and vain.

It's amazing how fast we went from checking our looks in store windows to make sure our hair was laying as it should, to emptying catheter bags as we calculate what option would be the least nausea-inducing for lunch. From deciding how much pec cleavage to show to brushing someone else's teeth while singing along to Salt-N-Pepa.

And to be honest, you still can check out your hair along with your CD4 cell count.

I tell Live Eddie what I'm going to do before I do it. This Francesco taught me, because the sicker he got, the less people told him what was going to happen to him next, like his illness made him a lab rat, entitling others to poke or prod or shove a thermometer under his tongue or strap a blood pressure cuff around his arm or grab his wrist and count. I always go over the plays with my boys, like a gay John Elway on third and long. I tell Live Eddie I'm going to take one of the big pillows from under his head and shoulders so his upper body won't be elevated. I tell him I'm going to pull his sheet down below his feet so it isn't in his way, and when I do, he shivers slightly, in spite of the muggy August heat.

Live Eddie always wears thin sweatpants now, and it'd be easier if he wouldn't, but it's not my place to tell a grown man and my gay best friend that he should just wear a diaper. Francesco liked pajama shorts, the more retro the better. He loved 1950s snowflake patterns or little horses rearing up or burgundy-and-silver checkerboards. Even with PCP and CMV, he was in style—fashionable and a little ironic, his trademark look.

I tell Live Eddie I'm going to pull the sweats down, first just a bit from his stomach, and then I lift him ever so slightly and as gently as I can with one arm around his bony waist to pull the waistband down his backside. And so it goes, pull a little in front, pull a little on the sides, pull a little on the back, until the sweats are below his knees. If they're clean, I leave them around his ankles when I change his diaper.

His skin's loose and his thighs, those once perfect, mouth-watering rugby thighs, his pride and joy, Dead Eddie's pride and joy, Gay New York's pride and joy, are a pair of kindling waiting on the first match.

He needs new sweats. The old ones go in the hamper, lined with a black Hefty bag, the kind that makes me gasp for air.

I pull the tape off the diaper and stick it back on itself so it won't catch on Live Eddie's skin.

And now for the really awkward part—"graceless" was how Live Eddie himself put it when he was pulling off one of Dead Eddie's shitty unmentionables. He never called them diapers. It was always "briefs" or "shorts," or, if Dead Eddie could stand to be teased, "unmentionables."

This is how I announce the awkward part: I sing "Time to

Change." The Brady Bunch sang it in the episode where Peter's voice changes. I gently lift the front of the dirty diaper and place it between his legs. I wipe his balls and check his penis, the catheter, and wipe his thighs—the stool is really just brown and green water—and wad the wipes into the diaper.

He stares at the ceiling or keeps his eyes shut when I do this. Francesco wouldn't look at me, either. Later it didn't matter—he had visual-field loss and couldn't even watch TV anymore. He was plagued by floaters, so many he would weakly swat at them like they were a swarm of blackflies.

Cleaning Live Eddie up like this is a kind of intimacy we never could have imagined years ago when we'd lie in each other's arms and tell stories about who we were before we came out, how the closet was different in Atlanta compared to Minneapolis, actors we had crushes on as kids (Burt Ward in his Robin tights for me, Farley Granger in his tennis shorts for him), and who we'd end up with (whoever they were, they always had money, delicious bodies, and were completely devoted to us). When we'd finally stop talking, we practiced on each other: fanatical, long, hot-blooded kisses, along with tight, packed embraces and frantic groping.

But we never went all the way, just rehearsed as best we could. Live Eddie had more experience than I did in the bedroom, but he was more uptight about sex—well, just about everything, actually—than even this Midwestern Irish Catholic boy. I'd laugh when he'd rush to the store for milk and bread at even a suggestion of snow in the forecast. After one long make-out session as the snow fell in thick, wet drops on the slick Manhattan streets, we promised each other if we were both still single when I turned thirty—thirty being inconceivably old to me—we'd call it a day and live the rest of our lives with each other.

I tell him it's time to turn on his side and I help him roll, but today it feels like I'm just nudging him into place. I adjust his legs. He gasps, and his chest rattles softly. This position is the one I dread—it makes it harder for him to breathe—and as I hear his lungs rattle, I tell myself to stay calm, move quickly, don't panic.

It was the same when I turned Francesco—I was always afraid to roll him the last weeks. He had so much pain and weakness from his hips straight down to his ankles, along with a spasticity that always made keeping his legs positioned an ordeal. All I wanted to do was not hurt him, not cause him more agony than he was already enduring, just for the sake of a clean diaper.

I roll Live Eddie's old diaper in on itself, the dirty tissues bunched up inside. I lay one of the barrier sheets alongside him and tuck it in place, just in case he has more to do now that he's on his side. These are the sheets I soak in buckets of bleach before I wash them and toss them in the dryers, set at the machines' highest temperature.

Live Eddie's eyes—those huge, marvelous eyes that could spot a perfect ass from ten blocks away—face the window that looks out on West Twenty-fifth. I tell him, "I'll be quick, like Lady Bunny," but it's hard to be fast and feel like I'm doing a good job, and, well, his ass is covered in slimy, sticky shit, and it takes wipe after wipe after wipe to get it all off and not just spread it around. I grab a clean diaper, lay it out, double-check that the tapes are at the top, do a quick eyeball measure to see if I centered it okay. I have, so he can lie on his back for a moment before I roll him onto his other side. This way it's easier to remove the old rolled-up diaper that I toss in the trash. I double-check for any shit I might've missed, and he looks clean, so I put on some new gloves as fast as I can and softly apply Calmoseptine to his backside.

Brother, you shoulda seen it in rugby shorts.

He can lie on his back again. I tape up the diaper, tight, but not so tight it makes his skin more raw.

And now the good parts: I throw away my gloves, and I tell him we're nearly done. Up go the new sweats, soft and fresh and smelling like the detergent's promised country air, the sheet is pulled up and over him to keep snug as a bug in a rug, and it's a victory when I help him sit up a bit so the big pillow can go back under his head and shoulders, elevating him so we can both breathe a little easier.

I say, "And now for the pièce de résistance" as I put Farrell Furskin next to him.

He says, "Get that thing away from me. I grew up with rednecks."

I lean down and pick the bear back up. "How about some music?"

He says, "Yes. Something I can dance to."

I turn on a tape and we listen to one of his mixes: David Bowie, Madonna, Talking Heads.

He sees himself back on the floor under the strobe lights and takes in the aroma of poppers as he nods in time to the beat. I open the journal on the dresser that I share with his volunteer.

I write the date, the time, the color, and the consistency.

Live Eddie's mother is already back in town. When I asked her if she'd get in trouble for taking so much time off work, this proper "Atlanna" lady sounded like a streetwise Foghorn Leghorn when she said, "Fortunately for me, I don't give a shit." She reminds me a little of Aunt Nora, but American, of course, and everyone she bitches about—doctors, nurses, even the volunteer—she makes sure to bless their heart at the conclusion of her rant.

She also doesn't like sharing her son with me or Alex, the volunteer, while she's in town.

Since there's just the sleeper sofa at Live Eddie's, I'm spending nights at Laurie and Toshiro's in Hell's Kitchen. Their place is mostly one big room with a kitchen at one end and what could be a walk-in closet for a bedroom at the other. From their single window they have a panoramic view of a solid brick wall, and the wood floor needed to be refinished maybe twenty years ago. For all that, the place would be cozy if it was winter, but it's a miserable, sticky summer night in New York. Still, I can appreciate the white Christmas tree lights hanging above Toshiro's art on the walls, the tall parlor palms sitting next to the lonely window looking out at a wall, and the stacks of books from the floor nearly to the ceiling. There's a light aroma of cinnamon oil, which Laurie claims helps her de-stress, but in this heat I think it just helps cover up our stink. In one corner Toshiro has what had been Francesco's drawing table. Toshiro's was stained and warped, so I gave him Francesco's, knowing that he would lovingly preserve the little ink doodles of the mice and cockroaches that had shared our place on Avenue B.

Toshiro takes a break from cranking out consistent pages, grabs a beer, puts the Waterboys on the boom box, and sits next to me on the futon couch, my bed for the night. He places a slender arm around my shoulders, even though we're both sticky from the humidity. Laurie points the fan at us. Next she hands me a seltzer and pineapple juice in a tall glass tumbler, with a little toothpick umbrella and a red swizzle sticking out of it.

Something's up.

Laurie smiles sweetly at me and sits on the floor next to the fan, facing Toshiro and me. She sucks down her iced green tea like it's Dutch courage.

We sit and perspire.

I say, "This can't be an intervention, because I don't drink anymore. Besides, it was just grief alcoholism, not the permanent kind."

Toshiro laughs, says, "We're so proud of you" before he

takes a swig of ice-cold Corona from a seductively bead-
ing bottle. He holds the bottle up now, makes a toast: "To sobriety!"

Laurie hoists her tea in the mason jar: "Sobriety."

I look at my little umbrella. "You know, I was just in a really
sucky, painful place in my life. You don't need to give me a pep
talk every ten minutes, I'm not addicted to alcohol." I take a
swig of the pineapple and seltzer—a couple shots of Malibu
Rum would finish it off quite nicely.

Laurie says, "Oh, sure, tell me that after *you've* hauled *my*
inebriated butt to the emergency room not once, but twice.
Even if you don't believe you're an alcoholic, you have to stay
sober. If I'd woken up in a hospital after a bender that almost
killed me, I'd swear off the stuff."

"You're not me."

"And that's why I have a job."

I cringe. "If this is about me getting a job, you know I can't
start looking until . . ."

And the teasing stops. Toshiro gives me a squeeze, says, "We
know. You're taking good care of Eddie One. It's not about
that."

I will the fan to blow harder. "So we *are* having a talk."

Laurie says, "Yes."

I get nothing. "About . . . ?"

They wait each other out.

At last, Laurie says, "We want you to get tested."

Jesus. "Why? So they can put me on placebos?"

Toshiro says, "No, it's not about AIDS. I mean, that's a part
of it, of course. The issue is that we've been trying to have a
baby for a while now—"

Laurie interrupts, "We've discussed it, and we don't want to
do artificial insemination at a clinic. It's too expensive."

I put the toothpick umbrella behind my ear, have some more

pineapple-seltzer. "So get a turkey baster and do it like the lesbians do. Costs squat."

Toshiro frowns. "What is 'baster'?"

Laurie shakes her head, tells me, "It's not about a turkey baster, you moron, we're straight. We do it the old-fashioned way. What we need is . . ."

Toshiro says matter-of-factly, "Your sperm."

What?

Right now?

Laurie says, "Before you donate, we want you to get tested three times. Once this month, and once in three months, and again three months after that. There are some other tests as well, but the most important is the HIV test. You have to abstain from sex until after I get pregnant. Not that that's going to be a problem because . . . you know. Since Frankie died . . ."

Yeah, about that.

I look at Toshiro. He nods, unembarrassed. "It was the mumps, and I am, of course, the rare case that was rendered infertile. I've accepted it."

I look back at Laurie. She grins, says, "So, what do you think?"

What do I think? People die. They aren't born. Then the perfect solution comes to me: "Ask Tommy. He's one hundred proof."

Toshiro says, "Who's Tommy?"

Laurie says, "You met him at Frankie's funeral. Big burnout with a mechanic's license." To me, she says, "No."

I pull out the little umbrella from behind my ear. "Why me? Why not some straight guy? A straight Japanese guy, for that matter?"

Laurie gets up, sits on my lap, something she's never done, and it feels unnatural in so many different ways. She kisses me on top of my head, also something she's never done. "After

Tosh, you're the most important guy in my life. I don't want the donor to be some stranger."

I look at Toshiro. "Don't you want the father to be Japanese like you?"

He finishes his beer, says, "I want the donor to be someone we love. I honestly don't care that people will see I'm not the biological father. I was adopted myself. I'm half-Korean."

"You never said."

"There's nothing I care to say about it. Besides, I'm not sure you'd understand. In any event I'm a private person, Kevin. Not shy. Not unfriendly. Just private."

Laurie says to me, "You're tall, good-looking. And you've got good skin, hair, and teeth."

"Leave anything out?"

She has to think about it for far too long before she finally adds, "Oh! And you're very intelligent." We both know her eggs have more than enough brains to make up for my sperm. "So, reactions? Questions? Concerns?"

Me?

A father?

I mean, a biological father?

I mean, a sperm donor, I guess.

I say, "Laurie, you know I love you. You put me up when I ran away from Minneapolis, you supported me when I came out, and you and Toshiro helped me all through Frankie's illness. And let's face it, the two of you saved my life, probably more than once. So, why me? I'm a fuckup."

Our skin peels apart as Laurie gets off my lap and sits back down on the floor in front of the fan. She shrugs. "Because I love you."

"Why? I don't get what's so special about me that you'd want me to be the donor."

She frowns. "I don't know what else to tell you. For someone so vain you don't have much self-confidence."

I am *not* vain. "You told me you had a crush on me back in school. Do you still? Is that why?"

Toshiro laughs. "You're not her crush. You're her cause."

Laurie puts her head right in front of the fan and her hair blows around her face as she says, "That's not fair, Tosh."

I say, "I don't understand."

Toshiro says, "You know Laurie has her causes, and she's quite passionate about them. Feminism, environmentalism, fighting racism, gay rights—you're one of them. Maybe I am, too, I don't know."

I stare at Laurie. "You're friends with me *because* I'm gay?"

"No. Jeez." She shoots Toshiro a look, but he just smirks. He tells her, "I love you, Laurie, *because* you're so passionate about so many things. It's not a pose with you, like it is with some other people, who just want to impress. With you, it's authentic. It's nothing to be ashamed of."

I say, "So if I was straight, we wouldn't be friends?"

She pouts, something she rarely does. "So maybe, hypothetically speaking, I might have made a tiny little extra effort with you because, you know, gay people are so oppressed. I mean, gay sex was illegal in New York until 1980"—Great, now she's *educating* me—"and the city council only passed a gay rights law, what? A couple years ago? And with AIDS." She gets emotional. Finally she says, "I just want everyone to be treated fairly in life. I want a just world."

Another self-delusion shot to hell. I always thought she was still in love with me. Maybe she wants me to be the donor because she thinks homosexuality's inherited. Maybe she wants a gay kid so she can yell at straight people to stop oppressing her gay kid.

She says, "So, what do you think?"

Well, as long as we're all being so honest and aboveboard with each other: "I've had sex twice. Wait, just once, but it was amazing. The other time we just tried."

Laurie's face goes blank, but Toshiro tries to be encouraging. "That's . . . great. Is it your friend Tommy?"

I laugh and Laurie grimaces. "No, Tommy's as straight as they come. Besides, it'd be incest. This guy's in my survivors' group. His name's Dave."

Laurie asks, "Dave what?"

I say, "Larson. A good Minnesota Swede, just like you," although I can't think of two more different people for the life of me.

Laurie asks, "Are you practicing safe sex?"

Jesus wept. "Gorsh, no. He shoots his load up my ass as we share a needle. For Chrissake, Laurie."

Laurie says, "You don't have to be mean about it."

Toshiro says, "I don't see why this should change anything, honey."

Laurie says, "It just scares me a little."

Scares you? "I haven't even said 'yes' yet."

Toshiro closes his eyes, wipes his brow with his beer bottle. "It's too hot. Let's take some time and think about this some more. It's not necessary to make a decision tonight."

It's too muggy and hot in the apartment to sleep, and, anyway, I'm so wound up after our talk that while Laurie sits in a cold tub, Toshiro and I take the subway to Astor Place. We were going to catch an air-conditioned midnight showing of *Rocky Horror* nearby, but it's sold out, so we head toward Avenue B, because I want to visit Francesco's apartment, at least from the outside. Some days, when I came home from work, and our window was open because it was a muggy night like this one, I'd yell up from the street, " 'Yo, *Frankie*! Where's your hat?' " He'd stick his beautiful face out the window and look down at me, and ask, " 'Why do you wanna fight?' " And I'd shout back: " ' 'Cause I can't sing or dance!' "

Maybe whoever lives there now will tell me how much they love his murals, how they couldn't bear to paint over them. Maybe I can see them again.

Toshiro and I hear it before we see it.

Police are everywhere and the crowds on Avenue A—squatters, skinheads, homeless people, East *Vill-ahgers*—are chanting, carrying signs like GENTRIFICATION IS CLASS WAR and $TRUMP CITY$. Toshiro's intrigued, but we need to get the hell outta here. There are so many police, and cops in groups are never a good thing. One-on-one they're usually decent, but put two or more of them together—dozens or, worse, hundreds of them— and you have a mob hunting down fags like they did in the Castro after the White Night riots.

Here's what you need to watch out for: the moment they cover their badges, or take them off altogether.

You see that, you run like hell.

But it'll probably be too late.

At the corner of Ninth and First, we see a cop on horseback ride up alongside a young white man who's doing nothing, just walking, minding his own business. The cop on the horse grabs the guy by his hair and shouts, "Think it's cool to throw bottles at us?"

The man screams he didn't throw anything, but he's dragged by his hair to a group of cops who knock him into the side of a parked car and then kick him to the gutter. The more the man screams, the more the cops beat him with their nightsticks. It's a sickening, soft sound. People around us freeze or scream or run away.

More cops head down First now, clearing out witnesses with threats and clubs.

Toshiro shouts from our side of the street at the cops knocking the living crap outta the guy, "Leave him alone! He didn't do anything wrong!"

One of the cops stops beating the shit out of the guy and looks at us.

Fuckitfuckitfuckit.

I grab Toshiro's arm, "LET'S GO!"

But he just looks at me like I don't understand. He says, as if I'm a child, "But they're killing him."

And they're on us.

A mob, short blue sleeves, helmets, nightsticks, and one of them grabs Toshiro by the throat and slams him against the metal slats of a storefront and I hear him gasp and I hear the sound of his skull against the metal and I feel a nightstick land on my shoulder and there's a cop, short, mustache, gut, visor down so I don't jab, I knee him in the balls and he stoops so I stick him right in the side and they're all on me, and it's a red fog of boots and sticks and spit.

"Kevin, please, please, you must get up, you must get up now." It's Toshiro's voice, but he's out of focus. I feel his hand on my arm and taste blood on my lips. I can't open one eye all the way and I hear a helicopter overhead and I wonder if we're finally at war.

Other voices: "He needs to go to the hospital."

I mutter, "No, I don't."

"Yes, you do."

"Watch out for the blood."

"Don't call an ambulance—he'll be arrested."

"He shows up in the emergency room looking like that, they'll arrest him, anyway, ambulance or no ambulance."

"Dude wasn't even doing nothing."

"He got that cop right in the balls!"

"They started it."

"Yeah, like that's gonna matter."

"Lucky he didn't get a bullet."

Toshiro: "Help me, help me get him on his feet."

I'm up, Toshiro on one side, a skinhead on the other. Everything's blurry, like I rubbed Vaseline on my eyes.

Skinhead: "You live around here?"

Toshiro: "No, no, we're in Hell's Kitchen."

I blink hard, can't focus. "What happened?"

Toshiro says, "The police attacked us. They knocked you out."

I see hazy blue shirts everywhere, but they're not on us, and I feel like I'm walking underwater. People stand, but I can't make out their faces. Helicopter's making my head ache.

The skinhead says, "Take off his shirt and wrap it around his head—he's still bleeding."

"I am?"

Toshiro says, "Help me sit him down."

And I'm lowered back on the sidewalk. There's old newspapers. Looks like a *Village Voice*. My arms float up, and then down. My head. Pain. "*Ow! Fuck!*"

Toshiro says, in a squeaky voice, "Sorry, sorry! It's to stop the bleeding."

"That's as good as I can get it."

"Let's get him back on his feet."

I make out people and they're all watching me. Why? "What happened?"

"You were knocked out."

"Who knocked me out?"

Toshiro says, "Shouldn't we call for an ambulance? We should call for an ambulance."

The skinhead says, "I don't know where they're taking people. Anyways, I've seen a lot worse. It's just blood."

I throw up.

"Fuck, watch it!"

Toshiro says, "He didn't do it on purpose!"

I slump to one side. The skinhead says, "I'm washing this shit offa me. Good luck to youse."

"Who's he?"

Toshiro says, "I don't know, I don't know. Kevin, you have to help me. Can you straighten up?"

"Ha!"

I wipe my mouth and there's blood on my hand. "Hey! I'm bleeding."

Toshiro sounds desperate. "Just walk with me. Please walk with me."

We hobble down the street, and I start to feel better. Toshiro asks me if I want to go to the emergency room, but, Jesus, I'm not drunk, I don't drink anymore. How many times do I have to tell people? He knows that. He leans me against the slats of a storefront. He says, "Don't move."

I watch him at a pay phone. I slide down the slat and sit on the concrete. So tired.

We're at Astor Place Station. How'd we get here? People sleep on benches or are hunched up along walls. There's a beaver covered in graffiti.

On the futon couch. Laurie and Toshiro are fighting. They never fight! She says "emergency room" and "doctor," and Toshiro says "police" and "jail."

Live Eddie's volunteer, Alex, the former separatist but still lesbian, is taking care of him so his mother won't see me before she heads back to Atlanta. The cover story is that I was mugged. Alex thinks we should've said "fag bashed."

Live Eddie's doctor was so stunned by my appearance that after she was done with him, she examined me, too, free of charge. Live Eddie watched from his wheelchair as she had me look side to side while she peered into my eyes with her flashlight, checked my balance, coordination, and reflexes, and read me a list of items she asked me to recall a couple of minutes later. She wanted to order a CT scan, but no insurance. If it were up to her, I'd have one gratis, but the radiation technologists need to eat, too.

She said I didn't seem too bad off; then she asked me in her Indian accent if I wanted an HIV test. First Live Eddie, then Laurie and Toshiro, and now this woman. It feels like a conspiracy.

And now she's telling me, "It's better to know your status than not. A couple years ago I wouldn't have said that, but with AZT we can at least try to treat the virus rather than just the infections. And we can get you some low-dose Bactrim as a prophylaxis for PCP."

I sit on the patient table in the little examination room. "I don't have insurance. And I don't want to be blacklisted for insurance when I get a job."

From his wheelchair Live Eddie laughs a little, coughs a little. "You," he wheezes, "with a job."

I imitate his mother's accent: "You're a vindictive old bitch, bless your heart."

His doc says, "Don't worry about the test result following you. There's a way around it." She puts on gloves and prepares to draw my blood. "I give you a number, rather than use your name."

I hear Jonny Rivers sing "Secret Agent Man." "I haven't said 'yes' yet."

She has me sit on a chair next to her little desk, has me give her an arm.

What the hell? This way, if I'm positive, I can just tell Laurie and Toshiro that I don't want to be their donor. And Laurie won't have to know I'm positive. I won't have her hovering over me, waiting for my lungs to congest.

The doctor frowns as she taps, looking for the best vein. Next the cool sensation of the antiseptic and the pressure of the tourniquet. She doesn't warn me, just sticks me and takes off the tourniquet.

In the past, when I had to give a sample or get a shot, I always looked away, but now I watch the tube fill. There's nothing special about the blood pouring in, it looks like regular blood, and that's the kick in the ass. Who knows if there's a virus in there somewhere, some invisible thing that's eating me inside out? If it's there, my blood should look different somehow, like it's corrupted or spoiled, the way milk becomes chunky and discolored when it goes sour.

Am I looking at my killer?

I can't tell.

I want to give the blood a blessing, like they do for pets on St. Francis's feast day, or take it to a confessional, where all its past sins can be forgiven, and we're given a pass to go forth and sin no more. I guess it's like Aunt Nora says, "You can take the boy out of the church, but you can't take the church out of the boy."

She pulls the needle out, tells me to apply pressure to the puncture, then puts a Band-Aid on me. It seems so anticlimactic after all the arguments and debates I've had with myself— that we all had at the survivors' group. I wonder if I should've had it done sooner, if I'd been negative, maybe Francesco would've died a little easier, the way Dave's partner, Gary, did. Maybe I was selfish. But maybe I couldn't take care of Francesco and know for a fact that what was in him was in me, too, that I was seeing a future version of myself every time I washed his hair or squeezed an eyedropper as I counted the beads of morphine that fell onto his tongue.

She fills out a form, gives the sample a number.

Let it be a lucky number.

She gives me the paperwork that's wrapped with a rubber

band around—to my surprise—the vial of my blood. I frown like I'm afraid of infecting myself. "What am I supposed to do with this?"

She hands me a slip of paper with an address on it. "There's a little refrigerator in the lobby. Make sure the rubber band's on good and tight, you don't want the form to get separated from the vial. If the front desk tells you to sign the visitors' log, just sign it Frank Young."

It was strange taking Live Eddie home with a vial of my own blood in my pocket. He said he'd be fine on his own while I delivered my blood to the address the doctor had given me. It felt like I was in a horror movie and I looked for Freddy Krueger on the streets.

I was stunned that my destination was New York City's Department of Health building, an anonymous office tower off East Twenty-sixth and First. The security guy didn't give me a second look or have me sign anything when he saw the sample, just pointed me to a refrigerator near the elevators, where I put my blood alongside the other samples waiting to be tested. It was like a casino with me making the max number of raises and going all in at the same time. I wondered about the other tubes and whose blood it was, and why they had decided to get tested. I thought stupid thoughts, like if mine were negative, some other sample would have to be positive, because there's only so much luck to go around. How was this little refrigerator going to change my life? The lives of everyone whose blood was inside?

It'll be two weeks before my blood shows its hand. Two weeks to find out if I'm going to go through what Francesco went through, what Dead Eddie went through, what Live Eddie is going through.

With Francesco, it didn't begin with a test result. It began with the spot on his skin.

He had seen enough of them to know.

I told him it could be anything.

We held on to that for a while.

But then the spots grew bigger as they multiplied. And then the sores in his mouth. And then the fevers.

Then that afternoon, when the doctor sat behind her desk and looked him directly in the eye as she told us what we already knew.

But hearing it out loud.

From a doctor in her white lab coat.

That's when our world truly changed forever.

I remember he didn't cry, just politely thanked her for the death sentence. When we got up to leave, he stood numbly in my embrace as if I were some sort of vine that needed trimming. On the subway home, and then the bus, nothing. Not a word or a sigh or a tear. Just this blank expression, open and empty, as I wondered if I had given it to him. Or if he had given it to me.

When we got back to our tiny apartment on Avenue B, I asked him how he was doing. Stupid question, but I needed to hear his voice, listen to him as he said something to make sure he wasn't dead already.

He said, I'm worried.

I said, I know.

He said, No, you don't. I'm worried you won't be able to handle this.

It was the first time he ever broke my heart. I shook, sobbing, because I believed he was right.

He held me in his arms, apologizing. When I had calmed down, he stroked my cheek, saying, There's something I want you to do . . .

Inhale. Hold.

Exhale. Slowly.

*   *   *

Dave calls and tells me that Butch Bobbie Jo couldn't facilitate the most recent survivors group meeting because she came back from the Michigan Womyn's Music Festival with shigella, so now there's rumors that the government's decided lesbians are the next to die.

"That's stupid," I tell Dave.

"It makes sense. The best way to spread a disease among gay men is sex—among lesbians, music festivals."

I don't want to hear any more government conspiracy theories or government conspiracy theory jokes. "What else is new?"

He says, "I hate to tell you this, but Jeff died."

I flinch. Jeff, who was almost kicked out of the survivors' group for sexual harassment. "That was fast."

"If it were me, I'd want fast."

He's right. Better to die quickly than linger on a mattress as people changed me, bathed me, and popped me full of pills.

Dave clears his throat, says, "Have you ever done phone sex?"

"You've got to be kidding me."

"I thought we might—"

"No."

"Just hear me out."

"Okay."

"We were fairly vocal at the St. Paul Hotel, so I thought—"

"No."

Silence from suburban Minneapolis. Then: "I was just thinking we could give it a try, since you may be out there for a while."

I look over at Live Eddie, sleeping in his bed, and I wonder how long "a while" will turn out to be. "It just sounds so fucking stupid, bless your heart."

He's quiet for a moment before he says, "Okay, okay. Just an idea."

"Keep it that way." Why am I being such a dick? Oh. Right. "I had the test."

"Really? May I ask why?" There's caution in his voice, or maybe it's dread. Maybe he's worried I have symptoms. We were safe, but, still, the idea of having it consumes me; the idea of getting it must consume him.

"Some friends of mine want me to donate sperm so they can have a baby."

"Seriously, why'd you have the test?"

"I'm being serious. They can't conceive."

"You're going to be a father?"

Live Eddie wheezes, but then his breathing relaxes. "I'm just a donor."

"But you'll be the biological father."

"Donor. If I'm negative three times. And then if I actually donate my sperm. And I don't even know yet how any of this would work. I mean, getting it in her. The sperm, I mean. We're not going to a clinic."

"When do you get the results?"

"Two weeks from yesterday."

From Minnesota he considers this news for a few moments before he says, "I've never been to New York. Would it be all right if I visited?"

"You'd fly out here for my test results?"

"I want to support you whatever the result. And . . . as long as I'm there . . ."

"You're flying out for sex."

"I'd also like to see Times Square, Christopher Street, and the Statue of Liberty. And I want to leave flowers at the Strawberry Fields memorial."

Dermatology. Neurology. CT scan.

Live Eddie and I are in the waiting room, Live Eddie's in a wheelchair, I'm facing him in a regular chair. The wheelchair's an improvement over the cane; our last two times here, we couldn't find seats together. At first, the sea of sick and emaciated men at Live Eddie's clinic frightened me, it just never seemed so—*everywhere*—with Francesco, or even with Dead Eddie. At the same time the packed room has its own peculiar charms. Here we swap prognoses like recipes, we study the pamphlets and brochures that are meant to empower, inform, comfort. One booklet tells me: *Don't blame yourself for contracting AIDS. Until fairly recently, it was not even known how the disease was transmitted, and it can lie dormant for years.*

Which is why we all do the math.

I open *Giovanni's Room*, one of Francesco's books that I brought back with me to New York, and I take some comfort in the thought that I'm reading words and sentences he had read, that my fingers are touching pages he had touched. I make it to the part where the boys experiment during a sleepover, when Live Eddie's name is called. This appointment begins with a muscle relaxer. It's simply the latest in a series of needles. Before this needle there were the needles to draw blood, inject contrast dyes, and retrieve tissue samples, which were then delivered to the laboratory for testing and diagnosis.

They can't anesthetize bone, of course, so after the muscle relaxer has begun to do its work, they administer the minor, nimbler injections that numb Live Eddie's skin. Marrow will be extracted from two sites on either side of the small of his back.

The doctor instructs Live Eddie to close his eyes and rest his head in the crook of his arm. The doctor says, "Deep breaths. Breathe with me, in and out. In . . . and out."

Needle is forced through bone. This isn't what causes the pain, it's the moment when the plunger is lifted and the marrow is drawn up and out.

The team moves on to the other side, extracts more marrow and a core sample. In a few days we'll learn if the cancer has breached the deepest recesses of Live Eddie's body.

The doctor finishes collecting his samples and congratulates Live Eddie on his courage, but, really, what other option does he have? Being courageous, being afraid, neither of these things will change the facts.

I wheel him back to the waiting room, where he sits, like a confused old man or a lost little boy, never himself anymore. I make a call at the front desk, then talk with the scheduler about appointments and insurance and follow-up. When I'm done, I ask Live Eddie, "Where to, Mac?" like I'm a cabbie. He looks behind, sees me at the handles of his wheelchair, and tries to place me. Then he remembers and the confusion's gone, replaced by a grief-stricken look.

I say, "I called our volunteer driver and he's on his way. It's Terry, the one you think's so cute."

He faces forward now, coughs softly. "Okay."

Around us is gossip and silence and the *New York Native* and rage and boredom and resignation and terror. We wait here, in the midst of it all.

Alex is spending the night in Live Eddie's room so I can finally get some sleep on the couch. She told me I looked like the wrath of God before she took her copy of *After Delores* and headed into Live Eddie's bedroom, softly closing the door behind her. His mom arrives again tomorrow and I don't want to look like a deranged insomniac when I meet her at the airport. I think she might have quit her job; she's always here.

Dave's flight from Minneapolis arrives an hour after hers.

We've seen Ellis Island, the Statue of Liberty, and Times Square, which was not at all what Dave expected. For example, Circus Cinema was not showing *Die Hard* or *Cocktail* or *Vibes*. He rushed past Peep Land in disgust, and when he saw the entryway to Venus, New York's *most unique cinema with*

the best adult entertainment from the film capitals of the world,
he asked, "Why does it have a turnstile?"

He was unimpressed by the psychics and the tourist traps
and the electronics stores. He scowled at the men sitting behind
folding tables with their signs, AMERICA, JUDGMENT IS COMING,
REPENT and JESUS, THE WAY, THE TRUTH, AND THE LIFE. When I
pointed out the Howard Johnson's, saying how Francesco and
I loved to treat ourselves to the fried clams and people watch,
he said he wouldn't eat anything served in Times Square—least
of all, clams.

This from a man who eats lutefisk by choice.

So tonight he's treating me to dinner at Windows on the
World, atop the World Trade Center, a place I've never been,
and convenient to his hotel, which you can get to without even
going outside. Put another way, tonight will be fine dining, im-
mediately followed by fine sex without even time enough to di-
gest. For this occasion I'm in my ripped funeral suitcoat and
dress pants, and a shirt Francesco had given to me. The nonstop
elevator ride to the restaurant lasted an unending minute, making me dizzy and panicky all at once, but Dave was his usual
stoic self and put a hand on my back to reassure me. We shared
the elevator with tourists from West Germany, who timed the
trip on their wristwatches, and an older Australian couple who
smiled tightly as if the cable might snap, the car plummeting all
of us to our deaths.

At our table we can look out over the streets of Manhattan, a
quarter-mile below, and I can't take in the view for more than a
few seconds without the sensation that I'm falling. I want to get
on the floor, close my eyes, and crawl to the center of the
restaurant. There's really nowhere to look that you aren't looking outside. Dave is entranced by the views. He stares, points
out buildings, tells me their names. From the moment he
booked his flight, he's learned more about this city than I have
after living here for years. But then—as my teachers have com-

mented from kindergarten on—I have never lived up to my potential.

Along with the view, the menu's like nothing I've ever seen before, and I order the oxtail ravioli in soy ginger butter because I recognize the word "ravioli." Dave has the poached breast of pheasant, which he savors.

He asks, "How's your meal?"

I've done the math, and for what he's paying for just my dinner, we could have eaten deli for weeks. I try to think of something diplomatic to say. "Fancy."

He grins. "What does 'fancy' taste like?"

I point at my plate.

He shakes his head. "I know this isn't your sort of place, but indulge me, I'm a tourist."

"It's fine," I lie, already dreading the elevator ride down. Why didn't we have fried clams at Howard Johnson's, with ice cream for dessert?

He says, "Tomorrow's the big day."

When I don't reply, he sips some wine and I have some water.

"Have you thought about what you'll do if you're positive?"

Oh no, not at all. What gay man ever thinks about that? "I'll cope." As best I can when I look at Live Eddie and see my future.

"It's just that when Rob"—the look-on-the-bright-side macrobiotic advocate from our survivors' group—"told us at last week's meeting that he tested positive, he fell apart. I'm worried he'll do something stupid."

I find Rob shallow and annoying, bless his heart. "You got nothing to worry about with me. I've run out of stupid things to do."

"You know what I mean."

Around us diners speak softly in English and German and

Japanese. "Yes. I know what you mean. I thought I'd go bleed all over Cardinal O'Connor."

He looks at me seriously. "Please don't kid. I want you to have a plan in case you're positive. I've always found it pays to 'hope for the best, but plan for the worst.' "

I can't believe the things this guy says to me, both in the bedroom and out.

I watch the waiter refill our water glasses, and wonder how much the staff gets paid to work way the hell up here. I mean, the elevator ride alone. After he moves on to another table, I say to Dave, "You're the most sensible man I've ever had sex with."

He looks around to make sure no one heard.

Now I tell him, "Eddie told me I should have a plan if I'm *negative*."

"What sort of plan?"

"Go back to school. Get a degree in something marketable. Get a good job. Buy a house in the suburbs. Have kids. Retire. Move to Florida. Die."

He wipes just the corners of his mouth, returns the napkin to his lap. "Well, you're not going to be twenty-eight forever. Most people are on their career track by the time they're your age."

"And you're most people."

"Maybe we should change the subject."

"Maybe we should."

I look at my plate, thinking of all the burgers I could buy for the price of this one dish. By the time Dave pays the check and we emerge from the elevator and back down on planet Earth, I'm of two minds: one mind just wants to go back to Live Eddie's because Francesco never made me feel like I was a complete loser, and the other mind just wants to bounce around Dave's hotel room like a glitter SuperBall.

So we're in his hotel room and the moment he closes the door, I shove him up against it and lick his neck with just the tip of my *soy ginger buttery* tongue, and he tastes like salt and citrus. He strokes my hair and I close my eyes and I think how much I want my hands on him, and his hands on me, and tomorrow I find out if I'm going to live or die, so I grab him by the belt and yank him to the bed.

He says, "I've dropped some weight—did you notice?"

No. "Yeah, as soon as you got off the plane, you look so good, let's go," and I pull him on top of me and grab him by his ass as he kisses me hard, like I need convincing, and for good measure he grabs the collar of my shirt in a fist and pulls, and I shout, "Don't rip it," and he says he'll buy me a new one, but I let go of his ass and push him off me and I sit up to unbutton it, because Francesco gave me this shirt and I shouldn't have worn it tonight, but we were going to Windows on the World, and what the hell else do you wear to a place like that?

He watches and my fingers are clumsy and trembling a little.

He says, "Hey, let me do that."

Very tenderly he undoes each button as if he were petting Minnie the Moocher, just so, and gently coaxes the shirt out of my pants with small, cautious tugs. "It's a beautiful shirt. I didn't pay attention because I wanted to suck your tits so bad, and it was in my way." He pulls it off me submissively and folds it like it's a sacred thing, a flag or a vestment, gets up, places it safely in a dresser drawer. It's actually not that expensive or unique a shirt, just black cotton corduroy. In fact, it was kind of a gag gift; no one in the East *Vill-ahge* wears corduroy. I had complained to Francesco that all his "nonconformist" friends dressed alike, as if they had a school dress code all their own, so he bought me a shirt that would make me a nonconformist around nonconformists.

Dave says, "That okay?"

"Thank you."

He takes off his shirt now, lays it next to mine in the drawer, and I smile because his chest looks tanned and hairless. "You shaved your chest for me?"

He runs his hand over his skin. "Smooth and slick to the touch. Isn't that *la mode*?"

"*Oui, oui.*"

He says, "Close your eyes."

I close them. His footsteps hardly make a sound as he approaches. I wait for his hands or his lips, but I just hear him breathing deliberately. I'm being reckless, we both are. The test puts an edge on everything I can think of doing to him, no matter how safe, how in keeping with the latest guidelines. I hear his voice, it's singsongy: "I can tell you're overthinking this."

I nod. I hear his knees creak slightly as he kneels down before me.

His hands hold my wrists lightly and then they glide up my forearms and over the spot where the doctor inserted the needle to draw the blood. Now they reach my biceps and linger, slow squeezes of the muscles and I see myself sitting on the examination table, feel the cool latex of the gloves, hear a voice telling me to take deep breaths while a cold stethoscope is pressed against my back.

I lie back on the bed and Dave misunderstands and reaches for my belt buckle, so I say, "Don't."

He gets up and arranges himself beside me on the bed.

"Maybe tomorrow," I tell him.

He exhales deeply. "Give me your hand."

I do and he brings it to his lips, kisses it lightly. He says, "Tomorrow's going to be the most amazing monogamous, two-person gay safe-sex orgy ever."

I say, "I should really call Eddie's mom and see how he's doing."

* * *

The waiting room's full. Live Eddie's in his wheelchair, facing me, while Dave leans against a wall by the doorway, and I realize that having them both come was a mistake. I wanted Live Eddie to get out of the apartment, go for a cab ride, be there when I got my news. If it's good news, maybe a celebration afterward, a roll through Central Park or maybe a trip to Sheridan Square to watch the boys walk by. If it's bad news, his hand to hold, a chance for him to do something for me, because I can tell he's sick and tired of me doing things for him. If I were him, I'd want some equality back in our friendship—if nothing else, for nostalgia's sake and my own.

His mother thought it would be good for him to get out of the apartment, too. She needs a shower and has to get some groceries in. Plus, she hasn't quit her job, after all, and her office doesn't seem to care that her son's dying, so there are clients to talk to long-distance.

But bringing Live Eddie was a bad idea. I've broken a bond with him: Dave's proof that my life goes on without Francesco, while his life ebbs out, faithful to Dead Eddie till the end. With Dave here I've made Francesco someone in my past, dead and irretrievable. I'm so fucking stupid. The first cabbie that sped off once I wheeled Live Eddie to the curb was warning enough that I should have come here alone, without either him or Dave.

Maybe I shouldn't have come here at all.

Stupid, stupid, stupid.

Dave can't hear us from where he waits, so Live Eddie speaks freely in his raspy, congested way. "I don't like him."

"You don't know him."

"I don't want to know him. What does he know about you? About you and Frankie?"

I crack my knuckles. "He lost his partner to AIDS. We're not the only ones who ever shed a tear, you know. Besides, you told me I should make plans for the future. He might be part of it. I don't know, it's early days. Isn't this what you wanted? Me moving on?"

He gasps, spits out some phlegm. It takes me a moment to realize that he's crying. "You get to move on." He coughs, and I pull tissues out of the backpack we hang from the back of his chair. I lean in to dry his eyes, but he slaps my hand, tells me he can do it himself. He says, "All I want to do is go back to who we used to be."

"I know, sweetheart."

His large eyes widen as he looks at the young men who surround us, aged fifty years. His voice cracks: "I still can't believe this is happening to me. I look at myself, and all I remember is who I used to be. That's the real me"—he looks down at his own body—"not this. This isn't me."

I hold his hand.

He wheezes, shudders slightly. He says in a voice with phlegm he's too exhausted to cough up, "I don't want this. I can't believe Eddie's gone. I can't believe Frankie's gone. I can't. I just can't anymore. I want to go back. I want to go back to before."

I say, "Let's go home. I shouldn't have made you come with me."

He's weeping quietly. "No, I wanted to be here for you, but I just . . . I'm so tired."

I touch his cheek. "We'll go home and watch *Entre Nous*. Maybe have some chipped ice for your throat. We can cuddle on the bed."

He nods, wipes his face. "We can't disturb Mom, though."

"We won't. I'll be right back."

Of course Dave thinks I'm making a mistake. "I'll just wait out here with Eddie while you get the result. How much longer can it take?"

"We could be here for hours yet. Let's get Eddie home. I can make another appointment."

"Can't she just give you a call?"

"Face-to-face only. You flag the cab, *get in*, and then I'll wheel Eddie up."

He frowns. "We've been here so long already, what's the harm—"

"Will ya just do this for me, for Chrissake?"

He looks at his feet. "Sure."

Live Eddie's mother wants Eddie to herself, which isn't unusual, but her tone is sharp and I'm worried that she thinks I'm not taking good enough care of her son. She says she may as well just move here.

So I'm with Dave at his hotel, trying not to obsess that I'm letting Live Eddie and his mother down, but I still go through everything I can think of: the appointments, the meals, the pills, the drips, the hygiene, the ways I try to keep him entertained, and I don't come up with anything I've done wrong. It's not like I haven't done it all before.

Maybe she's mad it's her son dying in front of her eyes and not me.

Dave's hotel is near a gym, so I'm de-stressing my usual way: bench presses and squats. I spot him as he piles more weight on the bar than he should, maybe to impress me, maybe because he's still mad I didn't get my results and wants to work off his anger.

On the lift the bar wavers, his elbows flare out, and he raises his head off the bench. I grab the bar and set it on the rack, annoyed. "You're going to mess up your shoulders lifting like that."

He sits up, puts his elbows on his knees, and looks straight ahead. "Excuse me. Some of us can't spend all our time in the gym, because we work for a living."

Finally he's said it out loud.

I tell him, "I'm taking care of Eddie—not making the Cargill family another billion."

"So now I'm a corporate stooge."

"And *meat solutions*. What kind of job is that?"

"A good one."

I fold my arms across my chest. "Why don't you say what you're really mad about, and stop being such a goddamn passive-aggressive Minnesota bitch? How's about you do that?"

Again, without looking at me: "You used Eddie as an excuse not to get your results. I came out here to support you, to be there for you if you were positive, and to celebrate with you if you were negative, but you give up even before you find out. Is that why you can't hold down a job? Because you always give up?"

I load the bar as he sits there. When I'm ready to lift, I say, "Move."

We swap places. As I position my hands, he doesn't say *you got this* or *let's do it*. He just glares down at me, maybe hoping I'll drop the bar and break my neck. I don't ask him for an assist with the lift off the rack. I push myself hard, doing way too many reps, to show him up. I'm strong, you can see for yourself. I'm no quitter, no loser. After I set the bar back on the rack, I put my hands over my eyes and catch my breath. Finally I say, "Why does it even matter so much to you? You gonna dump me if I'm positive?"

"Is that what you're worried about? No. I'm not going to dump you, because we're not a couple."

"But you want to be."

He pulls my hands away from my face, looks straight down at me. "No. We're not a couple. We are two AIDS widowers who are friends and who have sex. Had sex. Amazing sex. We could have it again. Tonight. And as your friend, Kevin, I think knowing would be good for you. If you're negative, it'd be a relief, because the not knowing can drive you crazy. And if you're positive, we really need to figure out a health care plan for you. You're my friend, and you're stuck. Perhaps the test result will get you unstuck."

He lets go of my wrists and I sit up. "Maybe."

"How about we get cleaned up and grab something to eat?"

When we get back to his hotel, he asks me to shower with him. I don't say yes, just strip off my clothes, step into the stall, turn on the water. He throws off his T-shirt and shorts and jumps in, saying, "Let's get passive-aggressive, bitch!"

Then, true to form, he says a LOT more.

For our after-sex meal, Dave spares me a return trip to Windows on the World. The restaurant in his hotel feels more down-home, with a hanging block-and-grid quilt that makes me angry when I think of Suzanne Huntington-Conti's fake panel for Francesco. But then I see the display cases full of brightly painted wooden carvings of men, women, birds, bears, and wolves, and the moment passes. An enormous painting of fruits and vegetables makes a strong contrast to Francesco's works, which always featured men. Me, of course, but whole tribes of gay men embracing, dancing, holding hands. Celebrating life like it was meant to be celebrated.

I order the charcoal-broiled fillet of salmon. It has a pink center and is covered with juniper berries for some reason. The lemon mayonnaise doesn't help, and I fantasize about fried clams in Times Square, followed by my choice of twenty-eight different flavors of ice cream. I can see Francesco slip the coffee mug into his backpack before we leave.

The pharmacist told me quite sternly that the morphine drops are supposed to be used sparingly, and only as directed, due to the risk of addiction, which is the stupidest fucking thing I've heard in a long time, but Live Eddie's doctor told me to use my own judgment—make him comfortable, whatever the official instructions. She also asked me when I was coming in for my test results, so I lied, promised her I'd make an appointment.

Live Eddie's breathing was seriously labored and his fingers gray from lack of oxygen, and back when all this started, he'd told me the one thing he feared more than anything else, more than pain, more than paralysis, more than losing his mind like Dead Eddie did, was fighting to breathe.

Fighting to breathe.

I told him not to worry, this wasn't my first rodeo; I wasn't shy with the morphine, like the virgins are.

Morphine relaxes blood vessels, which means better lung capacity, which means more oxygen. Yeah, too much and he may stop breathing altogether, and, yeah, he can become addicted, but better he suffers? And addicted for how long, exactly? Who the hell cares? When my time comes, just give me a Super Big Gulp full of the stuff with a straw instead of an eyedropper.

And here's the deal: Live Eddie has rebounded. His fingers are flesh-colored again and he's breathing much easier.

He's sitting up in bed this afternoon, listening to Janet Jackson sing "Let's Wait Awhile."

"Now, she tells me," he says. He talks along as Ms. Jackson sings: " 'La da lee de da da de de de.' " And then he adds, "And so forth."

I'm done sorting his prescriptions in the plastic pill organizer, so I sit on the bed next to him. We can hear the traffic below, because I have the window open wide, and apart from the exhaust, it's nice to feel a little breeze. Live Eddie says, "Let me hold on to you."

I lie down and don't move until he finds a position that's comfortable. Only when I get the all clear do I put an arm lightly around him, making sure it doesn't rest on a rash or a sore. Back when we first became friends instead of lovers, lying in each other's arms was how we'd often spend our weekends. It was so exciting to hold on to a man, to have a man hold on to me. Yeah, we messed around, but mostly we just felt the loneliness and the isolation and the lies melt off us, one by one, until we were left with who we were meant to be. Hours and hours just like this, not talking, getting up only to go to the bathroom, or maybe grab a pop, dozing, holding, squeezing, messing around, and thanking God there was someone else on this planet who was like me.

Diana Ross sings "I'm Coming Out" through her nose.

Live Eddie says, "Ha. This song. They'd always play it at the Friday night dances at Columbia. Do they still have them?"

"Probably, but it's not an all-male college anymore. A shame. An all-male school is probably the only place I could actually finish a degree."

"You mean the last place you could ever finish a degree."

I sigh. "Oh, well, it was fun to drive the scrawny egghead college boys crazy."

Live Eddie shifts. "Not their fault, you always dressed like such a slut for those dances. And by the way, I was a college boy, thank you very much. Augusta State. Go Jaguars!"

"Yeah, yeah, yeah, you, Eddie, Frankie—all college boys. I was the only idiot in our foursome."

"You must be the smartest one of all. You're not dead, and you're not sick."

"Jesus, Eddie, don't say stuff like that."

He wheezes, but then it passes. "I'm sorry we're leaving you on your own."

I blink hard, inhale, hold. "Let's talk about the Friday dances at Columbia."

He touches the tip of my nose, says, "*Beep!* Okay. Tell me about the first time we went."

I exhale. "We were so excited—our first college dance. We both wanted rich Columbia boys who'd take us to Europe. We went to Trash and Vaudeville to get some new looks and the thighs were too tight on all the checkerboard jeans you liked. And I wanted a drop-sleeved tee to show off my arms.

We tried on a lot of different looks, and we didn't end up getting any, so you bought me a black studded belt so the salespeople wouldn't get mad at us.

"Then we went to Laurie's and my old place to get ready. I thought we'd choke on Aqua Net. Your hair got really crunchy, so you washed it again and started all over." I can almost see us now, checking out our looks in the mirror. "You cut big holes in your jeans to show off your legs."

He one-ups me: "You had to lie on the floor to squeeze into yours."

I kiss his warm forehead. "Laurie brushed our eyebrows with mascara. I liked how it made us look, a little dangerous and a little fey at the same time. We took the subway to One hundred sixteenth Street and it kinda scared me, because we had never been to Morningside Heights before, and I didn't know if it was a safe neighborhood. We walked the wrong direction down Broadway and had to ask a Barnard girl to show us where Earl Hall was."

He looks up at me. "How do you remember all this stuff?"

"I remember because it was a magical night. Going with my first, and best, gay friend to a gay dance. I felt . . . like maybe how straight kids do when they're all excited to go to a dance and hope to meet someone. A dance seemed so old-fashioned to me. Like I was normal."

"What did we do when we got to Earl Hall?"

"We scoped it out. It was so different from the bars and the clubs, so much more laid-back. Guys with glasses in long-sleeved baseball tees. A lot of people dressed like it was Saturday afternoon and they were about to do their laundry. I liked the way they checked us out. Like they were all Dilton Doileys to our Mooses."

Live Eddie says, "Mostly, I remember dancing with you. Every month we went, we'd dance with each other. Everyone probably thought we were a couple, like you and Frankie."

Outside, sirens.

He says, "You know, I think about Frankie a lot. I think about the night he died."

"I don't want to talk about that."

"Sorry."

"Let's talk about something else."

"Like?"

"Tell me about how jealous you were when I met Frankie."

He laughs a little. "I had Eddie by then. You were the one who was jealous because I met someone first. You know, I was so relieved that the four of us all got on so well. I was afraid I'd never see my best friend again after the two of you paired off. But Frankie was so easy to talk to. So genuine. He liked himself, and the rest of us had grown up hating ourselves. He didn't need other people to like him to feel good. And that's what made him so easy to love." He catches his breath, continues: "It's funny, he and Eddie were so much more creative than either of us. When Frankie'd drag us to a museum, he could lose himself in a work. I'd watch him, he was so engrossed, like he was peering into another dimension. He'd say to me, 'The references seem at odds with the subsidiaries,' and I'd just nod my head." A rest, some short breaths. "Then he'd laugh and tell me to slap him when he got too pretentious. But it never seemed pretentious with him—he was too earnest. I have to wonder where his art would've taken him if he'd lived."

"I always imagine he wins whatever the big awards are for art. Commissions, exhibitions, openings in Paris and London. And I tag along, hoping he doesn't replace me when I get too old."

Live Eddie shifts just a little. "Oh no, he would've never done that. Once he fell for you, he fell hard, and for all time. And no matter what the radical queens told us about how monogamy was counterrevolutionary, so they could get us in bed, he held tight. You both did."

His wristwatch on the dresser goes off. Time for a pill. I

carefully disengage myself, open the gallon jug of distilled water on the floor by the closet, pour it in a paper cup. I say, "You and Eddie held tight, too. Maybe that's why we worked as friends." I pick meds out of this afternoon's compartment of his pill organizer.

He says, "Eddie cheated on me."

I say, "Scooch up. He told me it was just sex. Not love."

"Nothing's *just sex* anymore."

He takes his pills.

I carefully rejoin him in bed.

He says, "Sorry I was such a dick about that Dave person."

"Sometimes people don't hit it off."

He rests his head on my chest, says to my feet: "I was feeling sorry for myself. You know, I still can't believe this has happened to me. To my body. My grandfather used to complain about getting older, but he had years to get used to it. We get what? Weeks? Months? A year? Two, if we're lucky. Christ, I'm falling apart. I think, tomorrow, when I wake up, I'll get out of bed nice and quiet so I don't wake up Eddie." He rests, catches his breath, continues: "I go for a jog, and if it's warm, skip the shirt, see who gives me the once-over." He catches his breath. "Then come back here, take a long shower, make some coffee, read the paper." Deep breaths. "That would be heaven . . ."

His hair is so thin and wispy that when I stroke it, I feel the skin of his scalp.

His breathing becomes shallow, rapid. ". . . and that's never going to happen. I'm never going to get better."

There's nothing to say to that. Too many people have died.

His lungs crackle slightly when he says, "You know why I didn't go back to Atlanna? Because I don't want my mom and dad watching me die. I can't do that to them. And now, I can't risk dementia. I don't want to be so out of it, I can't do it. I'm ready."

No need to ask him what he means. Too many people have died.

"I got enough Amytal. But just in case they don't work . . . I have a bag from the dry cleaner's."

I bolt straight up. "No."

He groans. He's rubbing his arm; I hurt him. I ask, "Are you okay?"

He's feverish today, so instead of a sweatshirt, he's in his HAPPINESS IS A WARM PUPPY tee. "I'm okay."

I lie back down. "Sorry, sorry."

He says, "I know it's a lot to ask."

I don't say anything.

"I want to die on my own terms. The way Frankie did."

Inhale. Hold.

"It should be easy. Peaceful. I just take the pills"—he gasps—"and fall asleep, and I don't wake up again. I don't wake up like I am now. I don't have to face this again. I want to do it while . . . I'm feeling kind of okay. While I still can."

Exhale.

"Are you listening?"

Inhale. Hold.

"Kevin?"

I get up, walk in circles so I don't run away. He watches.

"Frankie died on his own terms. That's what I want."

Walk. Walk. Walk.

"The bag's just in case."

Walk like a man. Walk this way. Walk the line.

"You probably won't have to do it."

There's things I *have* to do. The dishwasher needs to be unloaded, and the dirty dishes in the sink put in. There are rugs to vacuum. I have to enter the meds in the journal, I forgot to do that. What time was that precisely? Wait, it was right after his watch alarm went off. Easy. After the dishes are unloaded and loaded, and the dishwasher is making its sloshing sounds, and the carpets are vacuumed, and I've updated the journal, then he will look at me and say, *I've changed my mind, please forgive me for asking.*

"Kevin? Talk to me, please."

There are other things I could be doing today. Other people walk the city's streets without being astounded that they can put one foot in front of the other. Other people get upset when the pizza delivery guy's late, and the pie's cold, and the cheese has slid all to one side.

I'm a young man.

I want to be one of those people again.

I never was one of those people.

"Where are you going?"

"The dishwasher. The dishes are clean and I have to put them away."

"It can wait."

No, it really can't. Things have to be done, the apartment has to stay organized, and who's going to do that? Alex, the lesbian ex-separatist? The parents? They don't know where things are supposed to go. They don't know where things belong. And a week from now, or a month from now, it'll be easy to get it all packed up, hauled away, because I kept it all arranged, I kept us in order. I'm your best friend. Who else can do that for you? No one. Everyone who knew where things belong is dead.

Except me.

"Kevin, please come back."

This is who I will be. I'll be the person who puts the cups on the cup shelf and the glasses on the glasses shelf. The person who sorts the silverware, stacks the forks neatly in the fork compartment, stacks the spoons evenly in the spoon compartment, and does the best he can with the knives, laid together and with the sharp ends all pointed in the same direction. And if for some reason I'm not dead by the time I'm thirty, I'll become a bitter old queen who, people will say, used to be quite handsome, and who the staff at the video store know by name and dread, and who vacations alone in Sarasota every January, just as big a misery in the humidity as I am in the wind chill. This will be my life if I become an old man.

Because I will be so desperately lonely.

"Kevin."

Live Eddie's standing. In the kitchen. Holding his catheter bag.

"*Jesus!*" I tell him. "You'll fall down." I put an arm around him, lead him back to the bedroom.

"I'm seeing spots."

"I'm gonna pick you up."

It's a quick, painful motion for Live Eddie, and with an arm around his back, and another under his knees, I lay him back down on the bed in this universe that extends only as far as his bedroom door.

He's gasping. "Didn't know I could still do that."

"You scared me."

"How?" He breathes extra hard, like he's just finished running laps. "I was calling your name." More hard breaths. "It's like you were in another world."

"Yeah, I was a million miles away. Sorry."

He shuts his eyes, tries to slow down his breathing as best he can.

I lie down beside him, arms folded across my chest. "Do you want me to hold you?"

"No"—he is gasping—"I want you to listen."

"Okay."

"Just lemme rest a sec."

"Okay."

Live Eddie pants, like a dog. He weighs next to nothing. I try to imagine us in a parallel universe where there's no virus that kills men like us; where, perhaps, we never met Dead Eddie or Francesco; where I turn thirty and we settle for each other, like we promised we'd do. In this universe we have no idea how lucky we are; we can't appreciate the fact that we can breathe without pain or rattling or crackling, because we've always been able to breathe; we've never had the experience of struggling for air, or finding bruises that aren't bruises, or waking up with the sheets drenched in sweat. I wonder if we're good people in that universe, if we're kind to each other after ten or twenty or thirty years together.

Live Eddie says, "I want you here . . . when I do it . . . I need your help . . . if the pills don't work."

I shut my eyes. "I don't know how you could even ask me. It's too much."

"No . . . it really isn't. I don't want to be alone. I want you with me."

But once you're gone, I'm still here. Try to live with that.

It was what he wanted. It ended the unbearable pain. It was death on his own terms. It was something he wanted me to do for him.

The vodka hasn't made living with it any easier. Working out until I ached for days didn't, either. Even being with Dave . . .

I open my eyes, grunt. "The pills better fucking work."

"They will."

"I'm not doing the bag. If you wake up, you wake up, and you don't get mad at me."

"But I'll be sleeping . . . I won't even know."

Yes, you will.

I see him now.

I see him so clearly: He's not veiled through the haze of an all-day bender; I'm not trembling. My eyes aren't shut tight, my skin isn't covered in the sweat of another panic attack. I'm not fighting for air.

I see my beautiful Francesco, still sleeping.

Still inhaling and exhaling after his four-hour deadline.

I had put the Kliban comforter on top of him after he took the pills, and just his emaciated head peeked out of it. I double-checked with a spoon under his nose, and it fogged up beneath his warm breath. I had promised him. It was what he wanted. I couldn't refuse, because I loved him, because he had done so much for me, for both of us.

There was the bag, a Hefty garbage bag, the kind that lines the cans you stuff trash in, stamping down the rubbish with one foot as you balance on the other. It was on the floor, beneath a copy of the *New York Native*. He had been very particular about the type of bag, it had to be thick and elastic. No takeout bags. He had said, "I don't want to die with 'Thank You' covering my face."

Francesco, you always wanted me to believe that I was stronger than I really am.

I'm so sorry.

So very sorry.

I stood over the futon with the bag in my hand, watching him, waiting for God to send a messenger to tell me this was just a test of my faith. But no angel came, there was no miracle, only me kneeling on the futon, opening the bag, and sliding it over my Francesco's emaciated head—the hair that had been so Joseph Bottoms thick, the eyebrows dark, the Italian Catholic and Russian Jew in him making them nearly black, the nose that he swore grew every year until the day he'd look just like his father, the thick lips, the carved chin, the lean trapezius of his neck.

His head in a garbage bag, like a butterfly in the killing jar.

I didn't know he would struggle.

We had both assumed—for my sake and his—that the pills would work. Neither of us was curious enough to find out what would happen if they didn't.

He had wanted this over with, so in those moments, when his arms reached up, when his head jerked from side to side, I held him down, grabbed the bag around his neck, and kept it tight against his mouth.

I begged him to stop.

He couldn't hear, he didn't know what he was doing, but I begged him to stop and the thought that *he* was begging *me* to stop has been in my brain ever since.

Parallel Universe Number 263: The messenger of God appears to tell me it was just a test of my faith.

"Kevin, all you have to do is be with me."

Chapter 9

SEPTEMBER 1988: CELEBRATING LIFE (AGAIN)

September used to be the seventh month. This fascinated Francesco, who liked the fact that the Latin root *septem* meant seven. Of course, September is the ninth month now, and Francesco said it was like September was in the closet, pretending to be the ninth month in order to fit in, but in its heart of hearts, it really was the seventh month. These were the types of things that intrigued him, but then, just about everything intrigued him, he was so curious about the world, other people, and maybe his art was a way to make sense of it all.

Live Eddie died on the second day of the ninth month that's really the seventh month.

I held him in my arms and he didn't wake up.

It felt like an answered prayer when he didn't wake up.

Live Eddie, lying there dead, a sheet gently tucked around his body, his body in Dead Eddie's candy-striped nightshirt, the one he picked out before the pills and the water.

This is what an answered prayer looks like in 1988.

Live Eddie's family sits in the front row. I sit right behind them, beside Laurie and Toshiro. This isn't orthodox, or even conservative; it's a celebration of life, albeit in a church.

Live Eddie's parents, his sister, and his sister's boyfriend have come up to New York. There'll be no service in Atlanta, a place that—with the exception of his immediate family—only had painful memories for Live Eddie. He used to wonder which was worse: everyone assuming you were straight, like his friends did, and therefore hearing the hateful, vicious things they said about gay people; or having everyone assume you were gay and beating the crap out of you. Dead Eddie told him, "Take it from me, having everyone assume you're gay is worse." Maybe that's why Dead Eddie was the assertive one of the two: From kindergarten on, he was used to being targeted, harassed, attacked. As the years went by, he didn't give a single goddamn what other people thought of him.

Except his family.

Live Eddie's celebration of life is at Judson Memorial Church in the West Village, which was built with Rockefeller money, and during the Depression, homeless men would sleep on the pews. I wonder if some man with nowhere else to go once slept on the pew where I'm sitting.

It's warm and we fan ourselves with xeroxed programs that feature a picture of the Eddies after one of Live Eddie's rugby games. He's lifting Dead Eddie off his feet in a bear hug as Dead Eddie kisses him on a dirty cheek. They look so incredibly young; I'd almost forgotten how young they were. The Eddies found each other first, and I worried that I would end up alone, but then I met Francesco, and suddenly we became the foursome, doing almost everything together. Laurie felt ignored and sulked, until she and Toshiro got together.

Here's what the foursome did when there actually was four of us, before AIDS: a trip to Fire Island and dancing to Yaz and Tom Tom Club from Friday night until the Sunday tea dance, with the smell of poppers thick in the air, talking all night as we tried to sleep on the beaches and the dunes, too broke to rent a place, our bodies wrapped in towels, watching the Muscle Marys and drag queens walk by in a seemingly endless parade of gay men exploding in joy and jealousy and sex. Walking down Christopher Street to be with our own, feeling the electricity of watching and being watched, the men smiling at each other or maybe an intense scowl from the desperate-for-sex, catcalls, whistles, being with your first true friends, the ones who have only ever known you for who you really are. The ones you didn't have to start over with. If Dead Eddie picked what we'd do, we might get tickets to *Lena Horne: The Lady and Her Music* at the Nederlander; if Live Eddie picked, we might cheer on and check out the guys of the Old Blue Rugby Football Club; if Francesco picked, we might see the New York/new wave exhibit at the Museum of Modern Art; if I picked, we'd go dancing at Pyramid or Danceteria, maybe try to get into Studio 54 to see the celebrities—people I used to think were important, for reasons I can no longer remember.

We're invited to step forward and share memories, but it doesn't take too long, many in our circle have died and the gay men I see at funerals and memorial services and celebrations of life have run out of things to say—so much seems the same, as if the same person's dying over and over again. Mostly, it's Eddie's neighbors and former coworkers, who speak of his kindness, of his imposing size—before he got sick—and how intimidating his size was until you got to know him, got to understand that he was actually a Georgia peach who was a bit shy.

I don't speak, because I feel I've nothing left to say. When Live Eddie and I made our promise to settle down with each other, if neither of us was in a relationship when I turned thirty, it never occurred to us that he might not live that long, or that I may not, either.

The foursome's gone, but for some reason, I'm still here.

Inhale. Hold.

It'll pass, always does.

Exhale. Slowly.

Inhale. Hold.

It'll pass, always does.

Exhale. Slowly.

My straight female best friend sits next to me, holds my hand, whispers, "Look around. Catalog. It will pass."

This church has archways and columns and stained-glass windows with men in robes, but the statues I'm used to from Catholic churches are absent, and nowhere do I see Christ in his agony nailed live to a cross. Up front, there's a circular stained-glass window with a cross at its center, but no one's being crucified on it.

Everything here is premised on an afterlife. Aunt Nora says we'll see our dearly departed in heaven, her priest tells me the same thing, and if you allow just for a brief moment that they're right, that I will see Francesco again, how do I explain Dave?

This one passes easily, quickly. Laurie squeezes my hand.

The celebration of Live Eddie's life nearly ends just as solemnly as it began. Not the celebrant's fault, because as we celebrate ever more lives, we mourn our own. But then Alex, Live Eddie's GMHC volunteer, takes the microphone. She's a small woman who looks big in her SILENCE = DEATH T-shirt, jeans, and biker boots. She's one of those lesbians you might see at a gay bar and check out, until you realized she wasn't a real cute boy, but a real cute girl.

Her voice is unsteady: "Eddie was the first person with AIDS I was assigned to work with. I was scared, I have to admit. Not of AIDS. But that he wouldn't like me. Some of my friends were surprised—my straight female friends, I mean. They'd known me back in college when I was a radical sepa-ratist, raging against the patriarchy, and now here I was, doing the girly thing, taking care of a man. One of them asked me, 'Do you believe for even one second gay men would volunteer to help lesbians if the situation were reversed?' This is a woman who used to love to go to gay bars and dance with 'her boys,' but doesn't anymore because she's afraid of AIDS. So, do you know what I told her? I told her to fuck off. Because this ain't political, it's personal."

Live Eddie's family flinches, they're still new to this community they've found themselves in. They don't know that celebrations of life are rated R, for mature audiences only.

Alex looks down at the floor, and then back at us. "You know, I never really had any gay male friends until I volunteered at GMHC, until I met Eddie. Lots of us never had gay male friends, lots of gay men never had lesbian friends. We stuck to our own worlds, by and large. I am so sorry it took this disease to bring us together, but I am so damn proud of all that we've accomplished, together. We are fighting for our lives, together. All our lives. And I'm so overwhelmed sometimes about all the work we still have to do. But then I see a flyer, like *Our Boys Need Our Blood*, and go and donate, because I understand that this isn't just a movement, it's a war, and there's no time for the healthy to wallow in self-pity, too many of our brothers are dying. Women like me aren't volunteers, we're warriors.

"I told Eddie once that I felt guilty—it can seem like lesbians are immune to AIDS. He told me not to feel that way, because when the assholes say AIDS is God's judgment, we just say that means lesbians are God's chosen people."

The people who have never heard that before laugh, the rest of us smile.

"Eddie was a funny man. I took him to ACT UP once, and there was this speaker complaining about how white and how male ACT UP was. So Eddie shouted, 'We're dying faggots, what more do you want?' "

Some of us laugh.

"I asked Eddie once how he could be so brave after losing his partner and having to face this disease alone. He told me he wasn't alone—he was lucky, he still had his parents, his sister, and Kevin and his friends, who loved him. And then he told me"—here her voice chokes—"that people like me gave him hope for the future . . . a future he wouldn't live to see . . . because even though we didn't have AIDS ourselves, we did everything we could for those who did . . ." Before she breaks down entirely, she manages to say, "I hope he knows how much he did for me."

And the celebration ends to a recording of Cris Williamson's "Song of the Soul." If Dead Eddie had picked the song, it'd be Sylvester's "You Make Me Feel (Mighty Real)."

I hug Live Eddie's parents, his sister, shake her boyfriend's hand. We'll see each other later today, there's a ton of logistics to sort out at the apartment, where we can speak freely now that Live Eddie's no longer there to hear us.

I look for Alex, but she's disappeared.

Outside on Washington Square I see Live Eddie's doctor. She's dressed in white, with a white scarf covering her black and prematurely gray hair. She walks to me like she's on a mission, maybe she's angry, I don't know her that well.

She says, annoyed, "Kevin Doyle."

I say, wondering what I did to piss this woman off, "Good memory."

Laurie holds out her hand, says, "Hi, I'm . . ."; the doctor ignores her, says, "It's actually quite easy to remember the only negative test I've had in months. You denied me one of the rare pleasures I had at my job, telling a gay man he's uninfected."

Laurie and Toshiro look at each other.

She says, "You needn't lecture me on my ethics. Getting the result is supposed to be your decision, very true, very true. But I'm giving up my practice, so ethics are something I don't concern myself with anymore. This is my last funeral, excuse me, my last celebration of life. I can't do it anymore."

I say, "I'm negative? Are you sure?"

"Of course. A negative result is memorable. A true celebration of life."

"And you're sure?"

She says, "Get tested again in three months to be certain. That said, you've been given a wonderful opportunity. I see so few gay men who aren't sick and dying. Those of you who are left need to make sure the next generation knows how to protect itself, but, more to the point, gay kids need to know they have value and deserve respect. I wonder how many of my patients never knew that. Give me your word."

I take her hand in mine. "You got it."

"I wish . . . I can walk away, but my patients . . . but what good am I to them if I can't keep some semblance of professional distance, you know? I'm tired."

She looks lost. I say, "You did a great job with Eddie."

She blinks hard, says, "He was very patient with me, I kept him waiting all the time, I keep them all waiting all the time, and how can I keep dying men waiting? There are just so many . . . never mind me. He was very fond of you."

"Thank you for all you've done."

She lets go of my hand, says, "It's never enough," before she walks off alone with quick, deliberate steps through the crowd of mourners, across the street, and into Washington Square Park.

Now that they're both dead, *le pied-à-terre des les Eddies* has become a museum. Everywhere there are artifacts of the Eddies and their life together. It feels like it should stay this way forever, a shrine to two men finding and loving and taking care of each other. I look with the fresh eyes of a tourist at the framed pictures and flyers and photos and magazine covers that span the floor to ceiling on a living-room wall. A flyer for the tenth annual Lesbian and Gay March that started in Sheridan

Square and ended with a rally in Central Park. The GAY AMER-ICA cover of *Newsweek*, with Bobbi Campbell and Bobby Hilliard. A *Christopher Street* cover with two men holding hands as they share a milkshake. A picture of the Eddies and Francesco and me drinking wine and sharing a pizza in Little Italy. The Eddies with Live Eddie's family atop the Empire State Building. And nothing with Dead Eddie's family.

I still sleep on the couch.

The phone.

Dave.

"How was the funeral?"

"Celebration of life."

"Makes it sound more like a 'hello' instead of a 'good-bye.' We had a 'funeral' for Gary at St. Paul-Reformation."

"Don't care."

"I'm sorry, I didn't mean to make light. I know he was a good friend to you."

"He was. They all were."

"What will you do now?"

"I'm going to pack up his things and ship them down to Atlanta. I can stay in his apartment until the end of the month."

"And after that?"

"Beats the hell outta me."

He says in his quiet, serious voice, "You should come back to Minnesota. You can move in with me. We should live together. I think it makes sense. But you have to get a job. You don't have to pay half the mortgage, but you could make enough to cover some of the utilities. It makes sense, financially—until you get a degree, you won't be earning much. You should know I'm willing to cover all the housing costs if you do go back to school full-time. I can help you with the student loan applications. Plus, we're sexually compatible."

"Is this a proposal?"

"No. Even if we could get married, like in that universe you imagined . . ."

Jesus! He remembers everything.

". . . I don't want to. This isn't love, it's companionship. I think we would be good companions for each other, Kevin. I had Gary, you had Francesco, and this way, we're not trying to replace what we had. We both understand that. I think that's a solid foundation for living together as companions. Plus, we can have sex with each other, so we don't have to look for partners. We don't have to take that risk."

"Oh, stop, you old honeydripper. I'm blushing. I'm turning red. You're embarrassing me."

"I'm being serious."

"You don't have to tell me twice."

"I had the head-over-heels love of my life. I'm not open to that again. I . . ."

I can hear his voice crack from Minneapolis. "Dave?"

He regains control. "I'm never going through that again. I almost didn't survive it."

"What do you mean?"

Another long pause. "You weren't the only one sent to the emergency room. After his funeral I overdosed on Gary's morphine."

"On purpose?"

"No. I didn't want to die. I wanted the pain to stop."

"I get it."

"I know you do. That's why we make sense."

Pete from the publishing company called, relieved to hear I couldn't work up the energy to give even one more damn about *Our Sacred Journey Together*. When I told Pete about Live Eddie dying, he asked me what I was doing Monday night. I told him, "The same thing I do every night since Eddie died— sit alone, stare at the wall, and feel sorry for myself."

He said, "Oh, so you have plans. Maybe some other time, then."

Then he said he was coming to Chelsea Monday and personally escorting me to an ACT UP meeting, dragging me there if necessary.

The meetings are held at the Lesbian and Gay Community Services Center on West Thirteenth, and the place is a dump. Like almost everything in New York, it used to be something else (in this case a high school), and it's covered in graffiti and the windows look like they might drop off the building at any moment and land right on your head. Inside, you have to walk by a huge reception desk that reminds me of my high-school principal's desk. His name was Mr. Rogers (no joke) and the only reason I ever met with him was to explain myself, like I feel I should at this desk, but Pete whisks us past without a word. The cracked and split linoleum in the hall that leads to the assembly room sticks to my sneakers, and the assembly room's floor is even worse, with all the cigarette butts. The fluorescent lights, the fans, and the wires crisscrossing the ceiling make me think this place could go up in flames at any moment.

We sit in folding chairs, and some of the late arrivals stand along the walls as the room fills. This seems to be a group of extremes: The AIDS-thin men scattered among the young men in tight jeans and tighter T-shirts that highlight their biceps. I was going to make a comment to Pete about how they all looked the same, until I realized that my T-shirt was stretched taut, and my jeans make me look like I'd been dipped in blue latex from the waist down.

Along with me, and the very quiet Pete, there's HIV in this room, and AIDS, and rage, and lust, and fear, and self-righteousness, and dedication, and passion, and some batshit crazy-ass people, too. We sit next to Pete's friends, a man and a woman, who both look like they should be studying for the big algebra test tomorrow. She's tall and in a white tee and jeans; he's small and wears a black tee and jeans. They kiss each other on the lips dramatically, but passionlessly.

The woman says, "You Kevin? Pete's told me all about you. I was really pissed about *Our Sacred Journey Together*. It's *so* unfair. I think we should have an action at one of her readings."

We sit, and the meeting comes to order with a man and a woman cofacilitating. There's talk of the attacks on gay men over the summer by wandering gangs of straight boys, and how the police have made no arrests, in spite of more than a dozen fatalities. There's talk of the Southern Baptist convention condemning our "depraved behavior and perversion," and it makes me think of "that son of a bitch, Charles Trevelyan, the filthy Brit." People propose die-ins, kiss-ins, fax zaps, they condemn Dukakis for opposing gay foster parents, but their sheer contempt is reserved for his running mate, Lloyd Bentsen, who voted for Jesse Helms's amendments to federal AIDS spending. They talk about how Atlanta police beat the shit out of activists during a kiss-in at the Democratic National Convention. At the Republican convention it was the delegates who attacked the kiss-in activists. There's no one to vote for, no one to represent us, but we should vote against Bush, the third Reagan term. It's depressing to realize you really have no one in power who gives a shit. As people speak or interrupt, I look at Pete, who listens intently to it all. New York, being out, it's all so new to him.

He's young, just twenty-four, but he seems so much younger, decades younger. He's a toddler, really, because he hasn't lost a single friend or lover to AIDS. And he looks like such a kid. He's pretty, in a skinny, goofy sort of way.

Francesco, you would be proud of me. Tonight I'm curious, not judgmental. After listening to what the people in this room have said, I think I finally understand that nothing will happen unless we make it happen.

Pete and I sign on for the October action at the Federal Drug Administration headquarters in Rockville, Maryland.

I also buy a T-shirt, one size too small.

A couple days pass, but they feel like weeks.

Laurie. Toshiro. Aunt Nora. Dave. Even Tommy, the ER veteran. Since Live Eddie died, they all want to make sure I don't "self-medicate," as Dave puts it, or "act a damn fool," as Aunt Nora puts it. Laurie stopped by *le pied-à-terre des les Eddies* to keep me socialized and to tell me how thankful she is that I'm negative—and I say, "At least according to the first test."

So I decide to call Pete, because even though I hardly know the guy, he's alive.

And, besides, Laurie's right, I need to be around other people, and I want to be around someone unfamiliar with the unfortunate events of winter, someone who won't look at me as if they're laying odds on whether or not I'll pour another handle of vodka down my throat, now that I'm the only one left of the foursome.

Maybe we could talk about something other than the plague. I have no idea what that would be, but still . . .

After Pete asks if this is to pump him for more information about *Our Sacred Journey Together*, and after I tell him no, I'd just like to see him, he happily accepts my invitation.

We're going to eat at a real restaurant and I'm treating, for once. Chelsea Place on Eighth was the Eddies' favorite, and the foursome always went there to discuss art, comic books, Broadway, rugby, gay clubs, and music. It was our secret place, and, no, I'm not kidding. To find it, you have to know exactly where you're going, it's hidden in the back of a used furniture/antique shop. Francesco said it was like being in *The Chronicles of Narnia*. In the back of the shop, there's a large wardrobe with mirrored doors that you open to get to the piano bar. Next go through the bar to another door, which opens up to a staircase that takes you to the dining room. There's a glass-enclosed garden with a totem pole in it and a pond with ducks.

Right here in Chelsea.

Pete's dressed smartly and reminds me of Francesco during his Teddy Boy days. He wears a light drape jacket and drainpipe trousers, along with desert army boots.

"Cool place," he says as he scans the menu. "And I love Northern Italian."

I smile. I realize that without *Our Sacred Journey Together*, I have no topics. I should've prepared some, because the only things I've been talking about the last three years or so are the same things I don't ever want to talk about again.

Pete looks around the restaurant in wonder. "This is why I love New York. Places like this." His enthusiasm's sweet, like a puppy with a new chew toy.

I say, because the Midwest is forever being trashed in this part of the country: "I'm sure there's great places in Kansas City, too."

"I tell you what, if you like steak and barbeque, KC's the place for you."

How did Dead Eddie put it? Oh yeah: "It must have other things to recommend it."

He looks stumped. After a moment he says, "Well, it *is* the largest city in the state of Missouri."

"Impressive."

"And it's the 'City of Fountains.' "

"Beats being the 'City of Crackheads.' "

"Lemme see. What else, what else, what else? Oh! There's a lot of people like you there."

What the hell? "You *are* gay, right?"

"Ha! You're funny. I mean Irish. You're Irish, right? I mean you've got those amazing blue eyes and hair like midnight, and with a last name like Doyle . . ."

"Mom was fresh off the boat and Dad's side came over during the potato blight."

"You mean the 'potato famine'?"

"In a famine there's nothing to eat. It was a blight, but the English made it a famine. Especially that son of a bitch, Charles Trevelyan." Aunt Nora would be so proud.

"Oh . . . okay. Good to know." He counts on his fingers as he says, "Lessee . . . I'm Irish, German, English, Polish, Italian, and French, with just a smattering of Spanish." He smiles. "And as far as KC's gay community goes, I have no clue."

"Really?"

"Came out in New York. Isn't that why you moved here?"

I nod.

"I'm so glad you called. I've been worried about you. Your friend Eddie's death must be so fresh."

I shrug. "You get used to it."

He looks at me seriously. "No one should have to get used to that. If I lost someone close to me—"

You're gay. You mean *when* you lose someone close to you. I point to the menu. "What looks good?"

We order pesto and risotto and polenta, and when I don't order wine or a cocktail, he doesn't, either. I struggle to think of something to say. The silence doesn't seem to bother him at all. He pulls a golf pencil and a little notebook out of his jacket.

I ask him, "Are you an illustrator?"

He looks up, grins. "Writer! When I get a good idea, I write it down so I don't forget."

At least he's not an actor. "Written any good books lately?"

"Not yet. To be a great writer, you have to read, read, read. That's why my job's so perfect, except it pays nothing at all. But I'm developing a network of acquiring editors at the big houses, and getting to know some of the best literary agents. My goal's to have America's first gay best seller by the time I'm thirty. *A Boy's Own Story* came close, but mine's going to be number one, and my protagonist will actually have a name. Then I'll adapt it for film and win the Oscar for Best Adapted Screenplay. Michael Schoeffling will play me. I mean, the fictional me. It's not a memoir, too soon for that."

You're gay. No, it's not. Around us, couples are chatting happily or eating their buttered bread in silence. "Good you have a plan. But you don't seem like a writer."

He tilts his cutie-pie head. "Why not?"

"You didn't order a double martini, you're not chain-smoking, and you haven't shown me pictures of your cats."

He says, "Alcohol makes me break out in rashes, ditto cats. And I will have you know, I was a peer educator at Mizzou. I told my peers not to smoke, drink, or rape."

"Oh."

"Literally a Boy Scout. 'All Out for Scouting!' How 'bout you? What were your college years like?"

He's a little hyper, never noticed before. College years. Time to lie? "Ummm. No college years and not a Boy Scout."

He looks at me sympathetically. "College was the best. Why didn't you go?"

Why lie? "I dropped out after two semesters because I was too stupid and too broke."

He blushes. "Sorry." Then he adds, real fast, "Not that you're too stupid. No, I mean, I'm not sorry you're stupid. *You're not stupid.*" Flustered, he leans in now. "So . . . when the rest of us were cracking the books, what were you doing for fun?"

I worked dead-end jobs, got high, and searched New York for my Francesco. "Uh. Concerts. Loved going to concerts."

"Symphony, chamber, or philharmonic?"

Jesus. "Ronstadt, Springsteen, and Petty."

"Nice! Love 'em all. But I'd have to say Tom Petty is my favorite."

"Really? Sing the first line of 'Refugee.' "

He freezes. "Ummm . . . 'I speak of love awake, I speak of love in my dreams, To the water, the shadows, the mountains, To the flowers, the grass, the fountains.' "

I clap my hands softly, tell him "It's like having him right here at our table!"

He giggles like Poppin' Fresh when he's poked, and I imagine having Tom Petty on the table.

I grab a piece of bread from the basket between us, pile on butter. "So, what's your best seller going to be about?"

He winks, says, "Promise you won't steal my idea?"

"I promise."

He looks at the other tables suspiciously, puts a hand up to his mouth, says softly, "It's a coming-of-age story about a gay boy from Missouri who moves to New York to become a best-selling author. Remember, mum's the word."

I smile. "I'd read it."

His eyebrows go up and down as he says, "I was hoping you would."

Oh.

He's so hyper 'cause he's flirting with me. At least I think he is. Either that or he's on speed. "Pete, are you flirting with me?"

He laughs, turns a little red. "Are there some new safe-sex guidelines I haven't heard about? No flirting on a first date?"

When I don't say anything, he asks, "This *is* a date, right?"

No. You're twelve years old. "I think maybe I gave you the wrong idea."

He slumps in his chair. "No, telling me I have the wrong idea's the wrong idea." He grabs some bread, butters it lightly.

I have some water.

The waiter comes by with our first course.

He stabs at his plate with a fork. "Why'd you ask me out to dinner if it wasn't a date?"

I look at him, my face all sympathy. "I thought it'd be nice to make a new gay friend. Mine are all dead. And to thank you for helping me out with Suzanne Huntington-Conti."

He's pouting. "I thought we weren't going to talk about her tonight."

I stare at him. "Do you like me?"

He drops his fork. "Is this your first day here?" Next he says very slowly, like English is new to me: "Yes. That is why I accepted your invitation to dinner. I thought it was our first date. I accepted because I like you. Anything else you want to know? Maybe the year or who's president?"

Those were questions they asked Dead Eddie at St. Vincent's. He got the year right, but thought Mondale was president. Or maybe he was too stubborn to admit Reagan won a second term. "I'm sorry. I like you, too. I didn't realize this was a date, though."

"Well, if you ever do, fax me the press release."

I say bluntly, "I'm doing you a favor, kid. I'm damaged goods."

He shakes his head. "Don't do me any favors. And I know this sounds harsh, but can you stop throwing your dead friends in my face, please? Can we just try to enjoy our meal, all right?"

"Okay."

He chews.

I say, "We're still going to ACT UP meetings together?"

"Yes." He grunts, adding, "It's a good place to meet hot guys doing the right thing."

"And the action at the FDA?"

"Yes." He grunts again.

He just keeps shoveling food in his mouth to get the evening over with.

I say, "Pete?"

He squints at me as he chews defiantly.

I say, "You're a great guy. Really. Cute and sweet and funny. You're going to make someone very happy someday."

"Please shut up."

Chapter 10

OCTOBER 1988: DIED OF INDIFFERENCE

I told Dave I need more time to think about his . . . proposal. Poor choice of words—what it was that he suggested in his own Minnesota Lutheran rational and pragmatic way. So I'm living on Laurie and Toshiro's couch, which isn't as bad as it sounds. She works a lot and Toshiro is like a piece of furniture, plugged into his Walkman and hunched over Francesco's drawing table all day. I work on my résumé, wondering how to finesse an average of three jobs per year with long periods of unemployment in between into a document that makes human resources think they must have me.

Oh, Lord, why? Why is looking for work so soul crushing? Why can't we all just have trust funds like Merritt the Wherret?

Tell me, Jesus, where's my trust fund?

Laurie gave me a daily calendar so I would write down a list of tasks for each day. This, she told me, was so I didn't just spend the day at the gym or sitting on the couch feeling sorry for myself. I'd have more options for how to spend my day if they had a TV, which, of course . . .

So, anyway, here's today's tasks:

1. *Wake up.*
2. *Protein for breakfast.*
3. *Shower and shave as if I had a job, like everybody else.*
4. *Don't go to the gym. Day passes too expensive.*
5. *Get a job that pays well and that I enjoy doing and that does good.*

I look over at Toshiro, cranking out consistent pages. Before he plugged into his Walkman, he told me that just because I don't have a job didn't entitle me to put myself down. I am not a loser and I should express my feelings in creative ways.

His answer to everything. Creativity. He never bitches or whines or complains because he's creative! One day he'll snap, climb a tower, and thin out the crowd.

No, be grateful. The man is letting you live on his couch.

So I have the action at the FDA, but that's still a week away.

Pete and I go to ACT UP Monday nights. He's really a sweet kid, even though he's still kinda mad at me.

Dave makes sense. An actual house to live in, and he's so vocal and uninhibited in the bedroom, unlike how he is everywhere else on earth. And I love dogs, and his sister, Tracy, seems nice. But it's still his and Gary's house. But I have Thursday Nighters in Minneapolis, and my Survivors Support Group is in Minneapolis, and so are Aunt Nora and Tommy, but once the baby comes, I probably won't see much of him. That is, if he's really serious about being a father this time.

And that bitch of an ex-stepmother won't even let me see my own sister.

What else? I did ask Laurie if I could sue Suzanne Huntington-Conti for something—I just don't know what, exactly—and she promised to ask one of the lawyers at her office.

So let's review. So far today I've been annoyed with Toshiro for no reason at all; discovered nothing on my calendar between this week and next week's FDA action; thought about moving in with someone I don't love, and who says he doesn't love me, either; and considered legal action against Suzanne Huntington-Conti.

And it's not even 10:00 a.m. yet.

Fortunately, Laurie did give me homework for her to review. I'm supposed to make a list of all the things I like about myself, including skills, personality traits, accomplishments, and successes.

Okay. Homework time. This is where I shine.

I lie on the couch, knees up, and put the pad of paper on my thighs. I start my list with:

> 1.

Good. Good start. Use it.

1. *I like the way I write 1.*
2. *I can bench-press my own weight fifty times in ten minutes.*
3. *My squats are flawless and I've never pulled a hamstring or herniated a disk.*
4. *I was a good partner to Francesco. I loved him completely.*
5. *I think I did a good job taking care of Eddie, even though I feel bad about getting paid to do it.*
6. *I let Eddie do what he needed to do and I was there for him, but I feel sick about getting paid for it.*
7. *I have good friends who I love and who love me: Laurie, Toshiro, Tommy, and Dave (though his love is just platonic and sexual).*
8. *Aunt Nora has always been there for me, no matter what, even when I thought she would freak out about me being gay, or when I told her Francesco had AIDS.*
9. *I love animals.*
10. *I am nice to people, so long as they are not being dicks.*

Yeah, I really do need to grow the hell up. There are plenty of gay men who work hard at their jobs, come home, take good care of their sick partner, pay the bills on time, and don't whine about any of it. I need to be that kind of gay man.

Besides, all I have to do now is find a job. And pay the bills. Because there's no one left to take care of.

Except me.

I tap Toshiro on the back and he screams, "くそ!" as he nearly falls off his stool. "Don't *do* that!"

I sorta laugh. "Sorry. You wanna go for a walk or something? Laurie says I need to go out in the world and stay socialized so I don't get weird. Weirder."

He looks at his consistent page, and then at me, and then back at his consistent page. He drops the pencil, says, "Okay, a brief one. I have much work to do. I need my camera."

It's a beautiful day, so we walk to Hell's Kitchen Park, a little green space that used to be a parking lot, and watch the skinny McThirsties lining up to buy their crack, moving along only when Guardian Angels show up. Crackheads squeegee windshields of cars stopped at lights or just stop traffic and start spraying.

Toshiro admires a mural of a giant baby in a diaper surrounded by pipes and vials. "This used to be a nice park." He shakes his head. "Let's continue." We walk Forty-seventh to Times Square in silence. Occasionally he snaps shots of signs and shapes that intrigue him, like the SIX BOYS FIVE TIMES A DAY sign outside the Gaiety, or the shell of the old Horn & Hardart Automat beneath a giant hamburger sign over Broadway, or the "Simple Simon and the Pieman" neon logo at Howard Johnson's. We stop for a pinball game at Playland, and Toshiro no longer seems to be in such a hurry.

On the walk back to his home and my charity couch, he says, "Francesco and I loved to walk the city and take photographs. Times Square was always the most interesting place. The lights and people and traffic. Very many superheroes live in New York or a version of New York, like Gotham or Metropolis, so the photographs were our guidebook for the Marvel and DC titles."

"I still have some of his photos if you'd like them. They're back in Minneapolis now."

He looks at me, smiles. "Thank you. I have much pleasant memories of our walks around Manhattan."

A block later he says, "Did Francesco tell you he kissed me?"

I stop. "No. He did not."

Toshiro stops, laughs. "It was nothing. We were working at the Strand bookstore. It was his first job after he moved to New York, and my first job in the United States. We talked about comic books and art and I guessed that he liked *Kamandi: The Last Boy on Earth* for reasons other than my own. When we discussed Kamandi's costume—the torn-up shorts—Francesco kissed me. We were very young."

"Did you kiss him back?"

He frowns. "No. I have never understood why one would prefer a penis to a vagina."

"*Jeez!* I didn't ask if you gave him a blow job . . ." Cars honk their horns as if that will get traffic moving, and people walk around us. "What did you do?"

"I told him I was flattered, but unable to return his feelings. He was disappointed, but understood. It made us friends. He got over his crush on me as he came out, and I had my first friend in this country. The only times I got mad with him, I'm ashamed to say, were when his pages outshone my own. And his murals in the apartment. The sketch of you. I was impressed, and a little upset—with him for being so talented, and myself for reacting that way."

A loud man grunts, saying, "You're blocking the sidewalk, assholes."

I'm about to tell him to fuck off, but Toshiro says, "Sorry," because things like that don't get under his skin the way they do mine. We walk.

I say, "I had a straight guy pity-kiss me once. Boy, did that not work."

"Francesco was lonely. I went with him to gay bars a few times."

"That he did tell me. He said all the boys made a fuss over you."

"He was lying. They made a fuss over him. He went a little wild, I think."

At a traffic light a gust of wind blows his long black hair in front of his face and he pulls it back behind his head. He says, "I miss him. I wish there was something I could do for him. For his art."

I remind him of the promise he made to Francesco to take care of me after he died. Toshiro says, "You've gone through a lot. You take care of yourself now."

Our goal is *drugs into bodies*.

It's a long bus ride down to the FDA in Rockville, Maryland, and to make use of the time, we study our *FDA Action Handbook*. Pete and I share one, as do Laurie and Toshiro across the aisle. Our list of demands includes:

1. *Shorten the drug approval process.*
2. *No more double-blind placebo trials.*
3. *Include people from all affected populations at all stages of HIV infection in clinical trials.*

From time to time Pete closes his eyes, asks, "Do you mind, platonic homosexual friend?" as he puts his head on my shoulder. He's letting his hair grow long on top of his head, and it swoops down over his eyes. The sides are buzz-cut short. He looks a little like a Muppet, with his big head of brown hair and stick arms.

From her seat across the aisle, Laurie mouths, *He likes you. He really, really likes you.*

I mouth back, *He's too young.*

She just shakes her head. She taps Toshiro and points at me and Pete. Toshiro's expression is hard to read.

Every once in a while, Pete sits up, rubs his eyes, and gives me a goofy Muppet smile, with his mouth wide open. Then he pats my shoulder, like he's fluffing a pillow, asks, "Do you mind, platonic homosexual friend?" and puts his head back down and an arm around my waist.

Can't help it.

I like this feeling.

I want to protect him. I want to keep him safe.

When we assemble at All Souls Church, there's more than a thousand of us from all over the country. We shout where we're from, the East Coast, mostly, but also the South, the Midwest, and the West Coast. The moderator tells us we're beautiful, that everyone here loves everyone, and strangers hug strangers, men kiss men, women kiss women, women kiss men. Pete puts his arms around me and I keep him close all night. Live Eddie had told me holding on to each other's the healthiest thing we can do.

It's after daybreak when we arrive. I don't know what I was expecting when we got to the FDA building. Maybe a medieval fortress, with giant gray stones illuminated only by the occasional flash of lighting, or maybe some sort of antiseptic *Logan's Run* institute. In reality it's just a giant block of glass in the burbs.

Hundreds of us walk toward the building's main entrance. Pete's brought a thermos of coffee, and the four of us pass it around like a Communion cup.

Police are everywhere, but so are cameras. The white and black men and women in their black jackets and tan pants are silent and stare straight ahead, like mannequins. The police who attacked me were in blue short sleeves and looked right at me. These police don't cover their badges. They wear gloves. And while they have on helmets and visors, something about them feels different to me, and for whatever reason I don't think they'll try to kill me.

Laurie reads my mind. "You doing okay with all the cops here?"

I nod.

"No panic or anxiety?"

"Don't jinx me," I tell her.

Pete gives me a hug. "Don't worry about the cops. I'll protect you."

That's so cute. Christopher Robin protecting me.

From behind Pete, Laurie puckers her lips and pats her heart. Toshiro turns away, takes photos of the crowd.

We're wearing our WE DIE—THEY DO NOTHING T-shirts. We have bail money with us; well, at least Laurie, Toshiro, and Pete do, and I'm thinking Pete brought enough for the both of us, but these cops are very hands-off in the face of the demonstrators, so we probably won't need it.

We ring the glass block tower that is the FDA, and block employees from entering.

We chant, "Forty-two thousand dead from AIDS, where was the FDA?" and draw chalk outlines of our bodies on the sidewalks. A pretty boy in a bandana jumps up on the awning over the main entrance and unfurls a SILENCE = DEATH banner, white letters, black fabric, pink triangles. Smoke rises from where he stands, and from our vantage point, I can't tell if he's lit smoke bombs or if he's started a fire. Some of the demonstrators—the ones blocking the entrance—are dragged away by police to the waiting buses. We blow our whistles, chant, "We're gonna seize control, we're pissed!" and "No more deaths!" We hold up our signs for the camera crews, green pictures of Reagan with pink eyes, stamped with the caption AIDSGATE. Hundreds of us, over a thousand, hear the helicopters overhead as we see FDA employees staring out the windows of their eighteen-story tower, confused, scared, and annoyed.

Laurie shouts, "What does AIDS stand for?"

We shout back: "America Isn't Doing Shit!"

Another group chants: "History will recall, Reagan and Bush did nothing at all!"

Gay men and lesbians sit down in the street in front of the building and hold hands in a chain, so the police divert traffic.

"Ronald Reagan, you can't hide! We charge you with genocide!"

Employees are still arriving in vans and buses, so they're redirected—police won't let them attempt the main entrance we've blocked. Most of them huff and roll their eyes, some look frightened, like we might splatter them with infected blood.

"Arrest Frank Young!"

Police radio back and forth, trying to find a secure building entry for workers. We walk back and forth, chant, hold our signs up, look for people we may know. I keep my eyes on the police mostly, waiting for one to cover his badge, maybe take it off, but none of them do.

This is going to sound strange, but I'm sort of enjoying myself. The action feels good, fun, even. Pete keeps flirting with me and I like it. When's the last time I had fun? With Dave at the hotel? That wasn't fun, exactly, more . . . I don't know . . . necessary. Very, very necessary.

Francesco would've loved this action. He would've designed picket signs with Toshiro, elaborate ones, hand-penciled and colored. Their signs would've been in the papers and on the news.

Some of the activists do their best to get arrested, but the police aren't cuffing anyone. The faces in the windows over us seem to have lightened up, and a few people are smiling down at us and taking our pictures.

That's when I see a man standing in silence, not chanting, not blowing a whistle, just holding up a cardboard tombstone: *Died of Indifference.*

Live Eddie, I'm so sorry.

You told me it was genocide.

And I'm fucking crying again.

I don't understand how this just *happens.* I never even feel it coming. It's like I'm peeing myself all the time. I need eye diapers.

Laurie rubs my back, says, "We don't have to stay."

"I'm fine. Our bus isn't leaving for hours." And then I cry some more, because that's what I do now.

Pete hugs me from behind, and Toshiro takes off his black bandana and gives it to me so I can clean myself up. Around us the crowd keeps chanting, keeps moving.

"Seize control of the FDA, fifty-two will die today!"

"We need more than AZT, health care must be free!"

"No testing, no quarantine, no matter what it takes!"

Toshiro trades his SILENCE = DEATH sign for one with Vice President Bush's picture on it, along with Bush's own words: *Testing is more cost-effective than treatment.*

Pete takes my hand and we walk to a quieter spot and sit on a curb, watching cars turn around in front of the police, who are in front of the protestors who sit in the street. Some drivers honk their horns, but the police aren't having it, and they stop.

Pete lies back on the grass. "I'm glad we came. It feels good to finally be doing something."

I lie beside him. The ground is cool and I fold my arms across my chest, because, you know, just a tight tee on. "Me too."

He rolls over, faces me. "So, is this our first date, Mr. Damaged Goods? Or are we still platonic homosexual friends? No pressure. Seriously. I'm okay with being friends. But just thought I'd check, because, well, I kind of feel like I'm getting mixed signals."

What a long, long way gay men have come. A date used to be sex. Now it's a four-hour bus ride to Rockville with the possibility of arrest. I look at him. He's young, and he's cute, and he hasn't lost anyone close to him, and he hasn't even had his heart broken yet.

If I wanted to be with someone after Francesco, Dave's the sensible choice. Good job, nice house, uninhibited sex, a dog, and I know he's negative.

"Yeah, it's our first date."

"Whew!" He kisses me.

There's nothing logical about this. I pull him on top of me, put his head in my hands, and my tongue down his throat. It's just blood and semen we have to worry about.

He surprises me, grabs me by the wrists, and I let him pin me down as we make out, and he's kinda grinding on me.

We hear: "Hey, horndogs, get a room, why dontcha?"

Another voice: "Aw, leave 'em alone. I want to watch."

And then condoms fall on us like pennies from heaven.

We sit up. A couple of Delta Queens are tossing the rubbers like it's a game of horseshoes. One says, dramatically: "You! Yankee boys! Yes, you! Open your eyes and look at me. 'No, I don't think I will kiss you, although you need kissing, badly. That's what's wrong with you. You should be kissed, and often, and by someone who knows how.' "

Pete's laughing, but I don't get it.

I stand up, hold out my hand to him. "Come on. Let's shut this place down."

He smiles, looking up at me like I just said *let's go split a sundae*. He picks up a couple of the condoms and sticks them in his pocket.

By early afternoon the police start making arrests, upset by all the SILENCE = DEATH stickers we put on their squad cars. Pete and Laurie and Toshiro and I don't get arrested, most people don't.

This is gonna sound really stupid, but I do believe I have a big old honking crush on Pete.

What a magical day.

We should shut down the FDA more often.

Before we leave Maryland, our bus full of gay men and lesbians and everything else take over Jim's Roadhouse, a bar outside of Fairland, to watch one of our own on a cable news show discuss today's action at the FDA. A Confederate flag hangs behind the bar, and dangling from the ceiling are bras in various shapes, sizes, and colors. The only customers—a couple of old guys at a table nursing their beers—leave. The bartender says he won't serve us and we say good, we wouldn't drink his overpriced swill on a bet. He says he'll call the cops if we don't leave and we laugh.

A man with a stage lisp shouts, "You think we don't know from cops? Now shut the fuck up and turn on the television or I'll bleed all over your bar!"

He shuts the fuck up and turns on the television, his back to the wall, his eyes wide. Anyone who comes through the front door takes one look at us, and turns right around. Aunt Nora made me promise to call her after the action to let her know I was okay because I had told her about what had happened at Tompkins Square Park. I find the pay phone, and when she accepts the charges, she's wild with excitement. "Skip Loescher said on the five p.m. report that people were arrested! I was praying you weren't one of them!"

I tell her, "We shut the motherfucker down!"

"Language."

I see the pretty boy from the FDA awning on the screen, and I tell Aunt Nora, "We're on, love ya, gotta go." I rejoin the others as the pretty boy's being asked by an old man in a suit whether or not the FDA doesn't have a responsibility to keep quacks from prescribing useless, untested drugs to desperate people with AIDS. They gave us AZT, after all.

That's when I damn near drop dead: They cut to a new man, and up there on the TV for the whole world to see is Merritt the Wherret, the man who fired me and canceled my insurance. He's pointing a finger at pretty boy.

Laurie and Toshiro stare at the screen, frowning. Toshiro says, "He came to the hospital?"

I nod.

Pete says, "You know that guy?"

I nod.

Merritt the Wherret tells pretty boy that this will surprise him, but he agrees entirely with ACT UP. The FDA's rules and regulations are crippling the pharmaceutical industry, tying it up in government red tape that's costing Americans their lives.

Toshiro says in disbelief, "He's on *our* side?"

Laurie says, "He's on Wall Street's side."

A mealymouthed old guy tells pretty boy that our demonstration has done more harm than good, and how can we expect to change hearts and minds with chants and demands and flamboyant behavior? Before pretty boy can answer, mealymouthed old guy turns to a new guest to respond.

Pete says, "Oh, shit."

The subtitle beneath her giant face reads *Suzanne Huntington-Conti, Memoirist.* She says, "I have to agree that these sorts of demonstrations are counterproductive. They're stopping people from doing the very work that will save their lives. Now, I understand better than anyone here tonight the desperation, the hopelessness, and the heartbreak that is AIDS. In *Our Sacred Journey Together*, I recount our praying together for a cure . . ."

I walk out of the bar and into the Maryland evening. The traffic along 200 is light, and I breathe the outdoor air in hard, holding it, releasing it, holding it, releasing it. I feel a hand on my shoulder and I know it's Pete's.

He says, "Sorry about that. I had no idea they were going to have her on. She's everywhere these days. I don't even want to tell you how many copies her book has sold."

"What an ironic little world we live in."

He massages my shoulders, says, "We did an important thing today. Maybe now they'll actually try to stop the genocide."

I take his hand, put it up to my lips, and kiss it. "Thank you."

He turns me around, smiles, says, "For what?"

"I dunno. You're just so . . . young. No, that's not what I mean. You're so alive . . . I don't know what I'm trying to say. You have this . . . You're not defeated."

A semi rumbles by.

Pete looks at me, seriously. "Kevin, you're *not* defeated. You lost the one person you loved more than anyone else in this world. And some of your very best friends. And it makes sense that you feel like part of you died, too . . . and here we are . . . and it's a beautiful evening."

He hugs me tight and a driver honks his horn, why I don't know.

He looks up at me with a sly little grin. "You know what we should do, right?"

"No." Am I crying? I can't even tell anymore.

"We should get back on the bus before everyone else, and make out."

Yeah, this kid, he's just so, and when he smiles . . . This is so stupid . . .

Get me on that bus.

Halloween's tomorrow and I have to replace the candy Laurie bought. I finished the bag while she was at work today, and Toshiro didn't even notice. Besides, he doesn't like American candy, anyway. There are messages on the answering machine, which Live Eddie's parents gave me, which I regifted to Laurie and Toshiro. I bought a new tape for them to record their greeting; I couldn't erase Dead Eddie's voice. I keep his tape in my backpack.

I haven't been picking up because I don't want to talk to Dave. I've been putting him off; putting off telling him that I'm not coming back to Minnesota. And Toshiro never answers the phone when he's working.

"This is Laurie and Toshiro. Hold your nose, vote Dukakis, and leave us a message."

Dave's voice: "Hi, this is a message for Kevin. Could you call me, please? I really, really want to talk to you."

Tommy's voice: "Hey, I'm a dad! Little boy this time. We're going to name it Alf. Ha! Just shittin' ya! I'm thinking we're gonna get married, after all, maybe New Year's Eve so I can start 1989 as a family man. I still want you to be my best man, and I was thinking you could be godfather, too, 'cause my brothers are pretty fucking useless, and—*beep!*"

The phone rings. It's Dave.

I lie. "I was just gonna call you."

He says, "I should have waited for you to call me back, but you haven't returned my last couple of calls and I need to talk to you."

Oh, shit. That voice.

He's in love.

I try to lighten things up. "Not for phone sex, I hope. To-shiro's here and, even with you in Minnesota and him wearing his Walkman, you're pretty damn loud."

It gets me nowhere. "You know I've been waiting for a decision from you."

I sigh. "I know." I shake my head. "I'm sorry. That was rude. I just . . . needed time to think." I really don't want to break his heart. He's helped me pull myself together. I owe him.

"I've been waiting for you to tell me that you don't want us to live together."

I plop on my couch/official residence. "Sorry . . . didn't have the nerve."

He's silent for a moment before he says, "Never took you for a coward."

I don't know what to say to that.

"Because, the thing is, I'm seeing someone."

WHAT?! "You're *what*?!"

Another pause. "Aaron. From our survivors' group."

"Are you fucking kidding me? His partner just died, for Chrissake! We did that cradle thing with him and everything. He's off-limits."

Dave's voice remains as reasonable as ever: "This is why I wanted you to tell me you weren't moving in with me."

"Jesus! This is grief sex."

More reasonableness: "If Gary's death has taught me anything, it's that life's—"

"Don't *even* with that shit! His partner's body's still warm."

Toshiro looks over at me, I'm louder than I think.

"His partner died in June. After you left for New York, Aaron and I started having coffee after the meetings, and it turns out we have a lot in common."

"Like what, sex? He better than me?"

"I have no idea. We haven't slept together. I didn't want this to happen. I fought it. I had my friendship with you, and I had made my offer, which I fully intended to honor. It's just that . . . Aaron and I can talk about everything. I mean *everything*. It comes so naturally, like it did with Gary. He makes me feel good about life, like it's not something to just struggle through. It just happened."

" 'Just happened'? Nothing like this *just happens*!"

He has the balls to say: "Oh. You're in love with me. You

shouldn't mistake sex for love. Remember how I was worried I might do that with you? You shouldn't do that with me."

"For Chrissake, I am NOT in love with you! What an ego."

Toshiro taps his pencil as he looks at me, a blank expression on his face.

"I'm glad. And I hope you can be happy for me."

"*Happy?* Haven't you listened to a word Butch Bobbie Jo has said?"

"Who?"

"Our facilitator! She warned us against this sort of thing. No impulsive decisions. No grief rebounds. No chugging the left-over morphine."

Another pause. "Yes. I've heard every word she's said, and they're wise ones. But if things with Aaron continue to go well, and if he continues to feel the same way about me as I do about him, then I'm going to ask him to move in with me."

I stare at the little window that faces a wall. "Glad you listened to her. *Jesus.*"

"He's positive, Kevin. I don't want to waste time."

He's what? " 'He's positive'?"

"Yes."

Quieter now, because Toshiro looks pissed, but it's still kind of hard to tell, I say to Dave, "You swore up and down you couldn't go through that again."

"I know. He's positive, he doesn't have AIDS."

I sigh. "I'm sorry. I mean about being a jerk just now. You're right, I didn't want to move in with you. And I was afraid to tell you, because . . . Well, that's beside the point now. Are you sure you know what you're doing?"

"Not at all. It terrifies me."

"Then why?"

"I'm almost certain I've fallen in love with him. You know, a meteor could wipe out all life on planet Earth tomorrow. I could get hit by a bus. We never know what the future will bring. Maybe it will bring a cure."

I close my eyes. "I dunno what to say. No, hang on, I do. You were a good friend to me when I needed one."

"I'm still your friend."

"Good," I say. "Good. I want you to be happy. I want all of us to have some happiness again."

Chapter 11

NOVEMBER 1988: THE ONLY GOOD THING

The only good thing about the election is that smug East and West Coasters saw that the biggest landmass on the electoral map that went for Dukakis was the Upper Midwest. Not all of it, just three states, but Minnesota was one of them, one of only nine that voted against a third Reagan term. That makes three times—three times—that Minnesota voted against Reagan. And the District of Columbia, which I always forget about. Take that, you *I don't even like to fly over the Midwest* New York snobs.

So that's the only good thing that's happened this month.

That, and Pete.

I feel like carving our initials on a tree in Central Park.

I want to slow dance with him as Etta James sings "At Last."

I want to lasso the moon for him.

So *two* good things, I guess. Don't tell anyone.

Oh, wait. I got a job. Alex, Live Eddie's volunteer, got me an interview at GMHC to work in development. Guess what I do? It involves gift acknowledgments for donors. But donors to something that matters. And that's satisfying.

So *three* good things. I feel bad about feeling good because we have four more years of Reagan via his lapdog, the blue-blood wimp who put his manhood in a blind trust.

But I feel good. It seems selfish, but I feel good.

Laurie takes complete credit for Pete, as she reminds me now, at the very diner where she first invited him to sit with us. Once she told me where to meet her, I knew she'd use the setting to bask in her own glory.

"You didn't want me to talk to him," she reminds me. "Remember? Remember how you didn't want me to talk to him? But you were staring at him. Did you even realize you were staring at him?"

"Yes."

"Because you were. You were staring at him."

"I know."

This time we each get our own dinner, because I have a job, but it's not like I'm rolling in it, so I get scrambled eggs, toast, and water, while Laurie treats herself to a half sandwich with the house salad and a seltzer.

She's in a vintage leather jacket, because even though she's an animal rights advocate—along with everything else—she couldn't resist, and, besides, it's vintage from a secondhand store, so the cow is long dead. She also has on Live Eddie's black-and-white checkerboard *shemagh*, which I gave her after his parents gave it to me.

I say, "You're looking very East *Vill-ahge* today."

"Funny you should mention it. You remember Cheri Hastings Andrew?"

"No."

"Trust fund mixed-media artist?"

"No."

"Has a gallery in your old neighborhood?"

"No."

"Friend of both Toshiro's and Frankie's?"

"No."

"Always in a black leather miniskirt, black stockings, and black beret?"

"No."

"Kevin, she was at your apartment a bunch for picnics."

Francesco and I hosted picnics on our apartment floor because we had so little furniture, and, besides, the place was too small for a table and chairs. He made dinner and I set the floor—red-and-white checkerboard tablecloth, along with a mishmash of dishes given to us or picked up at flea markets. He and Toshiro and Dead Eddie would talk art, while Laurie and Live Eddie and I would lie on the futon together and Laurie educated us about the El Mozote massacre or the Soviet war in Afghanistan or the Iran-Iraq war, but what could you expect in a world run by men, present company excluded (implication being, yet again, that we're not actually men).

I say, "Not ringing any bells."

She gives up. "That's probably just as well, she thought Frankie could do a lot better. She said you were just a shallow Muscle Mary without an original thought in your head."

"Still gonna have to narrow it down."

Our meals arrive. She looks at her half chicken salad sandwich guiltily, she was the one who always asked me if I knew how they breed and slaughter the animals we eat. Sometime during Francesco's illness, she fell off the vegetarian wagon, and has been struggling to get back on ever since. She takes a bite and rolls her eyes in pleasure.

"So about this 'artist' I have no memory of."

She covers her mouth, chews as she says, "She's closing her gallery and moving it to SoHo. She has a couple of weeks available in December before she moves, so guess what?"

"She's doing a Futura aerosol retrospective?"

"No, but I would actually go to that. No, she's agreed to let Toshiro mount an exhibit of his work—and Frankie's."

I tilt my head like the RCA dog. "Really?"

She beams. "Yes! Isn't it exciting? I felt we should celebrate with a dinner out!"

I load my toast with eggs, and in a few bites, I'm done.

She notices. "This is a good thing, yes?"

"Frankie didn't feel his work was ready for exhibit. Now he has no say about it."

Chicken salad sandwich finished, she starts reluctantly on the house salad. "Tosh told me you would say that. He feels Frankie's work was ready to exhibit years ago. He thinks the only one who got in Frankie's way was Frankie."

"What did he mean by that?"

"It was a confidence issue with Frankie."

"He was the most confident man I've ever known."

She reaches over, pats my hand. "Kev, he was a human being, just like the rest of us. Yeah, in the day-to-day world, he was a master of the universe, but when it came to his art? He was like every other artist—neurotic. He didn't share that part of himself with you, but he did with Tosh."

First he tells Aunt Nora my job surfing kept him up all night working, and now I find out it was Toshiro he talked to about his insecurities as an artist. "Why am I just hearing this now? Frankie could've talked to me."

"I guess it's something artists just talk to each other about. Did you encourage him to mount an exhibit?"

Well, there's a big old stinging slap right across my face.

She pats my hand again. "It wasn't an accusation."

"I know."

She sips her seltzer. "Tosh thinks this is a great way to honor Frankie, by honoring his work. Frankie was the first friend he made when he moved to the United States and they were both hustling their portfolios. Let him do this. Please."

"Why isn't he telling me this himself?"

"Well, you know he hates confrontations. Also, you're always at the apartment during the day, and it's starting to drive him crazy. That's the other piece of news. You have to move out."

I nod, look at the fat man reading the *New York Post* across the aisle. "I'll start looking. I'm grateful you've let me stay as long as you have. And you can have the exhibition." I add, with a sprinkling of bitchiness: "Obviously, Toshiro understands Frankie and his work better than I do."

"Oh, my God, don't sulk. They were friends before either of us came along. And you know you were Frankie's muse."

"He told me I was one of the nine sister goddesses presiding over art. 'Polymnia Doyle.' "

She slaps my hand. "There you go! You were his muse, and he discussed his art with Tosh. So, what's the problem? Art was their common thing, what they always talked about. Just like Minneapolis is our common thing."

"We never talk about Minneapolis."

She says, "I'm ordering dessert."

Today is Francesco's birthday. I don't go to Philly to visit his grave; in fact, I haven't been back since we drove off and left him there, all by himself. Part of me is afraid I'll dig him up. I can't stand the thought of him down there forever.

When I was in high school, I had an old neighbor whose wife died in their home. He never told anyone, just kept her body in a freezer in the basement so they could stay together. I think I finally truly understand why he did it.

I decided on Francesco's first birthday after he died that I would spend each of them at a museum. This birthday I'm at the Museum of Modern Art, a favorite of his. The exhibition I choose is drawings, for obvious reasons. The artist is Richard Diebenkorn, someone I have, of course, never heard of.

Francesco was a much better drawer. His people look like people, and there was never a naked lady's bush in the bunch. But, as Francesco insisted, I ask myself questions about the work rather than *judge* the work.

His motto: "Be curious first, judgmental a distant second."
Questions I ask myself about the work:

1. *How come a bunch of lines I could have drawn myself are on exhibit at the Museum of Modern Art?*
2. *Does this guy love vaginas, or what?*
3. *How much money does he make for this stuff?*

I was a bored child when Francesco took me to galleries and museums and exhibitions, and I'm still a bored child today, because though he tried, and tried hard, Francesco couldn't assimilate me into his world. The only time I sensed some frustration with my refusal to be cultured was when he'd softly sing, " 'Tis the gift to be simple, 'tis the gift to be free' " as I frowned at a painting, wondering what all the fuss was about.

But as I look at the drawings, there are some untitleds I like better than the women's pubic hair untitleds; for example, the tables that look like tables, or the portraits of faces, or the women with clothes on.

I check Live Eddie's wristwatch, which his parents gave me. I've been here one hour. That beats last year by a full twenty minutes. Maybe I am starting to get the hang of this.

Here's the other thing I do on his birthday: stop at a bodega, pet the cat, and buy a black-and-white cookie. Francesco loved them. He thought of them as a sort of edible art, and before taking the first bite, he would examine the line between black and white as if it were the most difficult stroke of a master's brush.

I regard the line carefully before I eat the cookie, looking for what Francesco saw.

Laurie offered to spend the day with me, and, of course, Pete, my cute new boyfriend.

Yes, *boyfriend.*

There, I said it.

But today is just for Francesco and me, and maybe by the

time I celebrate his fiftieth birthday, I'll look forward to these pilgrimages to art, seeing, perhaps, something of what Francesco saw. I'll assess the works through the lenses of imitationalism, formalism, and emotionalism. Then I'll go buy some comic books.

Black Friday, the day after Thanksgiving, the biggest shopping day of the year, and Pete and I are at the ACT UP demonstration in front of the 200-million-dollar Trump Tower, and its luxury brand stores for the richest of the rich. Laurie has to work, and Toshiro said he was going to be here, but never showed up at our meeting place.

The flyers we distribute tell people:

> *Donald Trump received a tax abatement of $6,208,773 to build Trump Tower. This money could have rehabilitated about 1,200 city-owned apartments. Instead, Trump gets richer while homeless people get sicker. The city favors private developers like Trump over small community-based organizations that are committed to providing low-income housing and housing for PWAs. The AIDS Center of Queens County, for example, never even received an acknowledgement of the proposal it submitted for twenty scattered-site apartments for homeless PWAs. Mayor Koch and the city allow Trump to displace people from apartments when he wants to build a building. Trump is symbolic of a system that lets the rich do whatever they want while letting the poor die.*

We're sick and dying of it.

There are thousands of people living with AIDS out on the streets, forced out of places like Tompkins Square Park, and this is what Koch, that closet-case little bitch, does—kisses trust-fund assholes, gives AIDS funding to Cardinal O'Connor's Catholic missionaries so they can serve the lepers and earn their place in heaven.

And where's our newspaper of record, telling our stories with *All the News That's Fit to Print? Avowed homosexuals* are not fit to print.

Some lives don't matter.

Live Eddie was right.

Aunt Nora was right.

We occupy the gold lobby of Trump Tower and our chants echo throughout the building. Shoppers, mostly women, some with children and nannies, retreat back into the extravagant shops of the atrium or escape out into the street in search of their cars and their drivers, but we've shut down the intersection of Fifty-sixth Street and Fifth Avenue and they don't get away so easy.

Pete and I join the rows of protestors sitting in the street, blocking traffic.

New York cops with gloved hands drag us, one by one, to the waiting police wagons. A woman shouts as she's hauled away, "Money for a cure, not for Trump!"

A man is dragged along behind her, chanting, "Don't be chumps, dump the Trump!"

None of the officers are covering their badges, there's too many people here, too many cameras, too many lesbian and gay reporters, too much lesbian and gay media.

None of them take off their badges.

None of them wave nightsticks.

I breathe steady. I don't allow myself to imagine men in helmets and blue short-sleeved shirts beating me. I don't taste my own blood in my mouth. Minutes and hours of my life don't go missing. Pete is next to me, holding my hand tight. I look at him, say loud enough so he can hear, "Hey, Boy Scout, what merit badge do you get for this?"

"Lifesaving!" Then he leans over and kisses me.

The lesbian on the other side of me, who I'd been holding hands with, lets go, is handcuffed, and dragged away.

And then it's my turn. I let go of Pete's hand, and he reluctantly makes his way to the sidewalks. Our plan was this: If he was arrested, I'd try to avoid it. If I was arrested, he'd try and avoid it. ACT UP has people ready and waiting to post bail, but we wanted to take care of each other.

Put another way, our dates keep getting stranger.

I do as we were told at the meeting: I go limp; I don't resist. The handcuffs are too tight and dig into my wrists, and as my feet and knees skid along the pavement, I look for Pete, but I can't turn around, and I'm stuffed into a wagon.

We chant, we sing, the wagon doors slam shut, and I feel the panic coming. I can't move my arms and there's too many of us in here. I can't breathe, and Laurie isn't here to hold my hand, to tell me, "It will pass, it always does."

I don't catalog my surroundings, as she always has me do. Instead, I close my eyes. I hear people laughing and congratulating each other and groaning under the pressure of their cuffs or the injuries sustained as they were hoisted up and dragged off, maybe dropped face-first a couple of times along the way. I hear the traffic outside, the sirens, the chanting. I hear the staticky voices of men over walkie-talkies.

I tell myself a story.

My favorite story.

Inhale.

It was 1981. The gangs, the homicides, the muggings, they were all a kind of white noise to me in this city I'd left Minneapolis for so I could get laid and fall in love. But after another breakup, with another man who thought infidelity was a

revolutionary act, a liberating blow against the heterosexist op-
pressors (the tired old battle cry of faggots who can't keep it in
their pants), I left the apartment I shared with Laurie and the
transient roommates who were in New York for internships or
to spend a semester in the United States or to try their luck in
the city before leaving in defeat.

Exhale.

I sat in Sheridan Square alone; Live Eddie had fallen in love
with Dead Eddie, and it made him stupid—and, for periods of
time, missing.

I was jealous.

Screw it, I thought, time for my own revolutionary act.

It was a tight little bar on Christopher Street, no dancing,
the kind of place men go to talk or get drunk or meet up before heading out to the clubs. It was crowded with young and
middle-aged men of all shapes and sizes and colors. The
smoke was thick, and the drinks outrageously expensive, even
for a gay bar. I ordered a gin and tonic and waited.

Inhale.

I noticed him before he noticed me. It was cold outside, but
he was wearing a crop top and denim cutoffs with a hole in
the back, where I could see a bit of cheek. He was outfitted like
the kind of guy who was good for a one-nighter and little else.
He looked sexy and he looked slutty, but then he turned and I
saw his face, and I thought for a minute he really was Joseph
Bottoms, the actor on the cover of my cherished *After Dark*
magazine.

Joseph Bottoms was here! To get laid! By me!

Exhale.

He noticed me noticing him. I looked away and then back,
and he was still staring. He smiled, made a production out of
eyeing my shoes before slowly working his way up my body to
my face, which was blushing deeply. Then he scrutinized me

from the neck back on down. When he smiled wide and I saw his teeth, imperfect, I knew he wasn't Joseph Bottoms, searching for me.

Inhale.

He walked up to me. I was used to guys being bold; it drove Laurie crazy in the early days when she would come along for moral support as I explored gay New York. She had said after a night that I had soaked up attention: "I've discovered the secret of invisibility—mammary glands." But Francesco was bold even by gay standards. He put a hand on my shoulder, leaned in, and whispered in my ear: "Would you like to make some bullshit small talk, or do you want to go to my place and fuck all night long?"

My last boyfriend, the liberated one who had lasted just under three months, had courted me with bullshit small talk. So, no, I did not want to make bullshit small talk.

We walked from Sheridan Square to Avenue B, and while he smiled and pointed out shops or buildings he found interesting—and to him, they all were—I was on tense alert, not for someone who might recognize me, like in Minneapolis, but for gangs who might bash me, like in New York. At his place on Avenue B, I worried the night might be fatal, not because of AIDS (it was 1981, after all) and not because I was "looking for Mr. Goodbar"—I knew I could beat the living crap out of him if I had to. It was the neighborhood, a far cry from Northeast Minneapolis and something I was completely unused to.

Exhale.

The walls of his apartment had been primed for the murals to come. There was just a bookcase, and a futon on the battered floor. On a shelf I saw framed pictures of people I would later come to know as Toshiro, his parents, his brothers. The books I was unfamiliar with: *Ernesto, Rubyfruit Jungle, Dancer from the Dance.* While I took inventory, trying to think of something to say, he took off his clothes, lay down on the futon, and

asked me, "Would you like to hug and kiss? Because I would."
I laughed. Men were usually so intense or so nervous or so de-
manding about sex. Francesco wasn't.

Inhale.

The morning was something I was unused to, too. Instead of
sharing our life stories, or him saying he had a really busy day
ahead of him, let's do this again, he said he was hungry and told
me to get dressed for breakfast. He put on his usual clothes, a
mishmash of postpunk and new wave, black and white (of
course), grabbed two copies of *New York Native*, and walked
us to a Ukrainian diner on Second Avenue, where he ordered
for both of us: coffee, eggs, toast, and bacon.

We read the papers in silence as we ate, and I think even then
I was in love, I just didn't know it.

Exhale. Breathe.

Pete's waiting for me when I'm released.
He has a cup of coffee and an egg-and-cheese bagel for me.

Chapter 12

DECEMBER 1988: ALL THE WAY OUT IN BROOKLYN

The gallery's a beat-up old East Village storefront covered in graffiti, and the owner, one of the countless friends of Francesco who thought I wasn't good enough for him, lives in what used to be the storage room. It's the last opening in this gallery before she moves to her new space in SoHo. I've told myself that I'm going to be pleasant to her, even if it kills me, because this is Toshiro's "coming out" party as an artist, and the first public exhibition of Francesco's work, organized in honor of their friendship, which predates both Laurie and me.

The title for the exhibition was a challenge. There are so many galleries in New York, with so many exhibitions, that Toshiro wanted his and Francesco's to stand out. He was tired of the usual titles, which he called, "*Self-Important Nonsense—* colon—*Pretentious Gibberish.*' " We had walked around SoHo and the East Village looking at exhibits with titles like *Breaking Sustainability: Post-Painterly Art of Change* and *The Bureaucracies of Ground? The Politics of Complacency* and *Desire of Relevance: A Retrospective of Social Identity.*

So his and Francesco's exhibit is *Drawings by 2 Guys, One Live, One Dead: Enjoy!*

The gallery's packed, with lots of East *Vill-ahgers*, comic book people in Batman and Superman tees, ACT UP people (I really plugged the show at the Monday meetings), and some of the Pyramid crowd, including a healthy representation of drag queens, one towering over the rest at six-four, plus heels.

But the biggest group is fans of *Our Sacred Journey Together*, who wanted to see art by Suzanne Huntington-Conti's brother-in-love. That was Pete's idea. He said the book should benefit Francesco somehow, so he had a colleague in marketing get the word out. Suzanne Huntington-Conti doesn't make an appearance, and for the first and only time, I admire her restraint.

Pete looks at the nude of me in sunglasses, which the comic book guys walk right past but some drag queens linger over. Then the tallest drag queen moves her group along as she says, "You're born naked, the rest is drag."

Pete points at the sketch, says, "Gosh." Then, "Gee."

I feel the heat on my face. "Frankie said it was dishonest."

Pete gets up close, lingers in front of it. Next he stands back, tilts his head, and squints his eyes. Finally he walks away from it and then walks back.

"Are you quite done?" I ask him.

Pete makes *hmmmmm* sounds, poses like an art critic with a hand on his chin, the other on a hip. "It's the glasses. You don't mind people looking at your body—in fact, you prefer they look at your body. But you're terrified of them peering into your soul, seeing the man behind the façade. Thus you conceal your eyes, the mirrors to your soul."

I smirk. "For Chrissake."

He smiles. "But it sounds like I know what I'm talking about, yes? I think, perhaps, I've got a knack for arts criticism."

Laurie materializes between us, a hand on each of our shoulders. Her eyes make her look like one of those Keane kids, an artist whose works I actually recognize. "Hilton Kramer's here. Hilton. Kramer."

Pete puts his hands over his open mouth. "You're shittin' me!"

Laurie gasps, says, "I wouldn't shit about this. You can see his giant ugly glasses from here. Oh, my God! Oh, my God."

Toshiro joins us, his arms folded, his head down. "信じられない!"

Laurie says, "You're speaking Japanese." To us, she says, "He said, 'I can't believe this.' "

Toshiro says, "I don't need a translator. Tell me our art is NOT trendy or fashionably political. Tell me Francesco and I uphold the highest standards of modernism."

Someone has to ask: "Who's Hilton Kramer?"

Pete says, "Umm, don't even. *The New Criterion*?"

I shrug.

Laurie says, "He used to be the arts critic for the *Times*. Now he edits *The New Criterion*."

I say, "Oh. Fuck the *Times*. AIDS is killing us and Abe Rosenthal couldn't be happier. So fuck the *Times*."

Pete says, "Max Frankel is head of the *Times* now."

I say, "Oh. Well, in that case, fuck the *Times*."

Toshiro begs me, "Please stop saying 'fuck the *Times*.' "

Laurie grabs his hand. She whispers, "Okay, okay. Let's all remain calm."

We look like we're huddling, or maybe praying. People have to walk around us.

She whispers now, "Let's just play this cool. Nonchalant. Bored even."

I whisper, "Why? Isn't this exactly what you wanted?"

Toshiro says, "No."

Laurie spells it out for me: "We disdain approval. Success is for sellouts. Now, Kevin, here is what I want you to do. I want you to go over to Mr. Kramer—the older gentleman with the giant ugly glasses—and tell him how much you admire *The New Criterion*. Tell him it's a beacon of hope in an arts world that seems to only value admission fees and cultural revolution. Then ask him if he would like to meet one of tonight's artists."

"You putting me on?"

Toshiro says, "No. Kevin, don't do it."

I say, "Thank you."

He says, "Pete, you work in publishing. It will make for a good introduction. Please tell him you admire *The New Criterion*."

Pete nods. "On my way."

And off he goes, parting the waters of comic book guys, and East *Vill-ahgers*, and book clubs from Greenwich Connecticut and West Chester County, and drag queens, and ACT UPers in their pink triangle tees.

When he returns with the critic, I go outside—the gallery's too hot, too packed with people, and the cold air clears my head. There are some smokers in black leather and retro jewelry. They look at me, but I'm not anyone that anyone's heard of, so they turn back to their conversation.

Francesco never felt ready for an opening, and now it's happening without him. I should feel good about this; he's living on through his art. Through his art, not some bullshit memoir by a woman who didn't know him at all.

I'll talk to Toshiro, find out how to organize these exhibitions. This is just the start, Francesco.

Pete finds me. "Do you always sneak out, or is it just when I'm around?"

This kid terrifies me. "Just when you're around. You scare me."

He grins, swaggers over to the curb, where I stand, my hands in my pockets. "I'm a big, tough, frightening sort of guy."

Petrifies me. "Thanks for coming tonight."

"You're kidding, right? I got to see you in the nude, at last." He slides an arm around my waist, says, "And I got to see Frankie's artwork. I finally feel like I've gotten to know him, just a little. He was very talented. I wonder what he would have thought about tonight."

Don't cry, ya big baby. "Me too."

He looks up at me. "I wish he were still alive. You miss him so much."

Tears. *Fuck-fuck-fuck*. "I'm learning to live with it."

He kisses me. "I hope you don't get angry with me, but I think part of what attracted me to you initially was your sadness. Do you remember when we met at the diner? I wanted so badly to take away all your pain. I was really hoping you would call me that night so we could talk. I was so disappointed when you didn't. Disappointed, and worried."

He was right to worry.

Another group of smokers down the sidewalk scream and then laugh too loudly. I say, "I hope you don't get angry with me, but it makes me feel even worse when people want to take care of me. It makes me feel like a failure."

Pete smiles. "Would it help to know that after that first dinner in Chelsea, I really and truly hated you?"

"A little. I prefer it to pity. I've overdosed on that more than vodka."

He doesn't look surprised.

"So Laurie told you all about that?" She tells everyone everything.

He gives my hand a squeeze. "No, Toshiro. On the bus ride back from Rockville, while you were sleeping. He thought it was important for me to know how far you've come. He didn't want me to screw it up. He said he promised Francesco he'd look after you."

I sigh. "So you know I almost died."

"Yes." Then he adds, "Did you want to die?"

I shake my head. "I just hadn't learned how to live without him. Spending all that time with myself . . . Well, I guess I hated myself, too."

"Why?"

"Story for another day. Let's just say I didn't believe anything good would ever happen again."

We stand there.

Finally I say, "We should go back in. I told one of the book clubs that Suzanne Huntington-Conti's just been diagnosed herself. I want to see if the news has spread."

He shakes his head. "If only you could sue her, get some of that money."

"Laurie already talked to one of the attorneys where she works. I have no standing."

"You do with me." He bows his cute little head, tells me, "I don't want to freak you out or anything. I mean, we haven't even slept together. But I already know I'm in love with you."

I grimace. "You're young. We hardly know each other. Don't mistake physical attraction for love."

He doesn't back down. "(A) Don't dismiss my feelings. I've sussed out that you have a good heart buried under there somewhere. And (B) I don't expect you to be in love with me, but I thought you should know, because, in case you don't see this leading anywhere, we can just part as friends, even though you'll be making the biggest mistake of your life."

Laurie sticks her head out the doorway, an ecstatic look on her face. She signals us to come back inside, but I raise my hand, Pete and I need a minute. "You think I have a good heart?"

"Yes." He looks up at the sky and then back down to earth. "If you don't feel like I do, I can go home alone and watch *Love Story* by myself, which I had the foresight to rent this morning, in case you dumped me. I love a good cry."

I put my hand on his cheek, lower it to his chin, and lift his face so he's looking right at me. He looks scared for the first time since I've known him, he wasn't scared at the FDA or Trump Tower. I say, in my gentlest voice: "Pete, you've been honest with me, so I'm gonna be honest with you. Please, just listen, this is hard for me to say." I put a finger on his lips, take a deep breath. "I don't want to hurt you, but ..." He looks terrified. Finally I say: "*Love Story*? You gotta be fuckin' kiddin' me."

He exhales, says, "God, you're *such a dick*."

"But I'm *your* dick." I stroke his cheek. "I love you, Pete."

WHAT?

I say: "I mean ... I think I do."

WHAT?

I say: "I'm pretty sure I do."

I just keep talking!

I say: "It's hard to be sure of anything."

He says giddily, "You love me! I knew it, I knew it, I knew it! Let's go back to your place."

Please let us be good in bed. "You mean the couch in Laurie and Toshiro's apartment? We should go back to your place."

"You mean the place I share with so many people I don't even know how many I live with?"

I pet his hair. It's not like Francesco's, but then, he isn't Francesco. And Francesco isn't him. He kisses me quick, says, "We should go back inside. I want to spend some more time with Francesco's work. Besides, Laurie looked like she's about to explode."

I can tell Toshiro's crabby, and it takes a lot for me to tell that Toshiro's crabby. The big art critic guy was very impressed, so I don't know why he's upset. And I've said I'd move out. After all, I have a job now. I have ... a boyfriend now. Because I'm ... in love now.

We're shopping for gifts for our respective sweethearts. Toshiro went all out and scored two tickets to *Les Misérables*, and I can't help but notice that in the first year after Francesco's death, he would've bought three tickets so I could go, too.

Now he's looking for stocking stuffers in a Village thrift shop, where I look for something for Pete.

My boyfriend. It's strange, it's nice, but there's a lot of the paranoia that comes with a new relationship. *Do I like him more than he likes me? Will it last? I don't want to get hurt.* That kind of stuff. It's like being in high school again, except this time I'm out and there's a plague. It's kind of amazing how we can go about our lives.

The tiny shop smells like Aunt Nora's cats, the mildew makes me sneeze, and you have to sort through trash cans full of clothes organized only by gender, and, even then, not exclusively. Still, the prices are right. I hold up a yellow-and-gold rockabilly bowling shirt, ask Toshiro: "Do you think Pete would like this?"

"Of course," he grunts, not even looking, as he picks up a cloudy snow globe off a dusty shelf and shakes it. A crackly "Baby, It's Cold Outside" is playing on a phonograph and I'm so sick of that song.

"Really?" I ask as I consider the shirt more closely. It probably isn't Pete's color. Dead Eddie told me yellow is tough to carry off if you have pale skin, like Pete does.

Toshiro turns, looks at me. "Get it or don't get it. Why ask my opinion?"

Jeez. "What's wrong?"

" 'I ought to say no, no, no, sir. (Mind if move in closer?)' "

He sighs, "Nothing, nothing."

I toss the shirt back in the can. "I swear to God, once I find a place, I'll move. I'm sorry it's taken me so long."

He turns, shakes a new half-full snow globe of Christmas

carolers. He says, "I know, I know. It's fine," in that tone of voice that lets you know it most definitely is NOT fine.

"No, it's not. I really appreciate everything you guys have done for me. I want you to know that."

He sets the snow globe back, considers a shot glass with a black stenciled flamenco dancer on it. "We know, we know." This is the other thing he does when he's upset—he repeats himself. I pull a plaid sweater vest out of the can. "How 'bout this for Pete?"

Toshiro says, his back to me, "Get it or don't get it." Then he says, almost under his breath, "Francesco loved Christmas. One year he gave me . . ."

He turns, faces me. He looks . . . stricken. "I thought I was ready for you to meet someone. I encouraged you. But now that you have, I think, perhaps, I wasn't being honest. Francesco was the best friend I ever had, Kevin. He loved you so much." He runs a hand through his long black hair. "I'm sorry. Pay no attention to me. He died, you didn't. You want companionship."

Inhale. "I'm not cheating on Frankie. If he were alive, you know I'd never leave him for anything." Then I can't help myself, I add: "Especially when he needed me most."

Toshiro's head slumps.

It was the three of us that night.

Toshiro was supposed to stay until the four hours were up. It was important to Francesco that I wouldn't be alone, if I had to do it.

But Toshiro couldn't bear it.

He left me alone with a man who hadn't died yet.

His eyes fill. "I'm sorry. I'm so sorry."

Exhale. "I'm not replacing him."

He nods, wiping his face.

He turns back to the shot glasses.

I decide on the plaid sweater vest, feeling, perhaps for the first time, that my grief is a selfish kind of grief, one I need to stop hoarding, like food during a blight.

It's the day before Christmas Eve. Christmas Eve eve. I'm with Pete and we've crossed the river to Brooklyn.

A place I've never been.

Tomorrow I fly out to Minneapolis to spend Christmas Eve with Aunt Nora, who sprang for my ticket, and her timing couldn't be better, because Toshiro and Laurie officially can't take it anymore. They came home early last night because *Rain Man* was sold out. They surprised Pete and me, and, well, we more than surprised them.

I still make lists, thanks to Laurie. Here's my list of things I will do in Minnesota:

> *1. Go to midnight mass with Aunt Nora at her affirming church with all the lovely gay lads.*
>
> *2. Spend Boxing Day, which I had never heard of before, with Dave and Aaron and Minnie the Moocher so I can catch up on all the survivors' group and Thursday Nighter gossip.*
>
> *3. Be best man at Tommy's New Year's Eve wedding, provided he really goes through with it. Do the godfather thing at his new kid's baptism.*

When I get back, there's gonna be a lot to do. I'll be processing what I hope will be a ton of year-end gift acknowledgments to GMHC. And Pete and I are going to dedicate more time to ACT UP, because there are people like Cardinal O'Connor appointed by presidents to oversee the plague: a man of the Middle Ages from a religion that blamed the Black Death on the sin of pride. A man who loves fags, as long as we're dying.

And then there's the president-elect, a man who was born with a silver foot in his mouth.

Farrell Furskin will be flying to Minneapolis with me. He's Sarah's Christmas gift, and Carol, nee Gunderson, married Doyle, nee Gunderson, will just have to deal with it. I've had two negative tests now, and long after she's dead and buried, good and deep, I'll still be around for my sister. Besides, we'll be even more related after I get my third all clear and Laurie pops out a kid.

So, yeah, I'm packing in a lot of living during my trip to Minnesota.

Even more when I get back to New York.

On January 2, in the new year of 1989, I start my new life with Pete. We just have to decide where we'll start it. Which is why we're here.

In Brooklyn.

He looks around the apartment. It's a dump, it's all the way out in Brooklyn, but it's cheap. It's not what either of us wants, and will probably be temporary until we can find someplace closer in, or cheaper, or rent controlled, or any one of the other kinds of places that New Yorkers fantasize about for their "next" apartment.

He says, "What do you think?"

Here is what I think:

1. *The bill collectors will find me if we're both on the lease.*
2. *I'm not emotionally prepared to join the bridge-and-tunnel crowd.*
3. *We're moving waaaay too fast, we hardly know each other, and I'm negative, and you don't know what you are, and you don't want to find out, and if you come down with it, I will die all over again, and who the hell needs that?*
4. *But, Jesus, when you smile at me.*

5. *I think Francesco would have liked you. You could've talked about serious literature together.*
6. *Maybe I'll be widowed twice, maybe you'll get sick of me and leave, maybe we'll grow to despise each other, but maybe we'll survive as gay men, as gay men in love with each other, who grow old together, who read the books you're supposed to read and watch foreign films with subtitles, and finally take that trip to Europe we've been talking about since forever.*
7. *Exhale.*

I tell him, "I think we're home."

Author's Note

On June 5, 1981, the U.S. Center for Disease Control published an article in its *Morbidity and Mortality Weekly Report* about a rare lung infection in five young, white, previously healthy gay men. All the men had other unusual infections as well, indicating a problem with immune system functioning. Two had died by the time the report was published. Hundreds of thousands would follow.

We think we know the rest.

Why revisit the trauma of the first years of AIDS in Gay America? After all, many gay men of my generation prefer not to recall an era when we were demonized by the media, religious "leaders," and politicians. An era when fully half of Americans favored quarantine for a disease that was not transmittable through casual contact. An era when the *New York Times* referred to us as "avowed homosexuals," as if we had publicly confessed to crimes against the state. An era when Rick Hunter and John Hanson were attacked by Minneapolis police in front of a gay bar, Charlie Howard was tossed off a bridge in Maine, and Rebecca Wight was shot to death on the Appalachian Trail.

To quote memoirist Roz Chast, "Can't we talk about something more pleasant?"

After all, antiretrovirals have been around for over twenty years. We can get married now. There are pressing injustices to address, like traumatizing "microaggressions" and the ever-growing number of "privileges" in need of checking.

Yes, I know I sound like a cranky old man, but it's not crankiness, and it's certainly not a nostalgia for the way things used to be. It's my desire to honor the heroes and heroines of the 1980s who fought a literal life-and-death battle against disease, hatred, violence, indifference, greed, and ignorance. And it's also a recognition that those of us who did survive often live with guilt and an empty space for those friends and lovers we will never see again.

I wrote *After Francesco* because as we approach the fortieth anniversary of the first CDC report, AIDS—as my generation of gay men experienced it—is becoming a footnote in some histories, and completely absent in others. The contemporary fiction by gay authors of the time is largely out of print, books such as *Facing It* by Paul Reed, *Eighty-Sixed* by David B. Feinberg, and *The Body and Its Dangers, and Other Stories,* by Allen Barnett. The gay writers we lost to the disease leave behind a legacy of what might have been—had this country decided that the lives of gay men mattered, had it dedicated the resources necessary to fight the crisis as it had done with Legionnaires' disease and toxic shock syndrome. I imagine the body of work created by Reinaldo Arenas, Steven Corbin, Melvin Dixon, John Fox, Robert Ferro, Bo Huston, and many, many others, had they lived. Had their own government and so many of their fellow Americans not turned their backs because they were gay.

As many continue to turn their backs today, because this pandemic is NOT over.

As I write this, much of the country is under quarantine to stop COVID-19, an infection spread by casual contact. And some of us are experiencing déjà vu: Anthony Fauci is back in the news, homemade cures are again being peddled, and we are protesting Donald Trump once more.

But the differences far outweigh any similarities: The national motto is "We are all in this together." Within months of COVID-19's outbreak, billions of dollars were allocated to fight the disease. The media is covering this pandemic, those who die are not being demonized, and the cause of their deaths are not shameful family secrets. Politicians are not debating whether or not the government has any responsibility to educate high-risk groups, and mainstream religious leaders are not calling COVID-19 the wages of sin.

When bitterness over these differences threatens to immobilize me, I look at a fragile sculpture made by my roommate, Paul, who died of AIDS in our Minneapolis apartment in 1991, a decade after the first CDC report. Paul was a visual artist from Minnesota's Iron Range, struggling financially like all artists, and waiting tables at an Italian restaurant to pay the bills. The piece is a tall, narrow vessel standing on six small, fragile legs. On one side a depiction of a man in profile, content, smiling, his skin tone a calm blue. On the other side—the side I don't display—a man enraged, facing you head-on. His dirty teeth are bared; his single yellow eye is wide open, looking directly at you.

Neither man has the self-pitying look of the bitter.

Brian Malloy
April 24, 2020

After Francesco

ABOUT THIS GUIDE

The suggested questions are included to enhance your group's
reading of Brian Malloy's *After Francesco*

DISCUSSION QUESTIONS

1. The book opens with a quote from Vito Russo, a gay film historian and author, who died of AIDS in 1990. What meaning do you take from Russo's statement that AIDS is *like living through a war which is happening only for those people who happen to be in the trenches*?

2. Have you experienced the death of one or more people whom you loved deeply? What immediate impact did their loss have on you? What longer-term impact? Did you find yourself sympathizing with Kevin as he coped—or failed to cope—with the death of Francesco?

3. There was no marriage equality in 1988. Since Dead Eddie died without a will, his savings went to his parents, not to Live Eddie. In addition to marriage equality, what other differences did you notice between 1988 America and the America of today?

4. For gay American men in the 1980s, AIDS was a defining experience. In his book *The AIDS Generation: Stories of Survival and Resilience*, Perry N. Halkitis describes this generation of gay men as the "bravest generation." Do you agree? Are there examples of courage in *After Francesco*?

5. "Gallows humor"—making fun of a horrible or tragic situation—is a common strategy employed by Kevin, Live Eddie, and even Dead Eddie in the flashback during the book's opening scene. How did you react to this humor? Are there some jokes that should only be told "within the family"?

6. Did Dave's idea of a strictly recreational sexual relationship with Kevin seem reasonable, given their circumstances, or was it doomed from the start?

7. Many of the events depicted in *After Francesco* are real. Were you familiar with ACT UP's actions at the FDA and Trump Tower, the first Minnesota AIDS Walk, or the Tompkins Square Park riot? Did you prefer ACT UP's civil disobedience or the AIDS Walk, in terms of how best to address the AIDS crisis?

8. Francesco's sister-in-law defends her fabricated memoir by claiming it's doing good by raising AIDS awareness, and changing hearts and minds. Do you agree? Why do you think she wrote the book?

9. What role does religion play in *After Francesco*? Do Aunt Nora, Father Michael, and Kevin share any common ground when it comes to faith?

10. Aunt Nora compares the government's handling of AIDS to the English government's response to the Irish potato blight. Is this a fair comparison? Are there other events that warrant comparison to the AIDS crisis of the 1980s?

11. Kevin's angry with the *New York Times*. In 2018, *New York Times* writer Kurt Soller addressed the newspaper's AIDS coverage: *Information about the spread of illness was often scant, judgmental or distressingly vague. The social and emotional toll of AIDS . . . were, when covered, often buried in the back of the newspaper, far from national news stories that were deemed important enough for the front page.* Did the media's failure to cover the crisis contribute to the spread of HIV?

12. Did the revelation of how Francesco died surprise you?

13. There are two depictions of assisted dying (also called "assisted suicide") in *After Francesco*. Assisted dying is now legal and regulated in Oregon and Washington. Should assisted dying be expanded to the rest of the country? Why or why not?

14. Kevin comes to think of his grief as a selfish kind of grief, one that he had to "stop hoarding, like food during a blight." Did you find his grief selfish? Why or why not?

15. Live Eddie resents Dave, and Toshiro admits he's struggling with Kevin's new relationship with Pete. Have you or someone you know encountered resistance from friends and family to a new relationship following the death of a loved one?

16. What do you think the future has in store for Kevin? Do you think he's equipped to handle what comes his way?

Want more of Kevin, Laurie, Tommy, and Aunt Nora? Read about their early days in the prequel, *The Year of Ice*.

Visit us online at
KensingtonBooks.com
to read more from your favorite authors,
see books by series, view reading
group guides, and more!

BOOK CLUB
BETWEEN THE CHAPTERS

Visit us online for sneak peeks, exclusive
giveaways, special discounts, author content,
and engaging discussions with your fellow readers.

Betweenthechapters.net

Sign up for our newsletters and be the first
to get exciting news and announcements about
your favorite authors!
Kensingtonbooks.com/newsletter